"We

"That was when I thought you a lad."

"What difference does it make? As long as I remain disguised as a lad there should be no problem."

He laughed again and pounded his chest. "I'll know you're a woman."

"Nothing else about me has changed. As you said yourself, my tongue is still biting. I still have skill with a bow and I still need to find my da."

Bryce stretched his hands out, as if he was about to strangle her, then pulled them back to rest fisted at his sides. "It isn't that simple."

"Why? And don't say it's because I'm a woman one more time. I can do this," she insisted, and stood much too suddenly. A foolish action. A wave of dizziness hit so hard she could barely see.

"Charlotte?" Bryce said, stepping toward her.

She reached out to him, his name the last word on her lips before she fell into his arms in a dead faint.

By Donna Fletcher

A WARRIOR'S PROMISE
LOVED BY A WARRIOR
BOUND TO A WARRIOR
THE HIGHLANDER'S FORBIDDEN BRIDE
THE ANGEL AND THE HIGHLANDER
UNDER THE HIGHLANDER'S SPELL
RETURN OF THE ROGUE
THE HIGHLANDER'S BRIDE
TAKEN BY STORM
THE BEWITCHING TWIN
THE DARING TWIN
DARK WARRIOR
LEGENDARY WARRIOR

Coming Soon
WED TO A HIGHLAND WARRIOR

DONNA FLETCHER

A WARRIOR'S PROMISE

AVON

An Imprint of HarperCollinsPublishers

AVON BOOKS
An Imprint of HarperCollins*Publishers*
10 East 53rd Street
New York, New York 10022-5299

Copyright © 2012 by Donna Fletcher
Excerpt from *Wed to a Highland Warrior* copyright © 2012 by Donna Fletcher
ISBN 978-0-06-203466-3
www.avonromance.com

First Avon Books mass market printing: May 2012

Avon Trademark Reg. U.S. Pat. Off. and in Other Countries, Marca Registrada, Hecho en U.S.A.
HarperCollins® is a registered trademark of HarperCollins Publishers.

Printed in the U.S.A.

10 9 8 7 6 5 4 3 2 1

A WARRIOR'S
PROMISE

Chapter 1

Charles ran like the devil was after him. His worn boots pounded the dirt, leaving a wake of dust in his trail. He couldn't let the soldiers get him. He couldn't. They would give him a thrashing for sure and then? He shivered as he ran, not wanting to think of what would happen if they discovered his secret.

He hadn't been able to help himself. Hunger had gnawed at his gut until it had pained him. It had been two full days since he had eaten, and he had to have food, even if it was a stale piece of bread cast carelessly to the ground by a noblewoman.

No sooner had he scooped it up than the woman had started screaming, "Thief! Thief!"

It had been little more than a crumb and done nothing to ease his pain. While the woman looked like she had not suffered from missing a meal in some time. It mattered not. Once the trio of the king's men had heard, they jumped into action and run straight at him.

He barely had time to put distance between them, and fright gave his bone-tired body the strength to flee. He dodged and darted in and around marketgoers and ware-barterers, slipped under makeshift tables, jumped over barrels, and yanked free of the hand that grabbed at the back of his wool vest. His skinny legs pumped as fast as they could to avoid the soldiers gaining on him, perhaps even toying with him, making him believe he'd escape them when he truly didn't have a chance.

His dark eyes darted in panic, desperate to find an avenue of escape. At the last minute, he spotted it: big, broad, and solid. Surely, he could take shelter beneath it. With all the strength he had left, he dove for the solid mass sliding along the ground and coming to rest on his belly between the two limbs that stood rooted to the earth. Then he hurriedly wrapped his arms around one thick leg and held on for dear life.

A quick tilt of his head had his eyes settling beneath the Highlander's plaid, and he gulped. Good Lord, he was a big one, which meant he was strong and could protect, and the lad needed protecting.

"*Please*. Please, help me," he begged, peering past the plaid to the giant Highlander, who stared down at him with a look of bewilderment.

"Hand him over," one of the three soldiers ordered, while almost colliding as they came to an abrupt halt.

The urchin hid a smile, relieved at their reluctance to approach the large man.

"And what will you do with him?"

The urchin liked the sound of the Highlander's voice; it confronted and dared all in one breath. He was not a man to argue with, but one to fear and respect.

"That doesn't concern you," the soldier said with trembling bravado.

"Why wouldn't it?" the Highlander demanded sharply.

"He stole from a woman and must pay the price," another soldier spoke up, not daring to step from behind the soldier in front.

"What is the price?" the Highlander asked.

"A good whipping and service to the woman to pay off his debt," the soldier in the front said, a bit more daringly.

"It was nothing more than a crumb off the ground," the urchin snapped. His dark eyes glared menacingly, while his arms clung tenaciously to the Highlander's thick-muscled leg.

"It wasn't your crumb to take," the soldier snapped.

"The lad looks in need of more than a crumb," the Highlander said much too calmly.

From the way the three soldiers took several steps back, each tripping and trying to get out of the others' way, the urchin knew that the Highlander must have sent them a menacing look.

"He broke the king's law," one soldier said from behind the other two.

"The king wants his subjects to go hungry?" the Highlander asked, his voice rising in anger.

Before the soldiers could respond, the woman whose crumb the urchin supposedly had thieved came upon them with laborious breath. Her large bosoms heaved, and she fanned her flushed face with her hand.

"That dirty little lad"—she stopped for a breath—"stole from me." She took another needed breath and stopped fanning. "Now he owes me, he does."

"What will you take for him?" the Highlander asked.

The woman stared down at the urchin. "He's worth a good amount."

The Highlander lurched forward, causing the soldiers and woman to retreat in haste and huddle closer together. While the urchin, having no intention of letting go of the intimidating Highlander's leg, was dragged along with every step he took.

"Don't think me a fool, madam," the Highlander snarled. "He's a skinny lad not fit for most chores. He isn't worth a pittance." And with that said, he tossed a meager trinket at her feet. "Take it and be satisfied."

The one soldier was quick to pick it up and hand it to the woman. She took it and, with a snort and toss of her head, stomped away.

"We're done here," the Highlander said.

Charles heard the tight anger in his tone, and, as the soldiers turned and walked away, he grinned. That is until the Highlander's large hand reached down, grabbed him by the back of his shirt, and lifted him clear off the ground to dangle in front of his face.

"Have you no sense, lad?"

A shiver ran through him. It wasn't only the breadth and width of the Highlander that intimidated, but his features as well. His long, dark hair, the color of the deep rich earth, was swept back away from a face with defined features. Wrinkles ran across a wide brow and at the corners of his light blue eyes. He had a solid chin that no doubt could easily deflect a hefty fist, and a nose so finely shaped that it proved he had been the victor of many a fight, for it looked to have never been broken.

"Answer me," the Highlander demanded, giving the lad a quick shake.

"I'm starvin', I am," the lad snapped.

The Highlander put him down, and fear crept over Charles. It was one thing to look the mighty warrior in the face, but standing beside him, the top of his head was level with the top of the Highlander's chest.

This Highlander warrior was the hero of legends that Charles's father had told him about. Suddenly, his hunger didn't seem important, and he choked back tears. He had to find his father and set him free. His father had told him not to worry about him, to run and stay safe; but he was his da, and he loved him with all his heart. He had raised him alone since he was barely five years, his mother having passed in childbirth along with the babe. He was a good, loving father. He would never leave him to suffer the king's torment. He would find him and set him free and then together they would go as they had planned to join those who supported the true king's return.

"I'll feed you," the Highlander said, casting an anxious glance over the marketplace grounds. "We'll get what we need and be gone. I don't trust the soldiers. They'll find more of their kind and be after us soon enough."

The Highlander was right about that, and Charles had no problem with filling his belly, then taking off on his own. He had a mission to accomplish, and he intended to see it done.

"Don't wander off," the Highlander warned. "Stay close to me."

Charles stuck to the warrior's side as he made a hasty round of the market, slipping Charles a hunk of cheese he traded for. He devoured the piece in seconds and hungered for more, but didn't ask. They would be done soon enough, and soon he'd be feasting, the Highlander having gathered more than enough food.

Charles had a feeling that the warrior was acquiring more than simply food. Whispers and mumbles were exchanged at most every place he stopped. Something was afoot, and he wondered if perhaps the Highlander was in some way connected with those warriors who fought to see the true king take the throne. A prophecy had been circulating for some time now about the true king, the king who possessed the inalienable right to the throne of Scotland. It was a prophecy his father had recounted many times to him until he could recite it by heart.

When summer touches winter, and the snow descends, the reign of the false king begins to end, four warriors ride together and then divide, among them the true king hides, when he meets death on his own, that is when he reclaims the throne.

His father had believed strongly in the prophecy and had claimed that the true king would one day appear, and his reign would bring peace and prosperity. Perhaps if the warrior was connected with those who fought for the true king, he could help Charles rescue his father and see them settled in a safe place.

Suddenly, Charles was glad for his near brush with danger, for it had provided him with an introduction to the Highlander and a better chance to free his father.

The Highlander dropped a sack to him with a warning. "Eat, but do not show your hunger. It demonstrates vulnerability."

Charles understood, and, though anxious to devour what food staples were in the sack, he reached in and tore off a hunk of bread. With hunger that crawled up and out of his mouth, he managed to eat slowly as he walked beside the Highlander, taking two, sometimes three steps, to the Highlander's one.

"Your name, lad?" the Highlander asked, as they approached the end of the marketplace.

"Charles, sir."

"Call me Bryce."

"Thank you, Bryce, for helping me," Charles said.

"Help you? I bought you, lad."

Charles stumbled, and Bryce grabbed hold of his arm. "Watch your step."

The Highlander kept a firm grip on his arm until the market was far behind them, and they entered the woods lush with fresh spring growth.

What a fool he was, not to realize that the Highlander had purchased him. He was now the warrior's property. And the strength of his grip had only served to remind him of the invisible shackle that duty-bound him to Bryce.

Questions assaulted Charles's mind and spilled rapidly from his lips. "What do you want with me? How long am I beholden to you? Where will you be taking me? Will we be going far from here—"

"Stop!" Bryce snapped. "You're a bit of a thing that not only needs feeding but help in growing into manhood."

"And what?" Charles halted in his tracks. "You expect to make a man out of me?"

Bryce peered down at him. "That's exactly what I intend to do."

He kept walking, and Charles had no choice but to follow, with only one thought in mind.

There was no way this mighty Highlander would ever accomplish making a man out of Charles, and for a very good reason.

Charles was actually Charlotte, a woman!

Chapter 2

Bryce walked them a good distance into the woods, finding a secluded spot where no sooner did the lad's small bottom hit the ground than his fingers dove into the sack and grabbed a hunk of bread. Chomping away, he again reached in and grabbed a sizeable chunk of cheese, breaking it apart and hastily offering Bryce the heftier portion.

Bryce took it, watching the lad devour the food. That the lad was starving and undernourished was obvious. Both his worn, green wool tunic and brown linen shirt beneath were a size too large for him, as was the patched gold wool vest he wore. His brown leather boots were well past worn, a small end toe peeking out from one of many holes.

He had wide, inquisitive, dark eyes with long lashes to match, a pert nose, and a round face that held not a scar or trace of ever having been in a fight, though it was smudged with dirt. His hair was a blend of colors from soft brown, to rich gold, to a deep honey color. And the length varied just as much as the colors, sticking out here and there and falling just below his small ears. It looked as if the lad had taken a knife to it in a fit of fury, yet somehow the crazy results fit him.

In spite of his skinny stature, the lad had been brave though foolish, his mouth speaking when it was better kept shut. But then, he was young and had much to learn, like all young lads. Bryce had been impressed by his courage and the common sense to latch onto someone larger than himself rather than try to outrun the king's soldiers. They surely would have caught him and treated him to a severe beating. And no doubt the woman who had accused him of thievery would have encouraged such an unfitting punishment. She had played the injured party well and seen a chance to be compensated; otherwise, she would have gladly seen the lad suffer.

"Where do we go from here?" Charles asked in between bites.

"That's a good question," Bryce said, thinking on what to do since the lad had unexpectedly happened into his life. He had a mission to accomplish, an important one. He and his three brothers, not by blood though as close, had been working and planning to see that the true king of Scotland was seated on the throne. They were growing ever closer to achieving that goal, and this mission Bryce was on could very well prove the turning point.

Did he continue on with it? Could he trust the lad enough to help him? Or would he prove a hindrance? The only way to find out was to learn more about the lad.

"Tell me of your family or where you come from," Bryce said.

"Why? What does that have to do with where we're going?"

He was a bold one, especially since he by no means

had the strength to defend himself. Bryce reached out and snatched a chunk of bread from the lad's hand. "It will determine where we're going."

"Wondering if I have the wit and strength about me to keep up with you?"

If the lad was larger, Bryce would have reached out and wiped that quirk of a smile off his face. But he restrained himself, reminding himself that he was a skinny thing a good wind would blow away.

Instead, he confronted the lad. "Do you?"

"I have enough sense to know when to avoid things, when to meld with the shadows, and when to hold my tongue."

Bryce chuckled. "You might want to practice that last one."

"And listen to those bigger than me sprout stupidity and ignorance?"

Bryce settled a cold, hard stare on him. "Do you think me stupid and ignorant?"

"Does it matter?"

Bryce could not believe the audacity of the lad, and he had to smile though his response reflected otherwise. "You will do well to watch that tongue and answer me rather than question."

"Or what?"

Bryce leaned forward, his voice low with a hint of warning. "Do you truly wish to find out?"

The lad swallowed hard, his wide eyes growing ever wider, and shook his head.

Bryce leaned back to once again rest against the boulder. "Good. Now tell me, where do you come from, what of your family?"

"There's nothing to tell," Charles said reluctantly. "I'm on my own."

Bryce admired his caution. No doubt he was doing the same as Bryce, trying to judge just how much to trust. Besides, there were too many lads like him forced on their own for various reasons, some having lost one or both parents, others a bad situation driving them away to survive on their own. He could continue to pry, but he doubted it would do any good. What he did learn, or rather confirm, was that the lad was a fighter, a survivor, and he just might be worth taking along.

"Your age?" Bryce asked, concerned he might be too young for such a risk though it seemed that past events and experiences might have matured him well beyond his years.

"Five-and-ten years," Charles replied with haste.

Bryce didn't believe that for a moment. "More like two-and-ten or three-and-ten years."

The lad's eyes blazed with anger, and he looked about to retaliate, but snapped his mouth shut though not for long.

"And you?" the lad asked boldly. "How many years are you?"

Once again the challenging smile surfaced, and Bryce suddenly realized that Charles reminded him of his brother Reeve. Not in stature, but in nature. Reeve believed himself always right and was quick to defend or fight, and fight he could, taking down more men alone than with his brothers' help. Charles had Reeve's confidence, and it made Bryce like the lad even more.

"My age is no concern to you," Bryce said, thinking it seemed like yesterday he was the lad's age, though lucky to have family who loved him. Now he was seven-and-twenty years, his family as strong as ever and growing. His brother Duncan and his wife expecting their first child anytime now, Reeve and his wife Tara happily wed. Trey having lost the woman he loved and vowing never to love again, and Bryce the only sensible one, avoiding love until their mission was complete.

"Forgot how old you are?" Charles asked with a chuckle.

Bryce ignored the jab. There were more important matters to discuss. "I'm more interested in your age and experience. Can you handle a horse? Are you skilled with weapons?"

"I sit a horse better than most, and while I can wield a sword, my skill lies with a bow."

Bryce liked that the lad did not boast, he simply stated fact, but there was one more question. "And women?"

Charles's chin shot up. "What about them?"

"Have you known many?"

Charles stared at him, chewing at his lower lip.

Bryce burst out laughing. "Your silence speaks loudly. You're a virgin then."

Charles took offense. "What of it? What difference does it make?"

Bryce went silent, his soft blue eyes turning icy cold. "It makes a difference. A lad who has never lain between a woman's legs can do foolish things when the urge strikes. And if I choose to take you along on my mission, I need to know I can depend on you even if you have the urge for a woman."

"What about your urges?" Charles asked.

"I'm a man with vast experience. I can control mine. You're just a virgin lad who probably will spill his seed before you can even get inside a woman the first time you try."

"Are you sharing that from *your* past experience?"

Bryce almost reached out and grabbed the lad by the neck. Then he could easily choke that stupid grin off his face.

"You don't have to worry," the lad said. "I don't want to just rut like most men do. I want to love the woman whose legs I settle between."

Bryce cringed. "That's even worse."

"You have no use for love?"

"Believe me when I tell you you'll rut before you find love. And as far as love? There's a time and a place for it; otherwise, it can rob your sanity and interfere with everything."

"You have loved?"

"Good Lord, no." Bryce almost choked, spitting the words out. "I have been spared, and I intend for it to remain that way until I complete the task that has been assigned to me."

"This task. You wish me to help you with it?"

"The thought has crossed my mind." And the more Bryce talked with the lad, the more he thought it could prove beneficial having him along. He was quick-witted, could run like the devil was after him, and if he was as good with a horse and bow as he claimed, then he definitely could prove an asset. Besides, if he was five-and-ten years, he was man enough to take on the challenge, gain the experience.

One uncertainty haunted him, and so he asked, "Can you follow orders without question?"

The lad's hesitation gave Bryce his answer.

"I do not know your nature well enough to answer," Charles finally said. "You rescued me, but for a price, and now I owe you and must work for my freedom. I am obliged to obey you, but without hesitation?" Charles shook his head. "It would depend on what you ask of me."

Once again, Bryce admired the lad. He was brave enough to speak the truth, an honorable trait for sure. This lad was trustworthy. There was just one last thing to ask, and though he might be taking a risk doing so, he didn't think the lad had any love for the present king, being he had been chased and threatened by the king's soldiers.

"Do you believe King Kenneth the true king of Scotland?"

The lad studied him with cautious eyes and turned the question back on him. "Do you?"

"I have my doubts."

The lad's face broke out in a wide grin. "You fight for the true king, don't you?"

"Would you fight for him?"

"Aye, I would," Charles said, nodding vigorously.

"Good; then you now know that anything I ask of you will be for the good of Scotland."

"What do you ask of me?"

Bryce leaned forward and lowered his tone. "There is a spy in King Kenneth's court, and news is that the king knows of his presence though not his identity. The information this person has learned is vital to the true king, and he must be found and rescued.

The lad jumped up. "I will strike a bargain with you."

"A bargain?"

"Aye, I will gladly help you with your mission; do whatever you ask of me, if you will help me with mine."

"You are on a mission?" Bryce asked surprised and curious.

Charles nodded. "King Kenneth had his soldiers take my da prisoner, and I intend to rescue him."

"Sit," Bryce said, "and tell me what happened."

Tears were close to choking Charlotte as she sat on the ground, but she swallowed hard and forced them to remain locked away. She had to show this Highlander warrior strength, or he would never agree to take her along in exchange for helping to free her father.

"My father, Idris Semple, holds no allegiance to any particular clan. After mum died, we began to wander around Scotland. My da is a man of great curiosity, which has brought him great knowledge and with it a reputation that has caused problems. Many believe him a conjurer."

Charlotte paused, waiting to see if the mighty warrior would somehow display distaste or fear though she doubted he feared much. His strength was evident at a single glance.

When he showed no reaction, she continued. "His only powers are his vast knowledge, but the king believes otherwise. One day, my da was on his usual early-morning stroll when he spied a troop of soldiers. He hurried back to the small abandoned cottage we had been occupying for a few months and insisted I hide in the woods. He feared they would do me harm."

"He knew they were there for him," Bryce said.

Charlotte wasn't surprised at his perception. She had realized soon enough that the warrior was not only a man of strength but of intelligence as well, which was why she had to be careful, very careful. He was growing comfortable with Charles, the lad, even feeling him fit and worthy enough to help him with an important task. But if he discovered that she was Charlotte, the lass, she feared the consequences. Not that she worried he would harm her. He was an honorable man and would probably send her off somewhere safe, where she would be looked after and protected. And that would not do. She intended to rescue her da, and to do that, she had to keep her identity secret.

She nodded slowly. "My father is not a big man. He is short, though spry, and has not the strength to fight off a pack of soldiers; nor would he. He would reason it a useless action and find another way to deal with them."

"He went without protest?"

"Yes, he did, and all because of me," she said angrily.

"Yes, he did it because of you," Bryce agreed, "but not to protect. Think, Charles. Your da is a man of reason. And therefore he knew that if you were not captured, you would make every effort to rescue him, as well you should. I would do the same for my da."

This was good. To him she was a lad honor-bound to family. Yes, her masquerade would serve her well though her heart broke recalling how her father had, in the most authoritative voice he could muster, ordered her to seek safety with a strong clan and not worry about him. How could he think she would desert him? They had argued briefly, for there was no time to debate the matter, and before they parted, she had sworn to him that she would not let him suffer at the king's hands. She would follow and free him.

"Then you will help me rescue him?"

"I would be honored to help you and offer you and your da a home with my clan for as long as you like."

"Thank you," Charlotte said, choking back tears that wanted desperately to break free. And those tears weren't only because she was grateful for the help, but also the offer of a home. While she had enjoyed the many adventures she and her father had had, of late she had been longing for a more permanent dwelling.

"Do you know where he was taken?" Bryce asked.

She shook her head. "I followed but couldn't keep up with the horses."

She couldn't tell him the truth, that when the soldiers had disappeared from view, she had returned to the cottage. Quickly, she had shed her garments and slipped into her da's. She had taken a knife to her long hair, chopping at it until she felt she resembled a lad, gathered a sack of food, and was soon following the horses' trail. Her father had taught her to track, and she had been glad she had learned well the task.

"How far did you follow?"

There was no reason to tell him that the troop had divided along the trail. And she, not having known which path her da was on, had chosen one to follow that had proven to be the wrong one. So she told him the point where the path divided.

"It was near Loch Lochy, and I've had no luck in finding out anything about him since."

Bryce stood. "We have much to do. We must find out where your da is being kept and follow the leads I have discovered about the spy."

Charlotte scrambled to her feet. "Being small and thin, I can slip in and around places most cannot. I hear and see things while not being heard or noticed."

Bryce chuckled. "Good, for I cannot."

"You are a big one," she said with a smile, recalling the glance she got of him while holding on for dear life to his leg.

Bryce placed a firm hand on her shoulder. "Size does not matter."

Charlotte warned herself to hold her tongue, but she supposed she was too much like her father—curious. So she asked, "Then large bosoms don't matter?"

Bryce grinned. "Large bosoms matter, lad, they definitely matter."

It was good to know the warrior preferred large-breasted women. Her bosoms were barely a handful. It had taken only one strip of cloth to bind them. She had no worry that even if he discovered her secret, he would find her appealing.

She was glad she had gotten a look at his privates. He was much too large, and she too small for them to fit. She didn't know why she even gave it a thought. There were more important things to consider.

Charlotte hurried along behind him, which didn't help, the image of what lay beneath his plaid much too vivid in her mind.

Chapter 3

They had walked in relative silence for almost three hours. Charlotte could tell by Bryce's drawn brow and few remarks that he was deep in thought. So she felt it wise not to disturb him even though she was anxious to inquire about their destination.

There were more questions on her tongue, which she bit to keep silent, though for how long she didn't know. She knew that the rescue of the spy was more important than that of her da, but she trusted the Highlander's word that he would help her. She wondered if he had a plan or was just formulating one or perhaps adjusting it to include her father.

Then there was her worry of keeping up with him. While his powerful strides were not fast, they were anxious. And he did not allow the rocky and hilly terrain to deter him. She, on the other hand, accustomed to traveling leisurely on foot, taking time to not only regard but learn from her surroundings, found the pace fretful.

How would they ever take notice of anything if they did not slow down and observe? What if there were signs they were missing? The thought that a broken branch, a misplaced rock, a footprint could help direct them finally had her losing her patience and stopping abruptly.

"Where do we go?"

Bryce did not glance back; he kept walking. "A small village about a day's walk."

Charlotte hurried up beside him, taking two steps to his one. "Why?"

"I've learned that the king's soldiers have been more active than usual in a particular area and that someone in the village might know the reason why. It's also not far from Loch Lochy."

He needn't say more; Charlotte was pleased that he was also considering her da.

"We'll find you a bow and arrows while there. What of a dirk? Can you handle one?"

"Fair enough," she said.

"Your father taught you the use of weapons well."

She grinned. Her father had insisted she learn the rudiments of handling a dirk, for her protection. And as for her skill with a bow, it had come easily, and her father had encouraged her as he always did. Knowledge, he had told her, gave one self-worth. And he had been right. She had the confidence to take on this task, and, while her ruse could eventually pose a problem, she'd find a way to handle it.

"We'll find a spot to bed down for the night, preferably by water. It's been a while since I had a dunk and could use one." Bryce shot her a glance. "You could use one yourself."

Charlotte just grunted. There was no way she was shedding her garments, and as for the dirt and grime?

They served a purpose. If she scrubbed herself clean, she'd have the fresh look of a pretty lassie, or so she'd been told by a few warriors in the various clans where she and her da had taken temporary shelter.

She hadn't encouraged them, not being at all interested. Her father had suggested she at least converse with them, see what it was she liked and disliked in a man. She hadn't bothered to tell him that with one look she could see that not a one was for the likes of her. While she admired strength and bravery in a man, she also looked for intelligence. Not that all the men who had approached her were dim-witted, they were fairly intelligent from the little she could tell of them. They simply were not interesting, unlike Bryce who, from the very moment she had latched onto him, proved appealing.

The thought gave her a start, and she almost tripped over her own feet. She glared at his broad back, her eyes traveling down the length of him, refusing to let her musing wander where it wanted to go, between his legs.

Between his legs.

Her cheeks flamed red, and she shook her head. Whatever was the matter with her? Where were these sinful thoughts coming from? She had *barely* laid eyes on this man—she almost groaned aloud. She had to stop thinking about what she had seen.

He was no different from most warriors. *Now there was a lie for sure.*

"Something wrong?" Bryce called out, not turning to look at the lad. "You're grunting and groaning back there."

She bit at her bottom lip, silently chastising her foolish rumination and upset that she had unknowingly been voicing her annoyance.

"Nothing is wrong," she snapped.

"Getting tired?"

"I'm fine," she insisted, though her legs were beginning to ache. She had covered a lot of land, at a far different pace, not only since early morning but since her father's capture a week ago.

"Good, for we have much land to cover before we stop."

She groaned inwardly.

"I heard that."

"You couldn't have, I kept it silent."

His laughter warned she had been duped.

"I can match your pace," she insisted.

"You'd better"— he laughed again—"for I don't want to be forced to carry you."

She hurried her steps, not doubting for a minute that the large Highlander would easily fling her over his shoulder and be done with it. What then? Would he discover her secret?

She wouldn't take the chance, and so, tired legs or not, she kept in stride behind him.

Bryce gave a slow stretch to the sky. "A perfect spot."

Charlotte dropped immediately to the ground, wanting to moan aloud with relief. They hadn't stopped once to rest, and she wondered where Bryce got his stamina. Not only did her body ache, but she was exhausted and wanted nothing more than to sleep. Even though the sun would not set for well over two hours, and her stomach protested in hunger.

"Let's have a dip before we eat."

Charlotte's head shot up to see Bryce already strip-ping off his clothes. "The stream is not deep enough for a dip or a dunk."

They had walked along the bank for some time, Charlotte hoping with each step that Bryce would stop. She could tell at a glance that the water might reach above her waist though not his.

"A splash then," he said, his garments tossed to lie beside his sword.

She couldn't help but stare at the spread of muscles across his broad back and how it tapered down to form a nice round, taut backside. And then there were his long legs, thick with solid muscles. Lord, he was a fine specimen of a man.

He turned around so fast that it startled her, and she jerked back. Not a good reaction. She was, after all, a lad and should be accustomed to the sight of a naked man.

Lord have mercy, he was one well-endowed warrior.

Eyes up. Eyes up, she warned silently. She obeyed her frantic command with haste.

"Disrobe and join me. You need a good washing."

The words shot out of her mouth. "I'm too tired; be-sides, the air has chilled."

Charlotte felt her heart pound wildly as he advanced on her, and she scrambled back.

"A little chill won't hurt you," he said, stopping much too close.

She fought to keep her eyes on his, a nearly impos-sible task since her face was even with his—

Don't think about it. Don't think about it, she cau-tioned herself repeatedly.

"I'm not dunking," she said, cringing and thinking of an entirely different dunk.

Bryce bounced down on his haunches, and she was grateful that their faces were now level.

"Charles, you may be a wee bit of a thing and need to grow sturdier into manhood, but do not let that stop you from doing manly things."

Bryce bounced up so fast that the rest of him bounced a mere inch from her face. Thank the Lord he turned around as quickly.

"Now come and join me."

Charlotte almost sighed aloud. For a moment, she had feared he would reach out and strip her. She was relieved for the distance he put between them. And she watched with even more relief when he entered the water and saw that it was deeper than she had thought.

It swallowed him to his waist and brought another sigh to her lips that she released aloud.

Bryce waved her in and for a fleeting moment she once again worried that he would force her to join him. But she was quick to realize he would not cause the lad embarrassment. If he had intended that, he would have done so already. He had given her due respect, leaving the decision to her though still encouraging.

The more she learned about this warrior, the more she liked him. And that alarmed her. Never had she found herself drawn to any man, and here, within only a few hours, she found that she liked this one. This was neither the time nor place for such frivolous thoughts.

Her father needed rescuing, and the warrior had his own mission to consider. There was work to be done for them both. She had to remember that, and, more importantly, she had to remember that to Bryce, she was the lad Charles, and, therefore, she needed to act accordingly.

Charlotte watched Bryce enjoy his dunk, and dunk he did, several times. It was when he made his way to the bank that she scrambled to her feet. She had no intentions of looking upon his naked, dripping wet body. She had seen enough . . . not really . . . she tried to convince herself she had.

"I'll get firewood," she called out.

"Good," he shouted. "You were right. There is a chill to the air and to the water."

Charlotte hurried around, collecting broken and dried branches, all the while keeping her eyes averted from Bryce. A fire, food, and sleep were upmost on her mind. She refused to allow any other thoughts to interfere no matter how hard they tried.

They ate in relative silence in front of the campfire, dusk settling quickly around them.

When they finished, Bryce said, "We must inquire with caution about your da. No doubt the king has him well guarded if he believes there is a chance of your father fattening his coffers."

"I thought the same."

"I've been thinking," Bryce said. "Your da no doubt believes you will attempt to rescue him."

He was right about that; though her father had warned against it, they had parted with him having no doubt that she would come for him.

"Since he taught you well about weapons, I assume he also taught you well his conjuring."

"My father doesn't conjure," Charlotte said. "He is a man steeped in knowledge, dealing with those who lack knowledge. He cares naught about wealth or power. Learning is his life; he believes humanity will not prosper without it."

"Does your father know you as well as you do him?"

She smiled. "Even better."

"Then I daresay your da would find a way to aid you in his escape."

His remark puzzled her for a moment, then she nodded vigorously, though annoyed with herself for not having realized it. "You're right. He would find a way of leaving a trail that no one but I would recognize."

"Is there anything that your da requires to do his conjuring or so make the king believe and to make finding him easier?"

Charlotte scrunched her brow, trying to recall something, anything that her da had mentioned of late that could prove helpful. To her despair, she could bring nothing to mind.

"Do not worry," Bryce said. "No doubt you'll realize something soon enough."

Her da had taught her that worry was a deterrent in solving problems. He had advised her that clear thought produced good results. She had to keep her thoughts clear. No matter how worried she was about her da's fate, it did no good to linger on it. She must think the way her da would. Only then would she recognize the signs when they appeared.

Charlotte was grateful to the Highlander warrior, for once again he had helped her. "I am indebted to you for rescuing me from the soldiers, but I am also indebted to you for helping me find my father. It is appreciated more than you know."

He glanced at her strangely, almost as if he wasn't quite certain who she was, then she realized. She hadn't spoken brash like the lad. She had sounded much too mannered.

She thought to correct her mistake but then thought better of it. Her blunder would be forgotten once she resumed the role of the lad.

"We struck a bargain, and so my word was given," Bryce said.

"Not all men keep their word."

"I do." He grinned. "My da taught me the importance of honor, and my mother taught me to heed a woman's word." His grin grew. "I prefer a woman who heeds my word."

"Then it's a mindless fool you want for a wife?"

Bryce laughed. "You have much to learn about women."

"Teach me," she challenged, curious to know his thoughts on women.

"You would be an old man by the time I finished," Bryce said, laughter coloring his words as he stretched out on the hard ground, crossing his arms beneath his head.

"One bit of wisdom?" Charlotte asked.

"Let no woman have your heart until you're ready to give it," Bryce said. "Now sleep. Tomorrow is a busy day."

Charlotte stretched out on the opposite side of the campfire from Bryce. She lay on her side, staring at him. He lay with his eyes closed, his arms still pillowing his head. His response had startled her. She had expected a humorous quip, not serious words.

Was that what he did? Did he hold firm to his heart when it came to women? Would he give nothing of his heart, not a bit, until he was ready? And if so, how would he ever know if he was ready to love?

One day, many years ago, she had asked her father about love. He had told her in his usual pragmatic manner that love could never be defined; it could only be felt.

Bryce had given a peek inside himself, and she intended to probe more deeply.

Chapter 4

Bryce stopped just before climbing the small rise and turned to Charles. "The people in this village no doubt will be leery of strangers. It seems that many have passed this way recently, and, being remote from common trails, it has the villagers curious and cautious."

"Is this the information your whispering got you at the market?" the lad asked.

"My whispers bartered for food, no more," Bryce snapped. The lad was more observant than he had realized, for that information was exactly what his whispers had gotten him.

"As you say."

"I say that you remain by my side and keep that tongue to yourself. You have a habit of speaking when things are better left unsaid."

"A loose tongue can help at times—"

"And other times it can bring trouble, and you—"

"Have to know which time is the best to let it loose," Charles finished.

"*Now* is *not* the time," Bryce warned. "Stay silent. Hear, listen and learn and keep alert."

"I can do that."

"See that you do," Bryce said, and began climbing the rise. "I don't need to be worried about rescuing you again when we both have missions to accomplish."

Bryce wore a pleasant smile as he approached the fields outside the walled village. He acknowledged the workers with a nod, and it was returned in kind though all eyes bore caution. It was the same beyond the wooden wall. Villagers nodded but remained vigilant.

The information Bryce had gleaned led him to believe that the smithy would be the best one to approach. Not wanting Charles to be privy to the conversation, he turned to the lad. "Go find the bowyer and see if he has a bow that will suit you. I will be along shortly."

The lad hesitated a moment though it certainly wasn't out of fear of leaving Bryce's side. More likely it was that the lad was more curious about what was to be discussed. But he took himself off without further delay, and Bryce regretted not reminding him again to be watchful of his behavior and tongue.

The smithy was short though solid with muscle. His hair was a garish red with two thick side braids. He banged at a sizzling-hot piece of metal on the anvil with a hammer, and Bryce said nothing until he clamped the piece with a set of tongs and submerged it into the water barrel, sending steam and sizzle rising.

"A bit of your time?" Bryce asked, and placed a trinket of worth on the corner of the anvil.

The man nodded.

Bryce didn't inquire as to his name. He didn't want to know; nor did he want the man to know his. He would rather it not be known he had passed this way. He wanted information, then he'd be gone.

"I hear the king's soldiers have been seen more frequently in these parts."

Again, the smithy nodded.

"Most are wondering why."

Another nod.

Bryce understood the man's caution, felt it himself, and proceeded slowly. The smithy's eyes suddenly turned wide enough to burst, and before Bryce could get his hand to his sword and turn, an arrow whooshed past his ear and stuck in the ground behind him.

He yanked the arrow out of the ground and turned to see Charles strutting toward him, a wide smile on his grime-ridden face.

Bryce marched toward him with angry steps. "You almost got me in the back."

Charles stopped and took a firm stance. "If I wanted the arrow in your back, it would be sticking there now."

Bryce halted within an inch of the lad, all but ready to wipe the smile off his face.

"It would be wise of you to speak with the bowyer before you talk anymore with the smithy," the lad said, keeping his voice low but his smile wide.

Bryce grabbed the lad's arm, his hand circling the whole of it, and hurried him to the side of a cottage out of the way of prying eyes. "The smithy was just about to tell me—"

"What the soldiers want inquiring warriors to know."

"What do you mean?"

"The bowyer says the smithy is not to be trusted."

"And how did you come by this information when

you were sent to do nothing more than find a bow to purchase?" Bryce asked.

"I asked if he saw an older man, white hair, small stature who had passed this way. He told me to be careful of whom I asked such information, and I simply replied, 'like the smithy?' and he nodded."

"Take me to the bowyer," Bryce said, releasing the hold he had on the lad with a slight shove, annoyed that the lad had disobeyed his orders yet pleased at what he had discovered. The lad just couldn't hold his tongue, and while in this instance it had proven beneficial, that might not always be so.

The bowyer showed his age in his stooped form and generous wrinkles though he was spryer than one would expect from his appearance. And though some of his fingers were gnarled, he worked on the bows with an agility that surprised.

"You would be wise to watch who you speak to in these parts," the old man said, continuing to work on a bow. "Too many new faces to my liking and some that call this home but show it no honor."

"It's hard to trust these days," Bryce said.

"A true Scot knows where his allegiance lies."

"With the true king," Charles chimed in.

The bowyer nodded. "It's brave you are to speak up like that lad. And when the true king takes the throne, you'll know a better life for it."

"Unless he's foolhardy enough to get himself killed beforehand," Bryce said, realizing he felt even more protective of the lad after getting a good feel of his scrawny arm. He simply did not have the strength to defend himself.

"Then he'll die with honor," the bowyer said.

"Not before I rescue my da," Charles said adamantly.

"A good son of Scotland the lad is," the bowyer said with a tear in his eye. "Defends his da and country."

"You have seen a man fitting his da's description pass this way?" Bryce asked, not wanting to linger too long, especially if the smithy wore eyes and ears for the king.

"Didn't see him myself, but I know someone who did," the bowyer said. "Elsa, a widow who has a croft not far from here. Many pass her way, and some seek shelter at her place for a night or two. She's a good, generous woman, and you'll probably take an instant liking to her, as most do. Tell her that William the bowyer sent you."

Bryce thanked him, then bartered fairly for the bow and arrows the lad had chosen, the old man refusing to take more than a fair share, insisting any extra Bryce had go to Elsa.

Not to place the bowyer in jeopardy, Bryce returned to the smithy to finish their conversation, sending Charles off with less valuable trinkets to purchase food and another warning to hold his tongue.

The lad took the trinkets though Bryce doubted he took the warning seriously.

Bryce directed the conversation in a way that could still possibly reward him with information but not reveal his true purpose.

"Heard the king's soldiers are collecting recruits willing or not to serve the king. Afraid my wife's brother may be among them," Bryce said, and gave a quick description of his brother Trey, knowing full well he was home recovering from nearly being killed by the king's soldiers.

The smithy shook his head.

"What's the best path to take to avoid the soldiers?" Bryce asked, knowing he would take the opposite of whatever the smithy suggested.

His directions were interrupted by a ruckus, and the smithy smiled and shook his head.

"Your lad is a fearless one. The soldiers would scoop him up fast enough."

Bryce didn't care for his comment and swerved around to see Charles locked in battle with a lad at least two sizes larger than he. Blood was already dripping from his mouth, and there was a welt beneath his eye that no doubt would encircle the whole eye soon enough.

As much as he knew the lad had to learn to defend himself, he just couldn't watch him take a beating. He silently cursed himself for feeling the need to rescue him once again. What would he do when he had a son of his own? He couldn't fight his battles for him. But then Charles seemed to come from frailer stock. His own son was sure to be a Highlander warrior just like him. But for now, his honor didn't allow for the weak to go unprotected.

Bryce worried that he wouldn't reach the lad before he suffered a few more blows from his opponent's meaty fist. Shock had him stopping in his tracks when suddenly Charles got in a sharp jab to his adversary's nose. The startled lad raised a cupped hand to it, and, in seconds, blood filled the hand and spilled over the sides.

The big lad's eyes turned wide while his face turned pure white, and, in the next second, his knees buckled, and he collapsed in a faint to the ground.

Charles picked up his bow and flung his cache of arrows over his shoulder. His foe was barely regaining consciousness as the lad stepped over him, and said, "Got what you deserved for trying to steal my bow." And with a strut of victory, he walked over to Bryce.

"You were lucky the lad had no stomach for blood," Bryce said, "or he would still be pounding on you."

"Luck had nothing to do with it," Charles said, and walked past Bryce, leaving him to catch up.

Bryce had the lad by the arm in no time and gave him a good shake as they left the village. "Disrespect me again, and it's my hand you'll be feeling to that scrawny backside of yours. Were you taught no manners?"

Charles bristled, though acquiesced. "I meant no disrespect. And manners I have—" He paused a moment and looked Bryce straight in the eye. "When called for."

Bryce was caught by the determination on the lad's face, and, for a moment, by his soft features beneath all the grime and spots of blood. There was not a single hard angle or line. It was as if delicate hands had sculpted his gentle texture.

He shook his head and released the lad's arm. Bryce didn't know what to make of him. The lad puzzled him. He was intelligent for one so young and inexperienced, though that could be attributed to his father's roving adventures. The lad surely had seen more than most, who never knew more than the place of their birth. Still, there was something about the lad that had Bryce wondering. He didn't know what it was, but something was there. Something he should know but couldn't quite grasp.

Before the lad moved away from him, he grabbed his chin, regretting his quick action when Charles winced. He hadn't meant to cause him pain. He just wanted to make certain his wounds were minor.

"The lip isn't split bad, but the eye is already bruising," Bryce said, taking a look at his injuries. "Your foe landed a good blow to your ribs. Does it pain you?" His hand fell away from the lad's chin, ready to examine his ribs, when Charles jumped back out of his reach, the cringe of pain on his face giving him his answer.

"Let me have a look at those ribs," Bryce demanded, his hand shooting out and catching hold of the lad's tunic.

"Not now," Charles said. "Please, we need to hurry to Elsa's house and see what I can learn about my da."

"You could be hurt badly," Bryce said with concern.

"Nothing's damaged, just bruised that's all."

"I'll take your word for it for now, but when we reach the croft, I'll have a look for myself."

The lad didn't protest; nor did he agree. He simply turned and walked off.

It took nearly an hour's walk to reach Elsa's croft, an hour where very little conversation was exchanged, and only one brief stop made. Bryce heard no complaint from the lad—he hadn't expected to. Charles was anxious to reach the croft and speak with someone who possibly could provide information about his da.

The croft was visible just over a rise and, on approach, appeared well maintained, not an easy task for a widow all alone. Her fields were tilled, ready for planting, and her kitchen garden was partially in bloom. Freshly washed clothes hung from tree branches, and a most delicious aroma had Bryce's mouth watering the closer he got.

A woman thick in size, though not in height, stepped out of the cottage, her smile warm and welcoming. Her gray hair was piled atop her head, and, as she watched their approach, she fought with several stubborn strands that refused to join the captured mass of curls. Her cheeks were flushed, her lips rosy, and her sharp blue eyes sparkled with a youthfulness that had long passed.

"I hope you're both hungry," she said in way of greeting. "I've got a stew cooking and bread baking."

"That's generous of you," Bryce said, "though William the bowyer did say you were the charitable sort."

"William is a dear friend and knows that those in need find their way here and offer to help me in return for my generosity. It is the way of things in the Highlands, is it not?"

"Aye, that it is," Bryce said. "And what is it that I can do for you, Elsa."

She was about to answer when her smile faltered, and she stepped to the side of Bryce. "What have we here?"

"Charles scuffled with a lad twice his size," Bryce said.

"And won I did," Charles said.

Elsa shook her head and looked to Bryce. "I'll tend Charles's wounds and you . . ."

"Forgive me, I should have introduced myself. I'm Bryce."

"Well, Bryce, I think some nice trout would be good with my stew. You'll find what you need on the side of the cottage by my garden, and a small loch is but a short distance beyond that grove to the west."

Bryce couldn't refuse the woman though he would much prefer not to leave the lad alone with her. With Charles's loose tongue, he was certain to garner information, and some of it could prove useful to Bryce. Not that he worried the lad wouldn't share it with him; he seemed honest enough. It's just that he wanted to hear it for himself to make certain he didn't miss anything.

He didn't have a choice, though; he'd have to trust the lad.

"Trout sounds tasty to me," Charles said.

"I'm sure Bryce will catch us some good ones," Elsa said, and reached out to slip her arm around Charles, "while I tend to you."

"I'll have a word with the lad first," Bryce said.

The strength of his command had Elsa nodding and retreating to wait by the door. Bryce stepped closer to Charles. "I need to know all you learn whether you think it important or not."

"I know we are on a dual mission. And I will not fail to relate all I learn."

"It is good to know you are a trustworthy lad and that I can depend on you," Bryce said. "And when I return, I'll have a look at those ribs. I want to see for myself that you incurred no serious injury."

He turned before Charles could argue with him and sent a smile to Elsa. "I thank you for tending the lad and will return with a fine catch of trout."

Elsa smiled and waved as Bryce disappeared around

the side of the house. Then she waved the lad over. "Come, Charles, we'll see about your wounds."

The lad hurried to her side.

She slipped her arm around him and gave a hug. "I'll fix you a nice brew, and we can talk. I would surely love to hear why a pretty lassie such as yourself is disguised as a lad; though more so, I'd like to know why the Highlander warrior doesn't realize it."

Chapter 5

Charlotte wasn't sure if she should be relieved or worried that Elsa saw through her ruse. It made it simpler that she had. It would be so much easier to tend her injuries, especially her ribs, which had been aching terribly. But could she trust the woman to keep her secret?

"I can see the worry in your lovely eyes," Elsa said, once inside the cottage. "I have no reason to tell the Highlander something he should see for himself though I am curious."

Curiosity Charlotte understood. Her da had taught her that it helped in gaining knowledge, and so he had encouraged her inquisitiveness.

"Sit," Elsa said, pointing to one of the four chairs at a well-worn table. "Share only what you're comfortable sharing."

Charlotte appreciated the woman's understanding and the brew that Elsa prepared for her before seeing to her wounds. She saw no reason not to share her whole story. After all, she was here to learn if the woman had seen her da and knew any more about his whereabouts.

Elsa finished with the wounds on the girl's face just as Charlotte finished her story.

"I have seen this man you have described."

"Where? When? How did he look?" Charlotte asked, anxiously, though she had hundreds more questions.

"About a week ago," Elsa said.

Charlotte clamped her eyes shut in disappointment. With a week's having passed, her father could be a distance from here by now. She opened her eyes, wiping away the dampness. "Tell me all you remember, please."

Elsa patted her hand. "Your father, though thin, appeared fit enough. His posture was strong, and he kept his chin up as though demonstrating to all his courage."

"That's my father." Charlotte smiled, relieved that it seemed he was well and keeping his determination strong. It made her wonder if he remained resolved because he knew she was coming for him.

"He was with three other prisoners, the lot of them tethered together and the king's soldiers more alert and guarded than I have ever seen them," Elsa said. "The soldiers were taking food from baskets of those passing through to the village Tine. I myself had baked two loaves of bread to bring to Joslyn, a new mother whose babe I helped birth."

"The soldiers took it from you?"

"Nay," Elsa said with a smile and shake of her head. "I know their tactics well, and my bundle of rags looked nothing more than that."

"Do you know where they were taking my da?" Charlotte asked.

"Gossip was more speculation than anything though I gleaned some information that may prove important from Old John. He's a man in the village Tine few pay attention to, stooped and battered by age and battle and thought not right in the mind. He says there is a secret place where the king's soldiers take prisoners, and they are never seen again."

A chill raced through Charlotte. "He didn't know its location?"

"I wasn't sure. How would he know of its existence if it was so secret—"

"Unless he'd been there himself," Charlotte finished. Encouraged by the news, she gave a slight jump and cringed, grabbing at her ribs.

"Let me have a look," Elsa offered.

Charlotte nodded. "Thank you. Having you tend my ribs would help me greatly."

Elsa helped her remove her vest and lift her tunic and shirt, and as she stripped the cloth that bound Charlotte's small breasts, she asked, "How so?"

"Bryce insists that he examine my ribs to see how severe the damage."

Elsa chuckled. "My, oh my, would he be in for a shock."

Charlotte laughed, then winced as Elsa gently touched the bruise beneath her right breast and asked her a few questions. "Seems like nothing more than a good bruise that will heal in time."

"Good," Charlotte said, relieved, as she raised her hands for Elsa to wrap the cloth around her breasts. "Will you tell Bryce that so he doesn't insist on seeing for himself?"

"Aye, I will." Elsa shook her head. "But I don't see how you're going to keep your secret from him for long.

He does not appear a dumb man. And for the moment, he sees what you want him to see. But I fear that will not continue for long. The truth might be better coming from you rather than having him discover it on his own."

"He trusts the lad . . ." Charlotte sighed, letting her words trail off along with her worry.

"You fear he will not trust the woman?"

"I tricked him, and he might not take kindly to that."

"He might understand why. A young woman alone is more prone to danger than an audacious lad."

"Though, would he favor an audacious woman?"

"It is his favor you want?" Elsa asked with a kindly smile.

"Nay. Nay, I meant trust, would he trust an audacious woman."

Elsa gave a comforting pat to the girl's arm before helping her into her tunic. "He is a handsome Highlander for sure. I imagine many a woman lost her heart"—she gave a wink—"and even more to him."

"I have no time for such thoughts, and, besides, he would find no interest in a scrawny woman who is forever curious, chatty, and strong in opinion."

"Perhaps," Elsa said, "or perhaps it is the type of woman he needs."

Elsa insisted Charlotte sit in the chair by the fire and rest while she busied herself with preparations for supper. Charlotte had offered her help, but Elsa would not hear of it. She was adamant about Charlotte resting to help heal her bruises.

Realizing that opposing the amiable woman was futile, she surrendered and curled in the wooden chair softened by a bulky blanket and pillow. It was like sinking into thick bedding, and she soon found her eyes much too heavy to keep open.

Her final thoughts were a bit chaotic as she drifted off to sleep, jumping from worries over her father to worries over Bryce's discovering her secret.

"Charlotte! Charlotte!"

"Da! Da!" Charlotte called out, frantic that she could hear yet not see him. She could barely see anything through the thickening mist.

"Help me, Charlotte. Help me."

She tried desperately to fight her way through the mist, but it surrounded her and held her firm.

"I'll find you, Da," she cried out. "I'll find you."

Charlotte bolted awake, jumping out of the chair and straight into Bryce's arms. The solid strength and warmth of him had her throwing her thin arms around his neck and holding on tightly. She needed to infuse herself not only with his courage, but the comfort his potent body offered.

It took only a moment for her to realize her mistake. She supposedly was a lad. Whatever was she doing hugging the large Highlander? She jumped back away from him, her bottom landing in the chair. The absence of his warm body left her chilled, and she wished she could return to his warmth.

He was hunched down in front of the chair, appearing a bit startled and glaring at her oddly. And why not? Flinging herself at him for comfort when she supposedly was a bold lad who could fend for himself hardly helped her disguise.

Then it dawned on her. Elsa had scrubbed her face clean when she had tended her wounds. The grimy lad's face was gone; with her mask removed, had she revealed her true self? Could he see that she was a young woman?

He gave his head a shake almost as if he was denying his own thoughts.

"Bad dream," Charlotte snapped, in an effort to misdirect his musings.

"You called out for your da," he said.

His eyes roamed over her face as he spoke, and she wished she had the capacity to know what he was thinking. Having no such power, she needed to keep his thoughts on anything other than her sparkling-clean face. And no doubt it did sparkle. Her father had always commented that she was at her prettiest when her face had been recently scrubbed. She had always graciously accepted his compliments, of which there were many, which was why she didn't pay much heed to them.

Now she wondered if there truly had been some validity to them.

"My da is waiting for me. He knows I'm coming for him," she said anxiously, though not as much for her da's precarious situation but for what could be her own.

"You miss him, don't you?"

He had just presented her with the perfect excuse for hugging him. "I do," she said, and let her head drop forward. "He hugged me when I needed it and sometimes when I didn't."

That was the truth of it, for her father had always been demonstrative with her, and she missed his warm, loving hugs. She had always felt good afterwards. Unlike now, an empty ache paining her. The big Highlander had felt better than she had ever imagined he could. And she wouldn't mind wrapping herself around him again.

She jumped, her eyes turning wide when he rested his hand over hers. His tone was gentle and sent warmth rushing through her, settling in her stomach with a flutter.

"I understand, Charles. And while I am not your da, I am your friend. And friends hug."

Charlotte almost launched herself into his arms. She wanted to feel the strength of his muscles wrap around her and, for a moment, feel safe and protected.

She quickly dismissed the dangerous thought and tossed her chin up. "I don't need no hugs."

Bryce smiled. "We all need hugs on occasion."

Charlotte didn't respond; she sat quietly, trying to contain the pain that radiated across her ribs. All of her sudden movements must have disturbed her injury, and she was suffering the results.

"Are you all right, Charles?" Bryce asked with concern. "You have gone pale."

Charlotte saw no point in lying. "My side hurts, but Elsa says I have no broken ribs."

"Perhaps I should have a look—"

"No," Charlotte said more vehemently than intended, and foolishly yanked back away from him. The sudden jerk sent an horrific pain shooting through her. She grew hot, her sight turned foggy, and she had no doubt a faint was about to claim her.

She didn't know why she did it, instinct or fear, but before she surrendered to the darkness, she reached out to Bryce. Charles slumped in his arms just as Bryce reached for him.

"Here now, I'll see to the poor lad," Elsa said, hurrying to Bryce's side.

"No," Bryce said, and scooped the limp lad up into his arms and stood.

"The bed," Elsa said, pointing to the narrow bed in the corner of the room.

Bryce carried Charles over to it, thinking how the lad barely weighed a pittance. Why, there was not a single thick muscle to him. He laid the lad down after Elsa pulled the wool blanket back.

Before Elsa could cover him, Bryce reached for the hem of the lad's shirt, ready to pull it up and examine the wound for himself.

Elsa grabbed his hand. "I bound the bruised ribs. It's best you do not disturb the wrapping."

Bryce ran his hand across the lad's ribs, felt the binding, and nodded. "It should help."

"Yes, and it should stay on for a while."

"I'll see that it does," Bryce said, "though the lad is a stubborn one."

"You admire him," Elsa said, retrieving a bucket of water and a cloth not far from the bed.

"It's a foolish undertaking he's chosen for one his slim size." Bryce reached out and took the cloth Elsa had dipped and rinsed in the bucket. He sat on the bed beside the prone lad and pressed the wet cloth to his head, his cheeks, and his neck.

"I believe his stubbornness is his strength," Elsa said, and walked quietly away to tend to the meal.

Bryce continued to press the damp cloth to the lad's face, a face that looked far different minus the grime. It was a pretty face and made Bryce wonder if the lad was younger than he had claimed. Add to that his scrawny body and short stature, and it would certainly seem so.

Charles started coming to, a moan drifting off his lips and his brow scrunching as if he fought his way out of the darkness. He certainly was a fighter and not fearful of taking on a larger one than himself.

Bryce did admire Charles. The lad didn't allow his age or lack of physical strength to stop him from attempting to rescue his father. He bravely pursued any and all avenues that might lead to his da. He was a good, trustworthy lad to have at his side, and though he would need extra protecting, Bryce didn't mind. He was finding that he actually enjoyed the lad's company.

Charles's eyes fluttered open and remained wide once they settled on Bryce.

"I fainted," Charles said. "I felt the faint coming on, but I couldn't stop it."

"You did the right thing; you reached out to me for help."

"You're a big one. I knew you'd catch me."

Bryce grinned. "And if it were the other way around?"

"I'd catch you and probably go down with you."

Bryce laughed. "True enough, but it's the thought that you would catch me regardless that makes all the difference. You're a true warrior at heart, Charles."

Elsa appeared by the side of the bed. "I assured Bryce that your ribs would heal as long as you kept the binding on."

"There'll be no arguing when it comes to that," Bryce said sternly. "I want to make sure you're well enough to rescue your da."

"For that reason, I'll make sure to keep it on," Charles said.

"Why don't we enjoy the stew while the fish cooks," Elsa suggested.

"I'm starving," Charles said.

Bryce reached out his hand to the lad. "Good. You need some meat on those bones of yours."

Charles's small hand was consumed by Bryce's large one, though it was with a gentle tug that Bryce helped him sit up.

"I'm like my da, small in size."

"That you are, small in stature just like him," Elsa agreed, as they gathered around the table.

"You saw his father?" Bryce asked, and Charles and Elsa shared with him what they had previously discussed.

"Would you know this secret place where the king sends prisoners?" Charles asked.

"I have heard rumors of such a place," Bryce said, "but there is no proof that it truly exists."

"Elsa and I discussed that, and the most logical conclusion would be that if such a place exists, then no one has ever escaped it," Charles said, "except possibly one."

"Tell me." Bryce listened as Charles told him about Old John. "It would appear that our next stop is the village Tine."

It wasn't until they were on the road again, Elsa having sent them off with a goodly amount of food and Bryce having dropped a trinket of solid value in her hand, which she accepted with a joyful smile, that Charles inquired about how this detour would affect Bryce's mission.

"Will you lose time going to the village Tine?" he asked.

"What we learn may just help me," Bryce admitted. "With all that I have garnered about this spy in the king's court, I've wondered if perhaps the king has discovered his ruse and has had him imprisoned. Elsa had spoken about two other men being tethered together. The spy could be one of them."

"The king will surely have him tortured to find out who he spies for." Charles's shoulders slumped. "My father will be tortured as well."

"How could a conjurer suffering torture serve the king?"

Charles's eyes brightened. "You're right. My da would be no good to the king if injured, though"—his shoulders slumped once again—"when it is discovered that my da cannot conjure, the king will surely make him suffer."

"We'll have found your da before then," Bryce assured with a strong pat to the lad's shoulder.

The lad looked up at him. "I am appreciative of your help, and though I do not like being owned, I will serve you well."

Bryce nodded and stopped himself from telling the lad that he was free, that no man was to be owned. But he worried that if the lad knew he was under no obligation to him, he might just decide somewhere along their journey to attempt to rescue his father on his own. And he wouldn't take the chance of that happening. Besides, the lad and his father needed a home, a permanent one, and with the lad obligated to him, it would force father and son to remain with the clan MacAlpin.

He would see the lad protected, whether he wanted it or not.

Chapter 6

Charlotte watched Bryce sleep. They could have reached the village Tine before nightfall, but Bryce had preferred they delay arrival so that they would have the day to explore the village and locate Old John and speak with him. And then they could take their leave, putting distance between them and the village. He didn't want to take the chance and linger too long in one place, and Charlotte had to agree with him. Asking too many questions in regard to the king raised suspicion.

So they bedded down a short distance from the village, enjoyed some of the food Elsa had generously shared, and while Charlotte wished to fall asleep as easily as Bryce had done, she hadn't been able to.

Her thoughts would simply not settle down. While she continued to worry over her father, Bryce crept in now and again. She couldn't seem to stop thinking about the Highlander, a brave man though, still, in a sense, tender. Never had she met one like him before. So wasn't it only natural that he intrigued her?

Her da would certainly agree and encourage her

to pursue her interest, see what she learned. And she would do that, though it wasn't only the Highlander that intrigued. It was how she was beginning to feel around him.

She almost snorted in disgust with even the mere thought that she could possibly find him attractive. She hadn't even known where the foolish thought had come from or when she had first realized it. But there it was; she found the mighty warrior attractive.

She rolled on her back, refusing to lay eyes on him any longer. That he was a fine-looking man was undeniable, but there was no time for her to be having such thoughts. Another time, another place, perhaps she could justify her interest in him, but not now.

Love waits for no one.

It seemed that every time there was a matter that concerned her, her father's teachings would pop up to guide her. But love and attraction were two different things.

It begins with attraction.

Her father enjoyed repeating the story of the first time he had seen her mother and how her beauty had drawn him like a moth to a flame. His appetite had waned, food of no importance to him, and he had stammered, unable to find the right words when he had first spoken to her.

That certainly didn't apply to Charlotte. She ate whatever food was offered, and she had no trouble speaking or voicing her opinion to Bryce. So she supposed she didn't have to worry about being on the precipice of falling in love.

She turned again, this time away from the fire, star-

ing into the darkness. It had been just her and her da
for so long that she could not imagine it any other way,
though . . .

She sighed. She would dream now and again of falling in love, and her da so often had encouraged her to
find love.

She had once asked him how she should do that.

He had scratched his head, then shaken it. "I do not
believe there is a satisfactory answer to that question."

She sighed again and turned around, her backside
toasty and her front needing warmth, a chill having
filled the night. She stilled, caught in the glare of
Bryce's wide-open eyes.

"Are you going to settle down now and sleep?"

"I thought you were asleep."

"Your whining interrupted my slumber."

"I was not whining," she said, though worried that
perhaps her sighs did sound more like whines.

"Then what was it?"

"Yawns," she said, thinking quickly.

Bryce eyed her skeptically. "Could be that your *loud*
yawns are keeping us both awake."

"And what about talking? Doesn't that contribute to
not being able to sleep?"

"You let your mouth run before you think. Not a
wise choice."

"Some things are so obvious they need no thought,"
she said with a smile.

"Your cocky confidence has already gotten you into
an altercation that left you bruised and—"

"Victorious."

"In pain," he corrected.

"That's to be expected when one defends oneself or another," she said, recalling the few altercations she had gotten into over the years, more so in defense of her father than herself.

Bryce went to respond, but Charlotte spoke up first.

"I'm tired, and all your chatter is keeping me awake." With that, she yanked the wool blanket up over her shoulders and shut her eyes. She waited for a reprimand, but none came though sleep came quickly.

Bryce had warned her repeatedly before they entered the village that she was to remain by his side. This time she paid heed to his orders. Neither the village nor the villagers were as well kept as the last one they had visited. Most eyed them suspiciously, and none offered a greeting.

Thankfully, there were no signs of soldiers, but how to find Old John when it didn't appear that anyone would be forthcoming with information was another matter.

"Not a friendly lot," Bryce muttered.

Charlotte recalled the reason Elsa had visited the village. "Elsa had come here to help a woman with a newborn babe." She thought a moment, then smiled. "Joslyn. If we find her and mention Elsa, she will trust us."

"We'll need to approach with cau—"

Charlotte turned and hurried over to a woman, one chubby babe in her arm and another clinging to her worn brown tunic. She spoke with haste to the woman and returned to Bryce's side before he could decide whether to follow or not.

"I found her. Follow me." And again she took off, without waiting for a response.

Bryce caught her by the arm, forcing her to walk at a less hectic pace beside him. "You need to be more cautious in approaching people."

"It stands to reason that if Elsa knows Joslyn due to a birth, then other women in the village know of her as well. Mentioning Elsa's name directly would alleviate any fear and result in an immediate answer. I know I take chances approaching strangers with questions, but what choice do I have if I want to find my da?"

Bryce shook his head. "One minute you sound like a foolish lad and the next like a wise one."

Charlotte almost bit her tongue for failing to keep to the lad's sardonic nature, but she quickly recovered. "Jealous of my wisdom are you?"

Bryce nodded. "There's the foolish one."

There was no more time to spar, the cottage just in front of them.

"I'll see to this," Bryce said, and gently shoved her behind him.

The door opened slowly, and a pretty young woman's head appeared from around it. Joslyn's cautious expression changed as soon as Bryce mentioned Elsa, and they were invited inside. The cottage was sparse though neat and surprisingly clean. A babe slept contentedly in a cradle a safe distance from the hearth. They accepted the hot brew the young woman offered them though graciously declined slices of fresh bread since it appeared it might be the woman's only food.

It didn't take long to learn the general whereabouts of Old John though it came with a warning.

"He talks crazy sometimes and doesn't trust many, so do be careful."

Charlotte wondered what Bryce whispered to the young woman as he pressed something into her hand. She supposed he cautioned her on letting anyone know whatever it was he had given her, but Joslyn appeared far too happy for a warning.

They left the village, following the directions Joslyn had provided, a chore for sure since there were no exact instructions to follow to Old John's secluded lodgings. It was more of a general area she had described.

"You'll do as I say when we find Old John's place," Bryce said.

"Don't I always?" Charlotte asked with a grin.

"You do keep me entertained," Bryce said with a laugh.

They found Old John's place after carefully scrutinizing the area. It was nothing more than a dilapidated shack with far too much debris surrounding it. Then it dawned on her.

"He's built a moat of sorts, a barrier to keep people out," she said.

"He's done a good job. There doesn't even appear to be an entrance."

"Shall we call out and see if he answers?"

"Someone who goes to this extreme to keep people out would already know we're here," Bryce said.

"What do you want from me?" the rough voice asked.

Charlotte jumped and cast anxious glances around her but saw no one.

Bryce remained as he was, not the least bit disturbed by the sudden, phantom voice, and answered, "A bit of your time in exchange for a trinket or two?"

"I need no trinkets."

Charlotte couldn't determine Old John's location. It sounded as if he were beside her and at the same time at a distance.

"Your help then," Bryce asked, "in exchange for mine?"

"How can you help me?" Old John inquired, strangely enough sounding hopeful.

"I can offer you a safe haven," Bryce said.

Old John appeared then, emerging from amongst the trees. He was as Elsa had described, stooped and battered by age and battle. But Charlotte noted something she doubted that many saw, his brown eyes, though framed by wrinkles, were sharp and much too aware for one supposedly crazy. His long, wild gray hair added to his air of madness as did his worn and layered clothing. For some reason though, Charlotte did not think this man as crazy as he led others to believe.

"What safety can you offer me when the king's soldiers are everywhere?"

"The safety of the MacAlpin clan," Bryce said proudly.

Charlotte caught the sudden broadening of Old John's shoulders though he remained stooped over some.

"The soldiers say the MacAlpins are fools; that there is no true king that will take the throne from King Kenneth. If there was, he would have made himself known by now," Old John said, shaking his head. "Why doesn't he make himself known if he isn't a myth? His people need him. They need to know someone fights for them."

"He will step forward when the time is right," Charlotte said. "If you know the myth, then you know it says 'when he meets death on his own, that is when he will ascend the throne.' No doubt meeting death means that he will face King Kenneth, and they will fight to the death. He will be victorious, and Scotland will have her true king."

"But King Kenneth does not fight fair, this I have seen with my own eyes," Old John said. "He will find a way to defeat the true king."

"Never," Charlotte said. "Evil and ignorance cannot conquer goodness and wisdom. The true king is good and wise and strong and courageous. He will defeat King Kenneth and ascend the throne, just as predicted."

"You are so sure," Old John said. "Have you met the true king?"

Charlotte shook her head. "No, but my father believes that his path crossed with his once many years ago. He says the Highlander was a man of keen virtue, kindness, understanding, generous and more courageous than he had ever known."

"And you, Highlander," Old John said, looking to Bryce, "you fight for a man you have never met?"

"If I answer that, it could prove not only dangerous for us all but for the true king himself."

Old John considered his words, then asked, "What do you wish to know?"

Bryce nodded to Charlotte, and she said, "My father has been taken prisoner by the king's soldiers, and we have learned that he may have been taken to a secret prison. A place the king saves for *special* prisoners."

"Forget him. He is lost to you now. There is nothing you can do."

"I will not abandon my da. I will find him and free him."

Old John shook his head. "No one escapes hell."

"You did," Charlotte snapped.

"And I'll not go back there."

"I don't need you to go back. I just need to know where it is," Charlotte said.

Old John suddenly sprang up, stooped no more, making him only a few inches shorter than Bryce. His eyes went wide, and he appeared to sniff the air.

"Others approach, soldiers by the smell of them." He turned wild eyes on Bryce. "They followed you."

He bolted, launching himself over the debris that protected his shack, grabbed a sack from somewhere in the midst of the mess, and took off.

Charlotte and Bryce barely had time to do the same, Old John's actions having been so sudden and fast.

Charlotte ran as fast as her slim legs would carry her, Bryce staying close on her heels. They were not, however, fast enough to keep up with Old John. And try as she might, Charlotte could not match his frantic pace. That was when she realized that Old John was not as old as he led everyone to believe.

She wanted to cry out to him to stop. He held the key to finding her father, and he was slipping away from her. Though she didn't want to, she clamped her mouth shut tightly. If she yelled out to him, she would alert the soldiers to their whereabouts.

It wasn't long before Old John disappeared from view, and though she and Bryce kept running, they never caught up with him. They stopped what seemed like hours later, though doubtfully so, fatigued and out of breath.

"We'll find him," Bryce said after regaining his

breath. "I think he knows much more than he shared."

"It may be too late by then."

"Your father is a wise man. He will find a way to survive until you come for him."

She had to believe that, she had to, or else she would go mad with worry.

Charlotte was about to ask what step they took next when she caught sight of a soldier running toward them, sword drawn. Drawing bow and arrow, she ran at Bryce and, with a hard shove with her shoulder to his gut, knocked him out of the way.

Chapter 7

Bryce couldn't believe his eyes. The lad not only felled the soldier charging at them, but drew another arrow with speed and precision and had it ready for the next soldier who appeared. He felled that one and was prepared for another before Bryce even drew his sword.

"We go now," Bryce ordered. "There's no telling how many follow."

The lad obeyed without question though he kept his bow tight in hand as they rushed through the forest.

After hours of endless running, they finally stopped and found safe shelter behind a cropping of rocks well concealed by a massive growth of bushes.

Silence settled over them, along with gray skies. Bryce watched the lad rub his arms rigorously and curl his knees up to his chest to keep warm. He knew why the lad shivered. It was likely the first time he had ever killed anyone.

"It isn't easy to take a life," Bryce said.

The lad simply stared at him, his eyes wide, his face pale, and his thin body shivering.

"When in the throes of battle or defending oneself, there is no thought to taking a life, it's an instinctive reaction. A warrior does what he must do, to not only protect those who cannot protect themselves but to survive."

The lad continued to stare.

"You not only reacted instinctively, but bravely," Bryce said. "And while I want to reprimand you for foolishly placing yourself in harm's way when you could have simply warned me of the soldier's presence, I cannot. Your quick reaction saved us both, and that is a sure sign of a true warrior."

The lad barely gave a nod and continued to shiver. Bryce knew the lad's reaction was part of a rite of passage for all young warriors. That didn't make it any less difficult for the lad, or for him to see the lad suffer. He might be thin and frail for one his age, but he was brave. He had wisely used his shoulder to ram Bryce out of the way, by no means disabling him, but getting him out of the path of danger and clearing the way to attack.

"You did well, Charles. I'm proud of you."

The lad nodded a bit more strongly this time and, to Bryce's relief, spoke. "Do you think more soldiers follow?"

"I'm not certain, but I was thinking that perhaps they were the only two and that they weren't interested in us," Bryce said, glad to see color slowly returning to the lad's face.

"You think they were looking for Old John?"

"I think the king doesn't want anyone to know where his secret prison is, and since Old John has the information, the king doesn't want him sharing it."

"You may be right. Old John had said that the soldiers followed us, but he never said they were looking for us." Charles shook his head. "You think the soldiers hoped we would find him when they couldn't?"

"It's possible though it seems unlikely that Joslyn would be the only one who knew the approximate whereabouts of Old John. Certainly the soldiers could have persuaded someone to be forthcoming with the information."

"Something is not right," Charles said.

"No it's not," Bryce agreed, worried that perhaps someone had learned about his mission and was actually tracking him. He had placed the lad in enough danger already though he had proven an asset. And the trouble they had confronted so far certainly was helping the lad mature as a warrior.

Charles hung his head, and Bryce knew why.

"We'll find your da, lad," he said confidently.

Charles raised his head, and Bryce was surprised to see that his eyes shone with unshed tears, though not a one fell.

"To find my da, we must find Old John, and seeing how the man sprinted faster than we did, I'd say that he isn't as old and feeble as he wants people to believe. Old John harbors more secrets than just the location of the king's secret prison."

"I was thinking the same myself," Bryce agreed, once again impressed by the lad's awareness and intelligence. It was an odd quality in one so young, and with time, his wisdom would grow even more, making him a distinct asset to the true king.

Hopefully, maturity would help him curtail his quick

tongue though Bryce was beginning to think it was part of the lad's nature. And he had to admire him, for it took courage to speak up, especially during these troubling times.

"However are we going to find Old John now?" Charles asked. "He'll no doubt bury himself somewhere so remote that no one will find him. And, not knowing if other soldiers follow, we can't take a chance of going back and trying to pick up his tracks."

"Right you are, but there are other contacts I am to meet who could possibly turn out to be helpful in finding your father."

"How?"

"The person I search for could very well be in the prison where your father is being held. Perhaps fate brought us together for that very reason."

"Do you believe in fate?" Charles asked.

"Every man has a destiny, and fate connects those who help to fulfill it."

"So we were meant to meet?"

"It would seem so"—Bryce grinned—"though I have no idea what fate was thinking when she threw you in my path."

"Attempting to guess fate's wisdom?" Charles asked, producing a wide grin of his own.

"I shouldn't—"

"But you cannot help it, can you?"

"No, I cannot," Bryce said, his smile remaining strong. "If it's help I need, why send me a skinny lad who doesn't know when to hold his tongue or obey orders?"

"And why would fate send me a big Highlander warrior slow in discovering information."

Bryce glared at the lad. "You're right. Fate had to have been deliriously insane landing you between my legs."

"Not a pretty sight for fate to show me." Charles smirked.

"The lassies don't complain."

"Not a one?"

"Not one," Bryce assured him. "Size and prowess speak for themselves."

"Bragging are you?"

"Stating the truth," Bryce said. "Don't worry; your time will come."

"I'm in no hurry."

Bryce looked at him strangely. "I've never known a young lad who wasn't eager to bed a lassie."

"I'm too busy, too worried about my da to think about anything else," Charles said, annoyed.

Bryce rested his hand on the lad's shoulder. "There is no shame in having a need for a woman even when troubles haunt."

"Are you in need of a woman now?" Charles boldly asked.

Bryce laughed. "A man is in need of a woman every day, lad. It's the way of things."

"So that's what your bit of wisdom meant, enjoy a woman but keep your heart from her?"

"That's right. Love and need are two entirely different things."

"How so?"

Bryce shook his head. "You do ask a lot of questions."

"It's the only way to learn."

"Your da taught you that?"

Charles nodded.

"He never taught you about the differences between love and need?"

"It's always good to get another opinion."

Bryce laughed. "Didn't care for your father's?"

Charles shook his head. "On the contrary, I haven't come close to finding any better than what he has taught me."

"Then it's you who should be teaching me."

"Anytime."

Bryce continued laughing. "You do entertain me, Charles."

"And I don't even try."

They were soon on their way again, Bryce insisting that they put more distance between them and the soldiers, and Charles agreed. It was several hours later, the darkening skies following them though not a drop of rain falling, that they finally stopped.

An old refuge that looked to have once housed animals was where they decided to settle for the night. It provided some shelter if it should rain, which no doubt it would, thunder having been heard in the distance.

A heavy chill claimed the land, along with the night, and Bryce and Charles were glad for the campfire they huddled around while they ate. Conversation was sporadic; both, it seemed, were lost in their thoughts. It wasn't until they settled down for the night that conversation took hold.

"I'm curious," Bryce said. "What did your father teach you about love?"

Charles didn't hesitate. "That it is a precious gift that should always be cherished. And what of you? How do you feel about love?"

"I'm not quite sure. I've been so busy with my missions that I have had no time to consider love. I meet a woman and enjoy her as she does me, and I take my leave. It is the best I can give at the moment. I have no time to worry over another's safety when I am fighting to bring the true king to the throne, a man who will be responsible for the safety and well-being of a country. It would be selfish of me to fall in love now. It would not be fair to the woman or to the king I fight for."

"What if love should find you?"

"I would have to walk away from it," Bryce said. "I have given my word and made a commitment."

"The true king is lucky to have such a loyal warrior."

Bryce ignored the compliment. He was never comfortable with them. He was a Highlander warrior raised on honor and duty, and that would never change.

"We need to find you a woman, Charles," Bryce said. "It's time you know what it feels like to bury yourself deep inside one."

"Does it feel different bedding someone you love?"

"A good reason to bed a few women so you will know for yourself whether it is love or not," Bryce said.

"So you would recognize love because you've bedded so many women?"

Bryce laughed. "I recognize what I want in a wife."

"I forgot. You want a wife who *heeds your word.*"

Bryce gave a sharp nod. "It makes for an easier marriage."

"Doesn't love make for an easier marriage?"

"You talk as if you've already been struck by love," Bryce teased.

"I have not," Charles snapped.

Bryce grinned. "You protest too vehemently. I think there is someone you favor, but perhaps you don't wish to admit it, not even to yourself."

"There is no one," Charles insisted.

Bryce stretched out on his back, folding his arms beneath his head. "Is she pretty? Does she have big bosoms?" He laughed. "Big bosoms are so much fun, as are full, round hips you can latch onto, two good qualities in a woman."

"Enough," Charles snapped. "I favor no one."

Bryce yawned loudly. "We'll get you bedded so that when you return to your special lass, you'll know if it's love."

"There is no special lass," Charles said through gritted teeth, and turned his back on Bryce.

Bryce's trickling laughter soon turned to a soft snore.

Charlotte wanted to punch Bryce, she was so angry. There was absolutely no one special. Of course, she thought he was attractive, but she wasn't the only woman who thought that. She had seen the way women gazed his way when they had entered the villages. She was no different; she was attracted to his fine features and nothing more.

Besides, he made it quite clear what he would look for in a woman when the time was right. She almost snorted with laughter.

When the time was right.

Love would not wait for him; it would punch him in the gut when it was ready, missions or no missions.

She could just picture the woman who would suit his needs, and she certainly didn't fit his requirements. Her bosoms were a mere handful, and she had only a mere curve to her hips. And obedient? This time she snorted with laughter.

It didn't wake him; he was too busy snoring to hear it.

She could never be obedient. Her father had raised her to think freely, and with that knowledge came more freedom, more curiosity, more need to live as she chose.

No laughter sprang from her lips this time though tears misted her eyes. She would never find a man who could accept her unconventional nature. And why did she even bother to concern herself with it now.

Like Bryce, she had a mission, and she would let nothing stop her. And like Bryce, she would not let love get in the way.

She forced her eyes closed and chased her nonsensical thoughts, but try as she might, sleep eluded her.

She made sure not to sigh though her chest weighed heavy with frustration. She didn't want to chance waking Bryce as she had done once before. She didn't need him staring at her, didn't need to be staring at him, didn't need reminding that he was attractive and that she was attracted to him.

Instead, she constantly reminded herself that she was not the kind of woman he would find appealing. And it was good that she was disguised as a lad and would remain so indefinitely around him.

She would not let him know, not now, and hopefully not ever, that she was a woman.

If she did, she feared he would simply laugh at her.

Chapter 8

Charlotte was relieved that the night rain gave way to clear skies. She kept pace with Bryce, eager to once again be on their way. When she had woken this morning, it was to gaze upon a stretching Bryce standing tall over her.

He was a size, so thick and hard with muscles and a face she not only found handsome but telling as well. Having been taught to be observant, she was beginning to realize that Bryce revealed many things with his changing expressions.

When he questioned something, his brow crinkled, when he worried, his soft blue eyes turned a tad darker, when he defended, his features turned menacing, and when he smiled and laughed, he was much too appealing.

She shook her head and forced her thoughts in another direction. Bryce had been right when he had told her that her da would no doubt leave signs that *only* she would recognize. She had to concentrate on what those signs might be. She could already be missing them.

They couldn't be the obvious, a broken tree branch,

a scrap of his garment, or stones in a pattern. No, her father would not choose the obvious for fear of being discovered. He would use something only she would recognize and understand. But what?

She tried to clear her head, but worry over her father's plight wouldn't allow it, and she grew frustrated.

"What's wrong?" Bryce asked as he dropped back a few steps to walk alongside her.

"Nothing," she said though worried that she was moaning or groaning with annoyance and hadn't realized it. It was something she had to remember not to do.

"You're mumbling to yourself."

She had forgotten about that trait. It only surfaced when she was very upset, and she hadn't been visited by it in years. She had to be careful. Not realizing she was doing it, she could very well mumble something she didn't want him to hear.

"Your da again?"

"Me," she said with a thump to her chest. "I'm trying to think what my da would do to leave a trail for me to follow."

"Don't worry. It will come to you," Bryce assured. "And shortly, I will need you alert to our surroundings."

"We're close to our destination?"

Bryce nodded. "It's a place where trading is done but not the fair kind. The warriors there owe no allegiance to clan or country. They sell information to you or on you and would just as quickly slice your throat as smile at you. The women among them are either slaves or whores, so keep your distance, stay close to me and"—he stopped and glared at her—"keep your mouth shut."

She nodded, fear rippling over her and leaving her

skin damp. This was no place for her true gender to be discovered.

Bryce started walking, Charlotte remaining alongside him.

"You'll need to dirty up your face. It's too pretty for a place like this, and they might mistake you for a lassie."

His words shocked her. He thought her face pretty? Her elated feeling soon burst, knowing that it had nothing to do with her being a woman, and she had to respond as a lad, or as Charles would.

"Pretty? And here I thought I was handsome."

Bryce smiled. "There are plenty of women who like pretty rather than handsome. Besides, being distinctly different means we'll never have to compete over a woman."

"Lucky for you, being I'd emerge the victor all the time."

Bryce shook his head. "Don't tempt me to prove you wrong, and enough of useless boasting from an inexperienced lad."

"Another thing the lassies might find appealing."

"I have to agree," Bryce said though not begrudgingly. "Some women love to initiate the young lads."

"So they would be wanting me instead of you, an old, overused lover."

"A handsome, seasoned lover," Bryce corrected with a smug grin, "which *many* women desire."

Charles scratched his head. "I don't know about that. Why would a young lassie want an old, overused lover?" She stretched her arms out and grinned, "When she can have a lad, pure, innocent, untouched, and belonging to her and her alone."

"You have a lot to learn."

"Maybe I've already learned, and you're the one needing lessons."

Bryce shook his head yet again. "Keeping your mouth shut starts now."

Charlotte laughed and nodded.

Charlotte knew that beyond the line of trees must lie their destination, Bryce's expression having turned hard and more menacing than she had ever seen it.

"Behind me," he ordered sternly. "And stay there."

She obeyed, and when they cleared the trees, she was relieved that his body shielded her. The small village was not unlike any other and surprisingly better kept than most, but it was the warriors themselves who gave one pause. Every one of them bore scars of heavy battle. And they were large, many almost equal to Bryce in size and width.

The women she did see, only two, kept their heads down and eyes averted.

Bryce stopped in front of an older man, his long hair gray and his many facial scars faded by the years.

"I look for Culth," Bryce said. "I have business with him."

A large man stepped out of the cottage, directly behind the old warrior, adjusting the leather strap that ran across his massive chest. A thick scar cut a path from his forehead down over his right eye to end at his jaw. His hair was black as night and his stance guarded. He was followed by one very large, black dog, with one scarred, floppy ear. He walked close to Culth, but to Charlotte it looked more from fear than respect for his master.

"I'm Culth."

The dog moved away from him to sniff toward Bryce and around him.

"I was told you are the one to see for information."

"For a price," Culth said, his eyes intent on the dog. "What are you hiding?"

"I hide nothing," Bryce said adamantly.

"Then let's have a look." Culth stepped around Bryce.

Bryce was quick to stretch his arm out protectively in front of Charlotte, and she prayed he'd keep it there. The warrior Culth frightened the wits out of her though not the dog, though he was massive. He looked sad to her, and her heart went out to him for what he must suffer at his master's hand.

"What do you want to know?" Culth asked.

His dark eyes followed along every part of her, lingering in intimate places and making her skin crawl. It was as if he could see beneath her garments and knew her secret. And strangely enough, the dog sensed his sinister thoughts, planting himself in front of Charlotte like a shield.

"Odin!" Culth snapped angrily, and the big dog crawled over to him. He gave him a kick and ordered him to stay.

"I have heard of a secret prison," Bryce said, moving to take the place of Odin and shield Charlotte. "And, with this land being yours, you would know if it is located around these parts."

"What's it worth to you?"

"What do you want?"

"The lassie," Culth said with a lift of his chin toward Charlotte.

"He's a lad," Bryce corrected.

Culth chortled, and so did the old warrior.

Charlotte nearly choked with fear. How did he know?

"That's my price," Culth said.

"Then I'll not be doing business with you," Bryce said, and slowly began to back away, his arm remaining protectively in front of Charlotte.

"I'll take that fine sword instead," Culth said.

"I'll not barter my sword."

"Then what will you barter?" Culth asked.

"Information," Bryce offered.

Culth laughed. "And what can you tell me that I don't already know?"

"Soldiers will dispense with you and your village soon enough, unless, of course, you wish to fight for King Kenneth."

Culth snorted. "If the king pays us, we fight."

"The king's wealth is gone."

It was obvious by the sudden widening of Culth's eyes that he hadn't been aware of that bit of news.

"How do you know this?" Culth asked.

"It's the information that's important, not where I obtained it. So if you were expecting payment from the king, it won't be forthcoming."

Culth nodded. "For that information, I will tell you that I too have heard of this secret prison, but if it does exist, it is not here on my land."

Disappointment settled in the pit of Charlotte's stomach, or perhaps it was fear. Their bargaining was done. Would the mercenary leader let them leave unscathed?

"We'll be going now," Bryce said.

"Be careful, *friend*," Culth said. "The woods hold much danger."

Charlotte's breathing was labored not from rushing, Bryce making certain they did not run but walked out of the village, but from the fear that choked like a hand at her throat.

"We need to put distance between us and this place," Bryce said once the woods swallowed them.

"He'll come after us?" Charlotte asked, though knew it wasn't them Culth was coming for; he was coming for her.

"Culth all but made it clear when he alluded to the danger in the woods." Bryce glanced around as if expecting Culth's men to already be surrounding them. He pointed in a direction. "Run and run fast."

They took off, Bryce remaining behind Charlotte and she running faster than she ever thought she possibly could. She worried that Culth would send too many of his men to defend against. And Bryce would certainly go down fighting, as would she, though no doubt Culth had ordered her to be taken alive.

Her anger built, for she knew if she did not survive to rescue her father, he would suffer and perish. But could she survive being taken captive by Culth, and, worse, could she survive knowing that Bryce had died protecting her?

Just the thought sent a chill through her and pained her heart. So strange since she barely knew the man, and yet there was something about him she favored. They had to survive not only to rescue her da but for her to discover what it was she was beginning to feel for the mighty Highlander warrior.

The attack came within a short time of their departure. Men rained down from the trees and rushed out from behind bushes. How they had gotten ahead of Bryce and her she didn't know, but she did react.

Her arrows were drawn in quick succession, felling three men, and still more came. Soon she would be without arrows though she had the dirk in her boot. But was she any match for the size of these mercenaries?

Bryce fought like a madman, keeping the men at a great enough distance for her to take aim and shoot. But he was one against many. It wasn't long before her cache was empty, and as soon as it was, she reached for her dirk.

With a solid prayer on her lips, she rushed forward with a battle roar.

She had always been limber rolling, tumbling, climbing like the squirrels that scampered about, her da used to say. And she used that skill now to avoid and attack her opponents. Time seemed to stand still. She didn't know how long she fought, nor was she aware of the blood that covered her. She simply knew that she must survive, must get to her da, and must not let Bryce die because of her.

Her anger fueled her strength and determination, and when no more men came at her, she turned, for a moment, thinking they had won, and saw Bryce battling three men. She ran and launched herself at them.

She landed with a solid thud on one's back, her dirk going deep, and he sunk like deadweight to the ground. She jumped up, and as she did, a fist connected with her face and sent her reeling backward.

The last thing she saw and heard before blackness

claimed her was a bloodcurdling yell from Bryce as he swung his sword at the two remaining men.

Bryce ran to Charles; blood covered him everywhere, and for a moment, he froze, fearing the lad dead. When he caught the rise and fall of his chest, Bryce scooped him up in his arms, and while it would have been easier to run with the lad flung over his shoulder, he couldn't take the chance. If his chest was injured, it would only worsen it.

So he ran, cuddling the lad against him, praying that the blood that covered him was not his. He needed to get as far away from Culth's land as possible. It would take time for the mercenary to discover that his men had failed, giving Bryce time to put good distance between them.

Bryce kept a quick pace, for how long he couldn't say, though when he realized that dusk was not far off, he knew he had been traveling for hours. There was a rise up ahead that Bryce decided would be wise for him to climb, then settle for the night on the other side.

If Culth did send more men, though he doubted he would, they would not attempt the hill at night.

Dusk was near to falling when he finally found a spot near the bank of a stream to camp for the night. He gently laid Charles on the ground, worried that he had yet to wake from that vicious blow he had taken to his jaw and it looked like his cheek as well since the bruise was spreading up along it.

He wanted to hurry and examine the lad to see how bad his injures were, but he knew he needed to get a campfire going first. He got one going soon enough, then wasted no time in ripping a strip of cloth from the sack of food and soaking and rinsing it in the stream before he once again scooped the lad up in his arms.

Bryce gently wiped away the blood and grime on the lad's face, the only color to it being the bruises, the fresh one darkening by the minute.

Bryce understood why Culth had mistaken the lad for a lassie. Charles was pretty, much too pretty for a lad. And being small and thin didn't help him any.

Once done with his face, Bryce decided it would be easier to simply slice the lad's tunic and shirt down the front to further examine him for wounds. He could always fashion a plaid around the lad with the extra blanket he carried.

He laid the lad on the ground near the fire, spread his vest apart, and sliced down the center of the blood-soaked tunic and shirt. He felt a catch to his heart when he saw the cloth that bound the lad's chest, to help heal his ribs, was soaked with blood. And he feared what he would discover beneath.

Bryce carefully sliced the cloth with his dirk, worried over disturbing a wound and hurting the lad.

When the lad groaned, he feared the worst. Had he disturbed a wound and brought him awake with the pain of it?

Bryce rushed to spread the cloth apart and see what damage had been done.

His hands stilled, his heart slammed in his chest, and his eyes turned wide.

Chapter 9

Charlotte felt a chill run through her as she fought her way out of the darkness. She struggled hard, knowing it was a matter of grave importance that she escape. And though it was an effort, a painful one, she wouldn't give up.

One last push had her eyes popping open, and it took her a moment to remember, to grasp hold of her surroundings and realize that Bryce was staring wide-eyed at her bare chest.

"You're a woman?" he asked incredulously.

"Being you're staring at my breasts, I would say you have your answer."

Bryce glared down at her. "Lad or lassie, your tongue remains biting. And you have much explaining to do."

Charlotte went to shove his hands away, but he stopped her.

"I want to make sure you have no wounds that need tending," he said, and took the wet cloth and began wiping the blood from her chest and midriff.

"I can do—" She winced as she tried to sit up.

"Don't dare move," he ordered. "I need to rinse the cloth, and you better be as you are when I return."

Charlotte watched him hurry to the stream, and she struggled to sit up, but a wave of dizziness gripped her, and she had no choice but to lie back.

"This may chill you," he said as he gently ran the wet cloth over her chest.

She shivered, and he reached for a blanket and covered her from her waist to toes.

"It doesn't look as if you were injured, except for the blow you took to your face. It's bruising and will probably grow worse."

Charlotte relaxed under his tender ministrations. She was much too sore and tired to worry that she was bare-chested in front of him. Sooner or later, he would have discovered her secret, even with her determination to keep it from him. What had she expected would happen when she rescued her da, and he claimed her, his daughter?

It was better Bryce knew who he dealt with, or at least she tried to convince herself it was.

He pulled her shirt and tunic together when he finished, tucked the blanket up over her chest, and sat staring at her.

Charlotte wondered why he wasn't raging at her for lying to him. Was the sight of her partly naked so disturbing that it had left him speechless? And then, suddenly, she was assaulted with memories of the battle, and fear raced over her.

"What are we doing camping here with a fire when we should be running from Culth's men?" she demanded.

"I have run for hours. We are far from his land."

"He'll send more men."

"I doubt it," Bryce said. "He took a chance with an attack close to home, but he won't want to risk sending more men and leaving his village vulnerable. Not now, not when he's learned that the king has no way to pay him for his services, though he may demand them anyway."

"He'll stay and protect what he has."

Bryce nodded. "Enough of Culth; tell me of your charade."

"Isn't it obvious?" she said

"A young woman traveling on her own is more vulnerable than a young lad," he answered.

"Precisely," Charlotte said. "Countless dangers await a young woman on her own, but a young lad"— she shook her head—"he can travel without incident."

"What is your name?"

"Charlotte."

Bryce rubbed at his chin while staring at her. She wondered what he thought now that he knew her a woman. She had her answer soon enough.

"This changes everything. I will take you home to my family, where you will be safe while I continue on my mission and search for your father."

"Not likely," she spat.

"You have no choice," he said sternly.

That he would even think that he could decide her actions infuriated her. "You'll not tell me what I can and cannot do."

"I can, and I will," he said, and stood.

Charlotte sat up slowly, not chancing any sudden movements. "We had an agreement."

"That was when I thought you a lad."

"What difference does it make?"

He laughed. "All the difference, and we can start with Culth since he obviously was more observant than I. It will be a constant battle to keep you safe when my time and worry needs attention elsewhere."

"As long as I remain disguised as a lad, there should be no problem," she argued.

He laughed again and pounded his chest. "I'll know you're a woman."

"And why would that make a difference?"

He raked his fingers through his dark hair. "Because it will."

"That is no answer."

"It is answer enough."

"Not for me," she said. "The only difference from before is that you know I am a woman. Nothing else about me has changed. As you said yourself, my tongue is still biting. I still have skill with a bow, and I still need to find my da."

Bryce stretched his hands out, as if he were about ready to strangle her, then pulled them back to rest fisted at his sides. "It isn't that simple."

"Why? And don't say it's because I'm a woman one more time. Since we met, I have proven over and over again my ability to defend and protect. I helped you in battle—"

"And suffered for it."

"That chance comes with battle."

"Not when you're a woman," Bryce said.

"I can do this," she insisted, and stood much too suddenly. A foolish action. A wave of dizziness hit so hard, she could barely see.

"Charlotte?" Bryce said, stepping toward her.

She reached out to him, his name the last word on her lips before she fell into his arms in a dead faint.

Bryce cradled Charlotte's limp body. He didn't know what else to do. He was at a loss. At a loss as how to tell her that he simply could not let a wee bit of a woman like her remain with him to search for her father. It was just too dangerous. And at a loss as to why he felt that he would miss her being alongside him.

He couldn't believe his eyes when he had cut open the cloth and found two handful-sized breasts staring at him, the nipples hard little buds. That he was shocked wasn't as bad as feeling a fool for not having recognized the lad as a woman.

Worse was that the sight of her bare breasts had aroused him. The thought had struck him fast and hard. He groaned, for he had nearly grown hard. But it wasn't only her near nakedness that had caused arousal. It was the thought that a petite woman like her was so brave and determined that she lived, acted, and fought like a lad to save the one she loved. And she had done the same for him in battle. She had lunged herself at a mercenary far larger than herself, her only thought to help him.

She was unlike any woman he had ever known. She had been unlike any lad he had ever known as well, but somehow he had gotten to admire and like the lad. And had found he thoroughly enjoyed his company.

Would he find Charlotte's company just as pleasing? But then, as she had said, she was still who she had always been.

He carried her, an effortless task, to the edge of the stream, and dipped his hand in the cold water to sprinkle on her face. As she began to respond, he moved back beside the fire though he kept her tucked in his arms.

He tried to keep the split tunic and shirt closed, but they stubbornly refused, and so her breasts remained partially exposed. Not that he minded, the sight of them was more than pleasing, and while he did favor large bosoms, he found he rather liked her small size. The whole of her would fit nicely in his hand.

Her eyes fluttered open. "I fainted."

"That you did."

"You caught me."

"I'm always catching you one way or another."

"Aye, you are," she said with a smile that soon changed to a wince.

"The bruise," Bryce said, fury racing through him that she had suffered such a blow while protecting him.

Her hand reached up to rest against his cheek. "Please, Bryce, don't send me away. I need to find my da."

A rush of heat ran through him even though her hand was cool against his skin. And he knew he would not deny her request. Not just because she asked but because he didn't want to send her away. God help him, he wanted her with him. As foolish a decision as it was, he simply could not help it. He wanted her with him.

He wasn't sure why, which irritated him all the more. But make no mistake, he would find out. He had to if he intended to keep his sanity.

"You'll obey my orders," he said.

"Don't I always?"

Her grin was small and impish. And he couldn't help but chortle. "You'll not go getting into trouble? You'll listen to my every word?"

"Haven't I been doing that?" she asked innocently. "Even when you spoke of bedding a woman, you had my rapt attention."

He cringed, recalling some of their conversations meant for men's ears alone. Then, suddenly, his brow knotted. "Is there someone who waits for you? Why didn't he come with you and help you search for your father?"

"What do you mean?"

"During one of our conversations you made it seem that there was someone you favored, someone special. Is there?" he snapped, trying to make sense of why the thought irritated him.

"There is no one," she snapped back. "Never has been and never will be until I find my da."

Bryce's brow relaxed. "That's a good choice when there is a mission to consider."

"And we both have missions."

"Our first priority," he said, once again being reminded of the urgency of his duty.

"Working together, I'm sure we can succeed."

"You know it will continue to be dangerous," Bryce advised.

"All the more reason for me to continue," Charlotte insisted. "What I have gone through is probably nothing to what my father is suffering."

"I owe your father a debt of gratitude."

"Whatever for?"

Bryce smiled. "I am grateful he allowed his daughter to gain talent in areas most women show no interest in."

Charlotte returned the smile. "My father had little choice in the matter."

"How did I know that was probably the way of it?" Bryce said. "Did you badger your father until he agreed?"

Her smile faded. "My father always protected me even if it meant suffering at the hands of some brute. It didn't take me long to realize that I could bear it no more. I could not watch my da ridiculed or tormented at the hands of ignorant men to save me. And so I learned about weapons and how to defend myself."

"And defended your father as well."

"There were times . . ."

Bryce didn't force her to finish. When the time came, if she wanted to tell him, she would, though now he had a better understanding of why her determination was so strong to find her father. She had been her father's champion for so long that she felt he could not survive without her. But a man as learned as Idris Semple no doubt could endure on his wit alone.

"You can let go of me now," Charlotte said, bringing an end to the silence their musings had fostered. "I'm feeling better."

"Are you sure?" Bryce asked, fearful she would once again pale and collapse in a dead faint.

"I am tired more than anything and could use some sleep."

"I can agree with that. My legs burn like the devil from the endless running."

"How long did you run?" she asked.

"I rid us of the last two men quick enough, then scooped you up and ran until just before dusk."

"Carrying me the whole time?" she asked incredulously.

"What else was I to do with you?" he said with a laugh. "Besides, you're a wee bit of a thing, weighing hardly anything. And you fit quite comfortably in my arms, so it was no chore."

"I'm grateful—"

"As am I," Bryce said, placing her on the ground by the campfire and covering her with the wool blanket. "If you hadn't attacked when you did, I might have lost my life."

"We make a good pair," she said, smiling.

"An odd pair, me being big and you being so small, but aye, a good pair."

"I can hold my own," Charlotte quickly defended.

"So can I," Bryce said, and stretched out on the opposite side of the campfire.

Nothing more was said, and soon, Bryce heard a gentle snore coming from Charlotte. He was glad. Sleep would help her regain her strength.

He glanced up at the night sky; clouds blotted the moon and stars. He hoped the rain would wait. Rain always made travel more difficult. And it was already difficult without it and would probably grow even more so now that he knew Charles was Charlotte.

If he had been wise, he would have insisted on taking her to the safety of his family. He would not have taken no for an answer. He would have forced her to do as he ordered, but he hadn't.

They both needed to attend to their missions, and

she understood that more than anyone. Though he had always been accustomed to traveling mostly alone on his mission, it felt good to have someone along who not only felt as he did, but bore the same determination.

That was probably the reason he had felt such a strong kinship to the lad. They shared common resolve. Lad or lassie, though, that resolve had not changed. They would see this through together. And then?

That was a good question.

He had bartered for the lad, and the lad owed him. But he certainly couldn't own Charlotte. It just wouldn't be right.

He cringed, just thinking what his mother would say. Being of strong opinion, she no doubt would give him a good tongue-lashing, perhaps even a slap on the arm or head. And then announce that Charlotte was free to do as she pleased—join the MacAlpin clan or take her leave, the choice was hers.

Why did that disturb him?

Chapter 10

Charlotte woke before Bryce the next morning, unusual, though he had run miles with her in his arms, which had to have left him exhausted. The thought that he had done that to save the lad warmed her heart. Bryce was a caring man more so than he wanted anyone to know.

One would never think of him that way with just one glance. He was so big and wide and imposing. He was a Highlander of legends, the type that battled to the bloody end, the one who would fight for the less fortunate, the one who would give his life for Scotland.

He was a man of courage, gentleness, and honor—a true Highlander warrior.

A tear tickled her eye. She was lucky to have met him, lucky that he had helped her and continued to help her, and ever so relieved that he wasn't sending her away.

Not that she would have gone quietly; she certainly would have protested. But that wasn't necessary. She would stay with him and be glad of it. After all, who would look after him?

He stirred with a groan and stretched awake, his glance settling on her as he opened his eyes.

"Sleep well?"

"I did," she said. "And you?"

He stretched his arms above his head and rolled his head from side to side. "Better than I expected."

"Our plans for today?"

"You don't waste time."

"There is no time to be wasting," she said, trying to avoid staring at the thick muscles that grew taut in his arms.

"Right you are," he agreed, and sat up, stretching his arms once again above his head, his chest spreading wide.

Lord forgive her, but she couldn't take her eyes off the way his muscles rippled over his arms. Whatever was the matter with her? Was it because she no longer needed to react as a lad that she allowed herself the pleasures of a woman?

She bolted up, annoyed with herself, then realized he was glaring at her almost as badly as she had at him. It took her a moment to recognize why, and when she did, color rushed to stain her cheeks bright red.

Charlotte quickly yanked her torn tunic together, holding it tightly so that her breasts didn't lie exposed.

Bryce, realizing his reaction, hurried to his feet and muttered something about finding them breakfast and disappeared into the woods.

She was glad for the privacy, though frustrated, for at that moment she knew that all had changed between them. She was now a female in his eyes, and he would treat her differently. She didn't know if she liked that.

She wasn't only used to, but she was comfortable with the camaraderie they had shared. She felt when he believed her a lad, he spoke freely about everything. She didn't think that would be the way of it any longer. And the thought troubled her.

She busied herself in wrapping the plaid around her so that it almost resembled the way Bryce wore his plaid. She would need to find other garments as soon as possible, but for now it would have to do.

Once done, she went to the stream to wash her face and run wet fingers through her cropped hair.

She would need to take a knife to it soon enough to keep it short and keep her looking like a lad. She couldn't allow a hint of her female nature from peeking through. She raked her raggedly cut, honey-colored strands with wet fingers.

Her hair had once been a pride of hers, long and silky to the touch. Yet the day she chopped it off, she hadn't thought twice. Her disguise was a necessary step in helping to find her father.

"Someday," she whispered, staring into the water at the reflection of the woman who no longer resembled her. Her hair was short, a bruise covered her eye, right cheek, and jaw and weariness plagued her soft blue eyes.

"You'll not take a knife to your hair again."

Charlotte turned with a start to see Bryce standing a few feet behind her.

"I will if it's necessary," she argued, and stood with a careful bounce.

"It won't be necessary."

"You can't be sure."

"Don't argue with me," he said.

"I will when it is a foolish thing you argue over."

"You are just as obstinate as the lad."

"You expected me to be different?" She laughed. "I am who I am."

Bryce grumbled beneath his breath before he turned and walked toward the campfire, and Charlotte was almost certain she had seen him smile.

She did, however, have no trouble hearing him say, "Take a knife to your hair, and it will be my hand you feel on your bare bottom."

"Not likely," she snapped back, which stopped him dead.

He turned and glared at her.

"You'll not be intimidating me with that look," she said, and gave a defiant toss of her chin. "I'm not afraid of you."

He walked over to her, but she stood her ground. His size alone could intimidate; add to that a knotted brow and piercing dark eyes, and there wouldn't be many who wouldn't scurry away in fear.

She wasn't one of them. She had gotten to know him over the last few days, and she knew that he would not hurt her. Threaten and bluster, yes, but never would the mighty Highlander do her harm.

He stopped right in front of her; another step, and their bodies would be touching. He peered down at her. "You might want to reconsider that."

Charlotte shook her head. "No, I won't be changing my mind. I'm not afraid of you."

"Why?"

"I know you won't hurt me."

"You're so sure?"

"That I am," she said.

He grabbed her so fast beneath the arms and swung her up to dangle in front of his face that she got dizzy. Pain followed, her head having snapped from the unexpected jolt, shooting a stabbing pain along her bruise from jaw to cheek.

It was intense, and she tried to fight against it though doubted she would have any luck.

"Charlotte," Bryce said anxiously. "What's wrong?"

"I think—"was all she got out before everything turned dark and her body went limp.

Bryce cradled her wilted body in his arms and cursed himself for his foolish actions. He should have never grabbed her the way he had. She had been through enough, suffered enough, and here he was adding to her burden.

Once again, like last evening, he went to the stream and dipped his hand in the cool water, then sprinkled some on her pale face, carefully avoiding the bruise that had darkened considerably overnight. When she didn't immediately respond, he silently cursed his stupidity once again. It had disturbed him when he had seen the way she had sadly fingered her hair. He could just imagine how glorious the three distinct shades had looked when long and tumbling in waves down her back.

He hadn't wanted her to suffer the indignation of chopping it short once again. Besides, he wanted to see her hair long, feel the silky strands for himself and . . .

He shook his head, letting his foolish musings

wander off. He had no cause to be thinking such thoughts. Charlotte and he were on a mission together, and nothing else mattered but that.

With Charlotte tucked safely in his arms, he returned to the campfire, where he had fish cooking. He continued to cradle her in his arms as he settled them near the fire. She roused not long after.

"Something smells good," she said as soon as her eyes fully opened.

Bryce laughed. "Only you would think about food instead of asking what happened."

"I know what happened," she said. "I fainted yet again." She shook her head. "I only faint around you."

"I have that effect on you, do I?"

Charlotte chuckled softly. "It would seem that way."

"Are you all right?" Bryce asked with concern.

"I am," she said. "It was the jolt that set my bruise to paining."

"I am sorry," he apologized, feeling terrible for being the cause of her suffering.

"That's all right," she said. "My da says I can test the patience of the Lord himself."

"I think I agree with him."

Charlotte laughed again. "I believe you and my da would get along well."

"I look forward to meeting him."

Charlotte's smile vanished. "Do you think we will find him?"

"I have no doubt we will," he said. "We're both determined."

She nodded and rested her head against his chest, as if it were something she had done many times before.

"I would suggest we stay here and allow you to rest a day—"

She was out of his arms in a blink. "We cannot lose one day, and I am fine. Besides, more soldiers could be tracking us. We must keep moving." She laid her hands on her slim hips and sent him a grin. "Unless you're too fatigued to go on, old man."

He shook his head and chuckled though it lacked a smile. "If it's a challenge you're looking for, be careful. This old man of seven-and-twenty years has more stamina than a lassie barely familiar with life."

She sauntered around the campfire. "Dare you say now?" She shook her head. "I'd not be spewing claims that have no substance. What match can you be for the likes of a lassie of only eight-and-ten years? No doubt I'll be tucking you into bed soon enough."

Bryce's brow narrowed. "It wouldn't be you who would do the tucking, my love."

His implication not only flushed her cheeks bright red but set a vivid vision racing in her head; Bryce and her completely naked in bed and him tucking himself deep inside her. Damn if it didn't heat her body and set it tingling.

Bryce stepped closer and leaned down to whisper in her ear. "See, I do intimidate you."

Charlotte went to respond, but his whispered warning came quicker.

"Open that mouth, and I'll kiss it closed."

She stilled, part of her not daring to test his threat and another part aching for him to do so. She kept quiet, reason winning out over desire this time. Finding her father was far more important than her craving to be kissed, though she wondered how long before that craving insisted on being satisfied.

Bryce stepped away from her. "Let's eat and be on our way. I got fish enough for the both of us. And we won't be having another meal until we settle for the night."

It didn't take them long to eat and be on their way, barely a word spoken between them until well on their journey.

"Do you have a destination in mind?" Charlotte finally asked from behind him.

Bryce didn't turn. He kept the quick pace he had set earlier upon departure. "An area more than a destination; we'll need to find those desperate to barter.

"Desperate for what?"

"Freedom from tyranny," Bryce said.

"And how do you propose to give them this freedom?"

"By welcoming them into my clan, where they will be safe until the true king takes the throne."

"You gather an army for the true king," she said.

"I gather those willing to fight for their freedom."

"Joslyn at the village Tine. You offered her a home with your clan. That's why her smile was so wide."

Bryce nodded and was about to answer when he heard a noise.

A sudden scurrying sound halted both of them, and Bryce reached his hand back, grabbed Charlotte, and yanked her next to him. He motioned for her to remain close to him, and they cautiously continued on.

They traveled an hour or so longer when they heard the sound again, only this time the sound didn't stop. It grew louder and louder as it got closer, and closer and closer. Before Bryce could warn Charlotte to run, a large animal burst through the trees and lunged itself at Charlotte.

Bryce was quick to draw his sword, but Charlotte screamed, "Stop."

He realized then that the animal was a big dog that was relentlessly licking Charlotte's face. And she was laughing and wincing when he slobbered his tongue over her bruised cheek.

"You know this huge mutt?" Bryce asked.

"Don't you?" she said between the dog's licks.

"*Odin*," Bryce said sharply, and the dog stopped and plopped down beside Charlotte.

She sat up and put her arm around the dog and gave him a hug. "You escaped Culth, didn't you?"

He answered with a big lick.

Bryce shook his head. "He cannot come with us."

Charlotte jumped up, and Odin growled as if he understood.

"He most certainly is coming with us," she said with a pat to the dog's head. "He's tracked us all this way, and we will not leave him on his own."

"He could have been followed or sent to find us," Bryce argued, though he wondered if it was a useless argument. The two already looked a pair, and he didn't think there would be a chance of separating them.

"He's much too fast. No one would ever be able to match his pace," she insisted. "Besides, you saw how Culth—" Odin growled at the mention of his name. "See, that answers it for you. He escaped the barbaric fool."

Odin barked, as if in agreement.

"So this large mutt suddenly decided to pick a new master and chose you?"

Charlotte rubbed behind the dog's ear. "He was waiting for the right person to give his heart to."

Bryce shook his head, annoyed that she threw his own words back at him.

"He's here, and he's ours," Charlotte insisted. "There's nothing that can be done about it." She turned and started walking, Odin following beside her.

Bryce kept shaking his head. The damn dog was bigger than she when he stood on his hind legs. And what did she mean by *ours*. The dog obviously looked to her as his master, and he and Charlotte were certainly not a pair, so how could the dog be *ours*?

He continued shaking his head as he walked, wondering over it.

Chapter 11

They came upon a small croft. An older woman, Glenna, lived there alone, and though age and toil marred her face and body, there was a vibrancy to her that was remarkable. In exchange for some repairs to her roof and door, the old woman agreed to give them food staples and repair Charlotte's shirt and tunic.

Bryce remained busy outside tending to the few chores. Odin was forced to remain with him, though not without a whining protest when Charlotte followed the old woman into the house, where she set to work, and she and Charlotte began to talk.

"Have you been traveling long?" Glenna asked, working her bone needle skillfully through the linen cloth.

Charlotte was surprised that the woman hadn't commented on her gender when she slipped off the torn tunic. She hadn't been the least bit taken aback. Had she known upon first meeting Charlotte? She hadn't seen any reason to hide her gender. The woman certainly appeared harmless enough though she had yet to ascertain who Glenna favored, the reigning king or the true king. But that wouldn't be hard to find out.

"A week or more," Charlotte said, wrapping the plaid around her. "That's how long I've been searching for my da." She didn't say anything about Bryce's mission as it was not for her to say. She watched closely the old woman's reactions as she continued on. "The soldiers took my da from our home, and I've since discovered that it's possible he's being held in the king's secret prison."

Glenna nodded, not showing an ounce of indignation or protesting the king's actions. That worried Charlotte. Could the woman be a sympathizer of the present king?

"Have you heard of such a place?" Charlotte cautiously asked.

"I pay no heed to petty gossip."

Did that mean Glenna had heard something but wouldn't share it? Charlotte wasn't sure how next to approach the matter. If Glenna was a king sympathizer, any more Charlotte said could prove to be dangerous for her and Bryce.

"It keeps one safer to mind one's tongue," Glenna said. "Though a man I once met told me that his daughter would not be able to hold hers if her life depended on it."

Charlotte's eyes popped wide. Her da had forever said that to her. A ray of hope set her heart pounding in her chest.

"Gave the man water one day when he passed through here," Glenna continued. "He looked tired and skinny, though his eyes were sharp as was his wit. He told me that he'd be seeing his daughter soon since she knew the way to him."

She knew the way to him.

Her father had sent her a message. What she didn't understand was why Glenna just didn't come right out and tell her. It made Charlotte wonder if the old woman feared speaking plainly, feared someone's hearing what she had to say.

It hit Charlotte like an unexpected punch. They weren't alone. Someone else was here with them, but where? The one-room cottage wasn't large, though there were dark corners and a bed to hide under. But who would hide?

She noticed that Glenna had stopped stitching even though she wasn't finished, the same moment she heard Odin whining and scratching at the door. Too late Charlotte realized why. Someone stood behind her.

Bravely, Charlotte said, "Is it friend or foe that hides here?"

"That would depend on which king you follow."

Charlotte went to turn, but the man behind her was fast and yanked her out of the chair, pressing her back hard against him, his lean arm settling tightly against her throat and nearly choking the breath from her.

"Damn it, Odin," Bryce yelled from outside. "You can't go in."

Charlotte wished Bryce understood that the dog was trying to warn him. In the next second, she discovered that he well understood Odin. The door burst open, startling all the occupants so badly that they all jumped, giving Charlotte enough time to stomp hard on her captive's foot and turn, swinging, connecting with the tip of the man's jaw, and sending him stumbling back.

Odin reached the culprit before Bryce and pinned

him to the ground with his large paws and a snarling growl that had the soldier trembling with fear. Bryce ordered the dog away and, with one hand, hoisted the soldier up.

Charlotte was shocked to see that it was a young skinny lad in soldier dress. He looked no more than four-and-ten years if that. His face was pale; his right eye bruised around the edge, and his lower lip was split and swollen.

He tried to fight Bryce, but it was a senseless struggle. The Highlander obviously had him well in hand. It didn't take long before his useless efforts ceased, and when they did, Bryce dragged him to a chair at the table and forced him to sit.

"What goes on here?" Bryce demanded of either Glenna or the soldier, his imposing glance darting from one to the other.

Glenna sighed. "He tells me he's escaped the king's soldiers, doesn't want to be one of them." She shook her head. "But how do I trust he tells me the truth? The king could be planting his soldiers to spy on us poor folk."

Bryce planted his hands flat on the table beside the soldier, who had yet to look at anyone. When he finally raised his head, tears shone in his eyes.

"I never wanted to be a soldier. The king's men came one day to my family's croft and dragged me off, telling me it was my duty to serve the king." He shook his head, and a tear fell. "I'm a farmer like my father. I want nothing to do with soldiering."

"It's a good story, but is it the truth?" Glenna said with a snort.

"What say you?" Bryce asked, looking to Charlotte.

"You see more than most. Do you think he favors us with truth or tale?"

Charlotte had first sympathized with the young soldier, being so bruised and battered, but the more she watched him as he spoke, the more she questioned. His hands showed no signs of farmer's toil. He did, however, bear the hardened mark on his finger of one who often used a bow. And it troubled her that he hadn't referred to his father as "da," a more endearing term than "father." Once being forced to sit at the table, he had kept his eyes averted from the three of them, and she wondered if he had taken time to conjure tears.

"Some things don't fit," she found herself saying.

Bryce's hand clamped hard on the soldier's shoulder.

"I thought the same myself," Glenna said, "him showing up here suddenly, weeping, yet forcing his way into my home."

"I was frightened, afraid you'd turn me away and not help," the soldier said, more tears filling his eyes, ready to spill over. "I don't want to be a soldier for King Kenneth; I want to be a soldier for the true king."

Charlotte realized his mistake as soon as the words left his mouth, and, surprisingly, Odin did as well. He moved closer, snarling at the soldier.

"You just sealed your fate," Bryce said.

The soldier's tears suddenly dried, and he paled, as if he knew that his ruse had been discovered; still, he didn't surrender. "How? I did nothing wrong. I want to fight for the true king."

Charlotte went to stand next to Bryce, her small shoulder brushing his thick-muscled arm. Odin moved to Bryce's other side, his snarling never ceasing.

"I am at the true king's service," the young soldier claimed much too anxiously.

Bryce laughed and looked to Charlotte. "He's like you, speaking before he thinks."

Charlotte punched Bryce in the arm though her small fist suffered for it, not that she let him see it, though he did grin; damn him.

"You want to tell him why his own words sealed his fate?" Bryce asked Charlotte, but it was Glenna who answered.

"The true king has no soldiers fight for him. Only those who wish to be free fight with him," Glenna said, her shoulders squaring and her chin high. "He is one of us, and we fight together."

Charlotte wanted to hug the woman, for her words echoed her father's sentiments and for a moment it was almost as if he were there with her. And in that moment she missed her da terribly. Without realizing it, she leaned against Bryce, and, without hesitation, he slipped his arm around her and held her tight.

How his arms could feel so familiar or so comfortable she didn't know and didn't care. She only knew that he made her feel safe and protected, and there was where she wanted to be.

"The truth," Bryce demanded of the soldier.

"I speak the truth," the soldier insisted.

"Then why did you grab the wee one here and nearly choke her?" Bryce asked.

Charlotte saw the soldier turn pale, and she quickly glanced up at Bryce. If he hadn't been holding her tight, she would have stepped away from him; his look was murderous.

"I-I-" the soldier fumbled, trying to explain.

"The truth comes easily when you're an honorable man," Bryce said, and the soldier paled to a ghostly white.

"They made me do it; I didn't want to," the soldier cried, tears streaming down his reddening cheeks. "I told them I wasn't good at lying, but they wouldn't listen. It was either obey or die."

"I don't trust him," Glenna said. "He lies and keeps lying. I tell you, King Kenneth is planting spies. He's desperate to find the true king. He knows the people are against him and that the true king will soon claim the throne."

Charlotte caught the sudden flare of the soldier's nostrils. He was angry with Glenna's words. He dropped his head to the table, and she assumed it was to hide his reaction, but then she noticed his hand inch down along his leg.

She shoved Bryce away from her just as the soldier flew up from the chair, dirk in hand, and lunged toward them. The tip caught her arm and would have sliced down the length of it, if it wasn't for Odin, who launched himself at the soldier. The force of his big body knocked the soldier to the ground.

Charlotte's eyes turned wide when she saw the soldier raise his dirk against Odin. She didn't think; she reacted. She was suddenly lifted in the air, tucked under Bryce's arm while he, with little effort, relieved the soldier of the weapon.

Odin stood guard over him as Bryce planted Charlotte in a chair, stuck his face in hers, and said, "Stay here; don't dare move." He looked over at Glenna, who had moved a safe distance away from the melee. "See to her arm."

The woman nodded and walked over to Charlotte.

Charlotte paid her no heed, her attention remaining on Bryce.

With a sharp command, he ordered Odin off the soldier. The dog obeyed immediately, and as soon as he did, Bryce grabbed the soldier by his tunic and tossed him toward the door. The soldier scurried to his feet, but Bryce grabbed him again before he could right himself.

Blood dripped from the various bite marks to his arms and near his throat. No doubt Odin could easily have killed him, but it seemed that the large dog had simply taunted him.

Bryce dragged him to the door.

The soldier's dark eyes glared with anger. "You will suffer for your foolishness."

Bryce yanked the soldier right up to his face. "You want to face me in battle like an honorable man, I'm ready, unlike your king, who kills without thought or reason."

He yanked open the door and tossed the soldier outside. He followed, Odin at his side and the soldier hurrying to get to his feet and lunging at Bryce.

Bryce deflected the young soldier with a simple shove.

He scrambled to his feet and rushed at Bryce again, and again Bryce shoved him aside. The third time he launched himself at Bryce with a fury and with a hard shove, the soldier stumbled and, unable to right himself, he fell . . . on the blade of the axe sticking out of a log.

"The fool was in a hurry to rush to his death," Glenna spat from the open door.

Bryce turned around. "A pity he gives his life for one who cares naught for him. King Kenneth would have seen him dead for failing his mission."

"The king is that quick to kill one of his own?" Charlotte asked with a wince, as Glenna returned to tending her wound.

Bryce walked over to her and hunkered down on his haunches beside her. "The king will not be so quick to kill your da, not when he wants something from him. There is time to save him."

He knew her worry well; she had voiced it enough times. And yet he patiently reminded her each time. She almost reached out to rest her hand on his face, so grateful was she to have him with her. And amazed at how only moments before his eyes looked ready to kill while now they were tender and filled with concern.

"Is the wound deep?" Bryce asked of Glenna.

"A scratch, nothing more," she said. "It's a brave one she is, defending you and the dog."

"More foolish than brave," Bryce said, and glared at Charlotte, their faces so close that she spotted the tiniest of scars along the top of his cheek, not at all visible otherwise.

"Aren't we all when we protect those we care for?" Glenna said.

Bryce and Charlotte quickly turned away from each other, Odin taking the opportunity to squeeze between them and rest his head on Charlotte's leg.

"That animal sure does love you," Glenna said, winding a cloth around Charlotte's injured arm.

Charlotte caught the hasty glance Bryce shot their way though he quickly avoided her eyes before they could catch his. She wondered what he thought, the look in his eyes foreign to her, though she had thought she was familiar with all his expressions.

"I better see to burying the soldier and getting those chores done," he said. "We'll need to be leaving soon."

"And I have her tunic to finish stitching," Glenna said, cleaning up around Charlotte.

"You," Bryce said, pointing at Charlotte. "Rest!" He shook his head, mumbling as he walked out. "Ribs, cheek, arm, what's next?"

"He favors you," Glenna said with a firm nod.

"We just met."

"As if that makes a difference."

"We don't know each other," Charlotte persisted in protesting.

"Give it time." Glenna smiled, her full cheeks flushing. "My William did more grumbling and mumbling around me when we first met, until he finally admitted he loved me."

"How long before he told you?" Charlotte asked, curious.

Glenna's grin grew. "Two weeks."

"My da knew he loved my mum as soon as he saw her."

Glenna nodded. "Love grabs hold hard and fast and won't let go. "Look at that dog of yours. He knew he loved you when he first saw you, and now he's yours forever."

Charlotte smiled and rubbed behind Odin's ears. "That's true."

"What of the Highlander? When did you know you loved him?"

"I don't love him." she said indignantly.

"Fighting it are you."

"I told you we barely know each other."

"And you told me that your da knew he loved your mum when first he saw her," Glenna reminded. "Are you like your father?"

In some ways she was; though when it came to love, she had no idea. She certainly found the Highlander appealing though she couldn't say she loved him. She did favor his company. And she certainly didn't care to think of parting ways with him; the thought actually upset her.

"Love will have its way, don't worry over it," Glenna advised.

But how could she not worry over it?

Chapter 12

Bryce was relieved Charlotte's tunic was mended. He didn't need any more distractions, and damned if her breasts hadn't distracted. It annoyed him that he couldn't get them off his mind. And it annoyed him even more that he found them appealing. He was usually attracted to more busty women, with wider hips, and tall, women more fitting with his own largeness.

Charlotte was nothing more than a wee bit of a thing. He had lifted her and tucked her under his arm without an ounce of difficulty, and carrying her as far as he had certainly had proven no chore. She just wasn't the type of woman he favored, yet she forever haunted his thoughts.

He kept walking, not looking back at her following, having left Glenna's croft over an hour ago. He had yet to warn her, and most strongly, that she was never to jeopardize her life for his again. It had been the second time she had done so, pushing him out of the way in the cottage as she had done when the soldiers had attacked. And while she had prevented him from harm and even possible death, she had also taken the risk of bringing both on herself.

The thought sent an icy shiver racing through him. He didn't want her suffering because of him. But more importantly, he didn't want anything happening to her. Or that dumb dog that had attached himself to her as well. They made a fine pair, they did, he being nearly as big as she was little. He did like that Odin protected her though she did the same for him. Now he would most certainly worry about her putting herself in danger for not only him but the dog too.

"Something troubling you?" Charlotte asked.

Bryce stopped and turned. "You take too many risks." He shook his head again. That wasn't what he wanted to say. He rubbed his chin. Damn, but he didn't know what he wanted to say, how to say it, or why he even should bother saying it since no doubt she would pay him no heed.

She stared at him but said nothing. Odin did the same.

"Did you hear me?" He nearly shouted though he caught himself before he did and, instead, kept his tone stern. "You'll not be taking any more risks with your life to save mine."

"Why?"

The one word shot from her mouth with the speed and force of the arrows she let loose from her bow, and when it hit, Bryce was almost compelled to take a step back. Instead, he took a firm step toward her.

Charlotte raised her hand, stopping him. "Say no more. I understand. It embarrasses you that a woman saves you from harm."

He raised his hands, then stopped himself from reaching out and grabbing her. He noticed then that Odin was snarling at him.

"Quiet!" he commanded, snapping a pointed finger at the animal. The dog instantly obeyed. Bryce glared at Charlotte. "Why can't you obey like he does?"

"Odin's afraid of you; I'm not."

"One of these days—"

"You will better understand the way of things," she said, and stepped around him to continue walking.

He walked up alongside her. "I understand well enough. It is you who do not understand."

"I understood the situation in the cottage most clearly," she said, stopping and turning to face him. "You"—she poked him hard in the chest—"would have suffered a dirk to your back if I had not pushed you out of the way. If your pride was hurt, I'm sorry, but I reacted as I did to save you from harm though now I'm wondering if it was worth it."

This time Bryce grabbed her and yanked her up, feet dangling, to plant her face in front of his. "You will not put yourself in harm's way because of me."

"Would you do the same for me?" she asked softly.

Her breath was warm and sweet against his face and her words tender. His glance settled on her lips, slim, pink, and moist—perfect for kissing.

The thought startled him, and it took a moment for him to regain his senses, and when he did, he grew annoyed. "You need to ask me that? Of course I would do the same. I would never let any harm befall you."

"Then why would I not do the same for you?"

"You're a woman."

"And why does that matter?" she asked.

He set her down on her feet. "You are a strange one."

"I am unlike most," she agreed. "Is that bad? To be different? To be who I am?"

He felt a twinge of envy. He had been raised for one purpose, to help the true king. His life had consisted of constant lessons so that he could grow into the mighty warrior that he was. There had been little time for anything else; though he and his brothers had made time for folly, more time was spent on being who they were—warriors.

"I am a warrior," he answered, as if it explained it all.

"You are so much more than that."

"How do you know?" he demanded, as if he needed her to define it for him.

"I see it in your expressions and in your actions. You can't hide who you are."

Her acute observations startled him though they shouldn't have. She had the remarkable skill of seeing people for who they truly were, though, with him and his brothers, that could prove dangerous.

And though he shouldn't have, he asked. "Who am I?"

"I will tell you what my father told me when I asked him that very same question," she said. "That is not for me to say but for you to know, for if you need to ask it, then you have yet to discover who you are."

"I know who I am," Bryce protested.

"Then why did you ask me?"

He couldn't admit that he wanted to know what she thought of him, so how, then, did he answer in a way that wasn't as revealing? "Your observations are keen."

"And you are curious as to what I think," she said with a chuckle.

"Your wit is too sharp at times," he said, annoyed. He should have known better than to think she wouldn't catch on to what he was up to.

"You knew this of me, but you asked anyway."

"More the fool me."

"Curious fools discover," she said.

"More of your father's wisdom?"

"Wisdom helps find answers." She continued walking, catching up with Odin, who had gotten bored and gone sniffing on ahead.

Bryce shook his head, trying to make sense of what she meant. He had been foolish for asking and foolish for being curious as to what she thought of him. It struck him then. Had he been looking at her to help him define himself more than looking for what she thought of him?

He was a warrior. What other defining did he need? He did what he had to do. What he had been raised to do. He had no doubt about who he was, yet he had asked her.

He pushed the annoying thought from his mind and marched forward. He'd waste no more time on such nonsense. He was foolish for having asked her in the first place.

She stopped abruptly and turned, forcing him to halt sharply.

"If the king planted one soldier amongst the peasants, then no doubt he planted more. We will need to be cautious."

"I thought the same myself," he said.

"And I didn't have a chance to tell you that my da passed Glenna's way—"

"Were the others with him?"

"It sounded as if he was alone, though I think Glenna purposely spoke that way, not wanting to alert the soldier that she spoke of the prisoners." Charlotte grinned. "But more importantly, my da sent me a message."

Bryce smiled. "He has no doubt you're searching for him."

"And no doubt he leaves a message where and when he can."

"What were his words?" Bryce asked.

"My da told her about his daughter who would not be able to hold her tongue if her life depended on it—"

Bryce burst out laughing, and through each burst, he said, "I can't wait to meet your da."

"Now that I have entertained you, do you want to hear the message?"

Bryce settled his laughing though a chuckle let loose here and there.

" 'She knew the way to him' is what my da said."

"You understand what he means?"

"I have thought on it, and I remember. When I was young, I wandered off away from my da and got lost in the woods. He found me huddled and crying beneath a large spruce. It was then he said he would teach me so that I would always know the way to him."

"What did he teach you?"

"To follow signs, as I thought, but it's what signs he's using that I can't seem to spot," she said frustrated. "I looked around Glenna's croft as we were leaving but saw nothing. And I've watched as we've traveled, and still I can see nothing."

"It will come to you."

"But I could be missing it, which means we could be traveling in the wrong direction."

"So far we have managed to keep a good trail," Bryce said. "And your father leaves messages when he can, and soon you will spot a marker that he has left. We do well, and we will continue to do well."

Charlotte smiled, and a tingle wound its way around and through Bryce. He had seen her smile so many times before, but this time was different. This time he saw that she was pretty. Not beautiful, like some women, but simply pretty. And it was impossible to stop staring at her. There was softness to her features, a gentleness that belied her nature. It was as though he was seeing someone different, someone he had yet to meet.

"You're right," she said.

She startled him out of his musings, and he wasn't quite sure what he was right about.

"My da would agree."

Her da and he would agree. But about what? Try as he might, his mind was too befuddled by her lovely face to think straight, and it frustrated him. He had to keep his mind clear. There was his mission, besides finding her da, that needed his attention.

That was it, finding her da, doing well, on the right trail. He almost sighed, his thoughts finally clearing.

They started walking, Odin keeping close to Charlotte, though sniffing ahead now and again.

"Where to now?" Charlotte asked.

"Another village about a day away that might prove helpful, and there are crofts along the way. Perhaps your da will have left more messages."

"And if not, then we travel in the wrong direction."

"Not so," Bryce said. "Your da may not always have the chance to speak with someone. Remember, he is taking a chance when he does, and having learned something about your da from you, I'd say he also watches and chooses the right people to leave a message with."

"You're right. Da would be watchful and choose whom he felt he could trust," she said, and glanced over at him. "I have been selfish concentrating only on finding my da when your mission must be just as important to you. We have yet to learn anything about it."

"Not true. We did learn there are other men being held captive with your father. Since the group is being taken to the king's secret prison, and from others things I've heard, there is little doubt left that one could very well be the spy. The king probably has plans to torture the poor man and see what he can learn."

"Does this spy know much?"

"I'm not sure. My brothers and I have only recently learned of his existence. He wasn't sent by us."

"Then by who?" Charlotte asked.

Bryce shrugged. "I have no answer to that."

"It might be an answer you want to clarify. I know people have faced danger to help the true king seek the throne, but to spy on the king on one's own?" She shook her head. "That doesn't make sense."

Bryce had thought the same himself when he started on this mission. His clan had had a spy in the king's court, Neil, and he had served them well. He was pulled out when it had gotten too dangerous for him to continue. While there, though, he knew of no other spy, but that didn't mean much since it would have been difficult to trust anyone, and it was better one didn't.

"Could it be a trap?" Charlotte asked. "Perhaps the king allows you to believe a spy exists so that he can capture someone of importance from your clan and discover what he can from him. From the gossip being spread, it seems the king grows ever more desperate."

"Time is drawing close," Bryce admitted. "Soon, the true king will need to reveal himself."

"Perhaps the king hopes to capture him before he can do that, and so he searches for one close to him. It is a thought you should consider and not place yourself in danger for a spy who might not exist."

"But if he does? What then? Do I leave an innocent man who believes in the true king to die?" He grinned down at her. "Besides, I cannot let you go off on your own."

"I can take care of myself."

He laughed. "It isn't you I'm concerned for. It's the ones who come across you."

She laughed along with him, and damn if the soft, tinkling sound didn't wrap around him and send a tingling through him. It didn't rush but crawled along slowly until it consumed every inch of him. Along with it came a heat that stirred and grew uncomfortable.

He knew damn well what he was feeling, but he'd be damned if he'd acknowledge it. There was no way, no way that he would admit it. He'd stamp it down and ignore it and force it away.

He wasn't successful, no matter how hard he tried. His body was in control and refused to obey him, just like Charlotte refused. The thought of her didn't help his predicament. He grew hotter, more uncomfortable. And still he fought against the obvious.

He stubbornly refused to accept what he felt. It wasn't wise of him to accept it. It would only complicate matters more. He had no time for it. Besides, Charlotte wasn't what he wanted in a wife.

Wife?

Where did that come from? He wasn't interested in marrying her. What he was feeling was simply pure lust.

He cringed. Damn it, he had admitted it. Now he was in trouble.

He lusted after Charlotte.

Chapter 13

Charlotte stared at Bryce's back. They had stopped and made camp a couple of hours ago, and as soon as they had eaten some of the food Glenna had packed, Bryce had turned on his side, his back to her, and gone to sleep.

The change in him since he had discovered she was a woman disturbed her. She missed the easy friendship they had shared and the conversations. He didn't talk with her freely the way he once had, and she partly understood why, but she had hoped that he had grown as comfortable with her as she had with him and perhaps–just perhaps–their friendship would not change.

It didn't seem that was the way of it, and she felt a twinge of loss. She draped her arm around Odin, who slept plastered against her. He had snuck in a crawl to plant himself between her and the campfire. Bryce had told her to make him move, but she didn't have the heart, he looked too comfortable. And it was nice to have someone to cuddle against.

She continued staring at Bryce's wide back, frustrated by the situation and not knowing what to do about it. Her father, no doubt, would tell her to let it be, let it resolve itself. Unfortunately, she wasn't very patient.

What bothered her most was that she felt as if she had lost his friendship. There had been camaraderie between Bryce and the lad that she had not only greatly favored but had never known. It had been hard to form a lasting bond with anyone through the years since she and her father never stayed long in one place. And there had been times they lived in remote areas, removed from people. She had grown accustomed to it, but now, having met Bryce, she didn't care to think that he was simply a passing friend. She hoped they could be . . .

She sighed. What did she truly hope they could be? That was the question that haunted her whether she wished to acknowledge it or not. When he had grabbed her and dangled her in front of him, a habit he was making of that, she had thought he would kiss her. She had been surprised she had even realized it, not having had much experience when it came to kisses. But it had been undeniable, she felt it. It was impossible not to, even to someone as naïve as she. And, Lord, did she want him to kiss her. Regrettably, it never came, it lingered between them in limbo—waiting.

She blushed, grateful there was no one to see her cheeks flame red.

"You're mumbling," Bryce said, startling her.

Why couldn't she rid herself of that trait?

"Did I wake you?"

Bryce turned to face her. "No. I haven't been able to sleep."

"Why?"

Charlotte was caught by his blue eyes. Normally soft in color, they were now the deep blue of a turbulent ocean. And she couldn't help but think of him that way, rough and tumbling, pounding to the shore and taking back with it what was in his reach: to protect and shelter.

She realized he hadn't answered. "Does something trouble you?"

He grunted. "Heavy thoughts."

"And I add to them."

"How could you? You're nothing more than a wee one. You could never be a burden."

Nor your lover.

Charlotte flopped on her back, shocked by her own thought. Whatever was wrong with her? How could she even think that? He certainly didn't find her appealing. She was much too *petite* for him. And he too large for her, and that was that.

Or was it?

"That wasn't a mumble, that was a groan," he said. "So what's troubling you?"

"Everything." She sighed, because it was the truth. Her life had been turned upside down so fast that she felt as if she had yet to take a breath. And it had grown more confusing and dangerous since the soldiers had taken her father.

"It seems that way sometimes, doesn't it?" Bryce said, turning to face her.

His gentle tone had her rolling on her side to lay eyes on his strong features. "Lately, it seems that way all the time."

"It is a difficult time, but it will pass."

"You sound so sure."

He grinned. "Working together—your tenacious nature and my patient one—there can be no doubt of it."

"Your patient nature?" she asked with a grin of her own.

"A virtue of mine and one you stretch to the limits."

She laughed. "Not purposely."

"And with no sound reason," he said with a shake of his head. "You simply forge ahead and damn the consequences."

"Confidence."

"Foolhardiness."

"Do you think me a fool?" It was more a challenge than a question.

He didn't answer immediately; he seemed to give it thought.

"You need time to think about it?" she asked, slightly offended.

"Time to explain my thoughts," he said. "You are different from others, and so it is hard sometimes to understand you. I dare say it was much easier when you were the lad Charles. He was someone I understood."

"Why?"

"That word forever spills from your lips."

"I'm curious."

"Another trait to add to tenacious," he said with a laugh.

"You avoid answering me."

"Charles reminded me of myself. I lost my parents when I was young, and it is a pain that never stops aching. I could relate to his need to find his da since

I never had the opportunity. I wished my parents had lived so I could rescue them. I would have done anything to save them just as Charles had been doing."

"Does it make a difference now? Charles and Charlotte are one. Do you not feel the same for me?"

"I feel even more need to help you, as you're a woman," Bryce said.

"It makes no diff—"

He reached around the campfire and pressed a finger to her lips. "It makes a difference to me that you are a woman. I was raised to protect women and those weaker who cannot defend themselves." He pressed his finger harder to her lips. "No protests. I cannot change who I am. I protect, and I will protect you."

Normally, Charlotte would have argued with him, but she found herself understanding, and so made no comment. It pleased her that they had talked, and she had learned more about him. And no doubt he felt the same, yawning along with her as sleep began to creep over them.

"I will always protect you, Charlotte," he said on a yawn once again, and stretched out on his back.

"And I you," she said, turning on her back.

Bryce was snoring lightly in no time, and though Charlotte's eyes grew heavy, she fought sleep. She wanted to linger in the feel of his warm finger pressed so tightly to her lips. She had imagined it a kiss, so solid and yet so alive.

She yawned, kisses were much too often on her mind, and with that thought lingering, she slipped into sleep.

* * *

They were up and on their way at daybreak, the early-morning mist fading as the bright sun claimed the land. It had been too long since Bryce had taken note of a beautiful day. He had been much too busy to take even a moment to think of anything else but his missions.

Why, now, did the loveliness of the morning strike him? He had to admit it was because of Charlotte. Her chatting started with the sunrise, only stopping when she spotted something that caught her attention. She'd run to unearth what had caught her eye, Odin right alongside her, then return to his side to either announce it was nothing or show him a plant and explain its properties to him.

She was trying hard to find any signs her da was leaving along the way, and he empathized with her frustration when something turned out to be nothing. But he admired her tenaciousness. No matter the disappointment, she didn't give up; she persevered.

"St. Bride's plant," she said, joining him once again.

"Roots and all?"

"Once the roots dry, they can be used to make a tasty drink."

"More of your da's knowledge?" he asked with interest.

"Just a small part of my da's vast knowledge."

"I have never known a man who pursued knowledge as his life's purpose," Bryce said.

"It seems odd to me that more don't."

"I truly look forward to speaking with your da. I think there is much I can learn from him."

She stopped abruptly and stared wide-eyed at him;

so did Odin. "Truly? You believe you could learn from him?"

"Why not? He is a learned man."

She shook her head and started walking again. "Most men think my da a fool. He carries no weapons, and yet he possesses the mightiest weapon of all . . . intelligence. I am pleased that you feel as you do. My da will enjoy talking with a man who seeks to learn."

Odin ran up ahead, then stopped suddenly. The two were quick to halt their steps and cast anxious glances around. In seconds, Odin relaxed his stance and scampered back to them.

Charlotte hunched down and hugged the dog, who planted lavish kisses on her. "Good work, Odin. Good work."

A twinge of jealousy struck Bryce, and he grew annoyed with himself. Whatever was the matter with him?

You want to lavish kisses on her.

He spewed a bevy of silent oaths. This was ridiculous. Whenever he had wanted to kiss a woman, he did just that. If he wanted to kiss Charlotte so badly, why didn't he just do it? What was stopping him?

He wished he knew. He wished he understood what made her different from other women he had kissed. And the thought that he believed her different disturbed him even more. Could it be that there was something special about her?

They continued their journey much as before, Charlotte hurrying off to investigate with Odin at her side, only to return to him delighted with found discoveries or disappointed there had been none. All along knowing she searched for clues that would lead her to her da.

The sun was still bright in the sky when they stopped near a stream to rest and satisfy their hunger. Odin no soon as gobbled down the fish that Bryce had caught, his catch more than adequate for the trio, when he was stretched out and was sound asleep.

Bryce and Charlotte continued enjoying their fare.

"We have been lucky so far, but I fear we may head in the wrong direction," Charlotte said, concerned.

"Perhaps it is not luck, but instinct that keeps us on the right course," Bryce said. "Your father could very well be relying on your instinct in finding him. Wasn't his message, *She knew the way to him*? Could your da having been talking about instinct?"

"It's possible, but I don't think that's what he meant."

Odin's head popped up, followed by his body, and he ran in front of Charlotte and Bryce, planting himself in a protective stance and growling.

Bryce was to his feet in seconds, his sword drawn. Charlotte grabbed her bow and readied it.

A young couple with a child no more than four years emerged out of the bushes. The trio looked exhausted and half-starved. The little lad clung to his father's leg, his eyes wide with fear as he looked on Odin.

Odin, sensing they were no threat, sat.

The father stepped forward. "We caught a whiff of your food and wondered if there was any to spare."

Charlotte put her bow aside and waved them forward. "There is plenty. Come join us."

Bryce sheathed his sword and welcomed them. "Yes, do come join us. We have more than enough."

The trio hurried over, the lad keeping his distance

from Odin. They were soon gobbling down the fish as fast as Odin had done, though it was the lad the da and mum fed first before taking any for themselves.

"I'm sorry," the father said. "I have lost my manners. It has been days since we have eaten." He wiped his hand on his dirt-covered garments and extended it to Bryce. "I am Ian, this is my wife Brigit and our son Thane."

Bryce admired the strong set of his handshake. Even though weakened, he demonstrated strength. "I am Bryce and this is . . ." He hesitated, not sure how exactly to introduce Charlotte.

She decided for him. "I'm Charles, and this big dog is Odin, friendlier than he looks."

The little lad giggled.

Odin, hearing his name and the giggles, positioned himself next to Charlotte though he extended his paw to the lad.

The lad shook it and giggled again. When he finished eating almost a whole fish, the lad took to playing with Odin. It was a game of fetch and catch with a stick that they both seemed to enjoy.

"It is good to hear him laugh again and have fun," Brigit said, tearful.

"We lost our farm," Ian said with a resigned painfulness. "The soldiers kept taking and taking until there was not enough to feed my family. And then we heard the soldiers were taking men old and young from their homes to serve the king."

"We had no choice but to leave," Brigit said as if in way of an apology.

Ian shook his head. "We still can't understand what

brought so many soldiers to our area. I believed we were too remote for them to have any interest in us."

Charlotte was quick to ask. "Did the soldiers pass your way with any prisoners?"

"No," Ian said. "We never saw any prisoners. I wondered if perhaps the king made use of the remote area to grow his troops without the true king finding out."

"That's where we go now," Brigit said. "To find safety with the true king's followers."

"We both are followers, and Bryce knows where you can go to be safe," Charlotte said.

Bryce liked that Charlotte didn't hesitate to offer them help, especially with her instincts about people being so keen.

A squeal from the lad had them all turning their heads. Odin was licking the lad's face clean, and the little fellow was delighted.

"Let me show you where to go," Bryce said to Ian, and took a stick from the pile he had collected for firewood and began drawing in the dirt.

The couple was eager to be on their way, happy that they finally had a specific destination to reach. And knowing that Bryce's clan would greet them with open arms only encouraged a speedy journey. Thane didn't want to leave, having made friends with Odin. Charlotte explained that where they went was Odin's home as well, and once the animal returned, Thane would be able to play with him as much as he wanted.

Thane gave Odin a big hug, and the dog gave the lad a sloppy kiss, which delighted the boy. He left with a wave, and called out, "I see you soon, Obin."

Bryce and Charlotte smiled at the way the lad pronounced Odin's name and waved as the trio disappeared into the woods.

"Time to go ourselves," Bryce said.

Charlotte turned to gather her things and went tumbling over Odin, who had circled behind her. Bryce reached out, grabbing hold of her and yanking her up before she could fall.

She landed so close to him that their lips almost touched. Their closeness startled them both for a second. And time seemed to stand still between them, as if each one did not know what to do.

Then Bryce did what he normally would have done with any woman he found attractive. He leaned in, ready to kiss her.

Chapter 14

Bryce's lips had barely touched hers when he suddenly found himself sprawled on the ground, Odin standing in a guarded stance, paws spread out, body down and head low, in front of Charlotte, and snarling.

"Odin!" Charlotte scolded.

The big dog refused to relent.

Bryce got to his feet slowly, dusting dirt off his plaid, then suddenly pointed a finger in Odin's face and warned firmly, "Enough!"

The animal quieted instantly and gave a small whimper though he remained in front of Charlotte.

"Odin must have thought you meant me harm." She shook her head. "He didn't understand that you only meant to—" She took a breath and looked as if she wasn't sure how to continue.

Bryce finished for her. "Kiss you. I meant to kiss you."

"Truly?"

Her bewildered tone confused him. "You didn't realize that was what I intended?"

"I thought it was, but I wondered why."

Bryce scratched his head, then shook it. "You wondered *why* I attempted to kiss you?"

Charlotte nodded. "It's a reasonable thought; after all, you have made it quite clear that I am not the type of woman you are attracted to."

"When did I say that?"

"Big bosoms," she reminded. "You favor big bosoms, and you saw for yourself that I don't have—"

"Enough!" he shouted, this time at Charlotte, though Odin whimpered. "You should not question a man when he wants to kiss you." He winced. "That's not what I meant. You should not question *me* when I try to kiss you. And your breasts are quite lovely."

"Truly?" she asked, a smile growing.

Bryce ran his hand down his entire face. "We should not be having this conversation."

"Why not? It clarifies things."

"Clarifies what?" he asked, throwing his arms wide. "I wanted to kiss you." He shook a finger at her. "Don't dare ask me *why* again."

She opened her mouth, and he stomped forward with a warning finger in Odin's face. "Don't dare move."

He took hold of her, yanked her up against him, and planted his lips solidly on hers.

She went rigid in his arms, though only for a moment. After his lips caressed and taunted her with pleasure, her body softened and pressed against his. The kiss startled him. It was unlike any he had ever experienced, and he had experienced his share.

The deeper it grew, the more deeply he wanted it to grow. It set his body on fire. Molten heat rushed through him, heightening every sensation and sparking new ones. He ached with the thought that the kiss had to end. He wanted the kiss to go on forever, this feeling to go on forever.

Cold, sound reason intruded and urged him to end it, or soon he would not have an ounce of sanity left. And he would, without doubt, do something he would regret. Something he wasn't sure either of them was ready for.

Bryce kept her held firmly against him. He might have relinquished the kiss, but he wasn't ready to relinquish her. He favored the feel of her in his arms. Light as a feather she was, he could hold her all day, and he would not suffer for it.

She sighed and rested her brow to his. A hint of a smile appeared along her plumped-with-pleasure lips, and a faint blush stained her cheeks; that she had enjoyed their encounter was obvious. And damn if he didn't want to do more than kiss her.

He warned himself to put her down, let her go, take a step away from her for sanity's sake. He didn't listen. He kept her close.

"That was most enjoyable."

Another wave of heat raced through him. Simply because she told him she favored his kiss? But then he had never had a woman say that to him. Kisses, touches, coupling. And it was done. No flowery words or praise had ever been exchanged. Though he had been told often enough that he was a big one, and the gleam in women's eyes when they had seen him naked had taught him at an early age that size was an attribute most women favored.

"I would enjoy having you kiss me again . . . some-time," she said softly.

He liked her boldness, her ability to speak her mind and tell him how she felt. It was refreshing to share such openness with someone and not be restricted by convention.

"I would enjoy the same." He brushed his lips over hers, and he nearly shivered from the pulsing heat that tempted. He had to keep rein on his senses when he said, "Don't dare say 'truly' or ask why."

With a tinkle of laughter, she said, "You know me well."

"I'm beginning to," he said, ready and willing to learn all he could about her.

It hit him then; his mission. It came first, it had to. And though he didn't want to, he reluctantly released her, placing her gently on the ground.

"I like being in your arms," she said, taking a step back away from him.

It was a mistake; he should never have kissed her. She was inexperienced when it came to intimacy, un-touched by a man, and she would expect more than he could give. It was not fair to her and to him, for he felt more than he wanted to feel for her.

For once, Bryce was relieved that Odin interrupted them with a low growl. Only this time he wasn't look-ing at them. His eyes were intent on a spot in the woods.

"Gather your things and ready your bow," Bryce or-dered in a whisper.

Charlotte had already started doing so and had ev-erything together, her bow ready in seconds.

Bryce pointed for her to follow him off to the left of where Odin kept a steady glare and snarl.

They had taken no more than a step when Culth emerged from the woods.

Odin continued snarling though he was quick to scurry behind Charlotte, and she was just as quick to draw her bow, aiming it at Culth.

"I came for my animal," Culth said with a snarl almost as vicious as Odin's.

"You've treated him badly," Charlotte accused.

"I do what I please with what is mine," Culth snapped.

"Odin no longer belongs to you," Bryce said. "And don't make me take your life to prove it."

"You dare threaten me?" Culth said, stepping forward.

Bryce didn't hesitate; he stepped forward, sword in hand. "No threat; simple truth."

"I could call my men from the woods—"

"If you had brought men with you, we would be dead by now," Bryce said. "You came to restore what respect you lost when not only your men were found dead, but your dog deserted you."

"You are a mighty warrior like me—"

"Bryce is nothing like you," Charlotte said, her bow remaining firm in her hand. "You respect nothing, not even an animal, and yet you demand respect. You are a man without honor and not worthy of being master to such a fine animal."

Culth laughed and shook his head. "I knew she was a spirited one. I will enjoy her after I kill you, though the animal will be severely punished."

An arrow whistled passed Bryce's ear and landed on the ground between Culth's spread legs.

"I would kill you before I'd let you touch me or Odin," she spat.

As if he understood, Odin barked in agreement, though he remained safely tucked behind Charlotte.

Culth's eyes narrowed. "You will pay for—"

"It is you who will pay," Bryce warned. "Unlike you, I not only protect what is mine, I do no harm to what is mine."

Culth laughed. "I'd say it's the wee lassie that is protecting and keeping you from harm with her bow."

"And it's a *wee* lassie who holds you at bay," Charlotte said with a smile.

"I'll cut that sharp tongue of yours from your mouth," Culth snapped.

"That makes no sense," Charlotte said, and Bryce waited to hear the logic she was about to inject into the altercation.

"In one breath, you say you will have me, which no doubt included you forcing kisses on me, and in the next breath, you threaten to cut out my tongue." She shook her head. "How enjoyable would kissing me be then?"

Culth glared at her, shook his own head, and turned a dazed expression on Bryce.

He explained, without Culth saying a word, "She not only has a spirited nature, but an inquisitive and intelligent mind."

"A waste of a beautiful woman," Culth said. "You can keep her, and as for your punishment for killing my men? I'll let you live. Having her as your woman is a more fitting punishment than death. I'll take my dog and be on my way."

"Are you deaf?" Charlotte shouted loudly, as if he were. "You'll not be taking the dog."

Culth glared at Bryce. "Do you truly want to fight over a dog?"

"I have met many idiots," Charlotte angrily spat, "but you are the biggest one yet if you believe this fight is about a dog."

Culth turned livid eyes on Bryce. "Her tongue slices as sharply as a sword. She needs to be taught a lesson."

Charlotte was ready to retaliate, but Bryce's hand snapped up, and she clamped her mouth shut.

"So she does obey," Culth said with a sneer.

"She does not remain silent out of obedience; she does what is wise," Bryce corrected.

"You both make no sense." Culth snapped his hand at the dog. "Odin, come *now*!"

The dog rested his big body against Charlotte's legs and whimpered.

"Odin!" Culth yelled.

The dog trembled and turned sorrowful eyes on Bryce.

"Stay, Odin!" Bryce ordered, pointing his finger at the animal.

"You fight for a dog?" Culth asked incredulously.

"I fight for what is right. You fight for gain."

Culth crossed his arms over his massive chest. "You are one of the true king's men, aren't you?"

"A spark of intelligence," Charlotte said. "Perhaps there's hope for him after all."

"Does her mouth ever cease?" Culth asked of Bryce with a grin.

"Only when I kiss her, and even then . . ."

While Culth laughed, Bryce wondered why he would tell the mercenary such a thing, though truthfully he knew. He wanted to make certain that Culth understood that Charlotte belonged to him. Realizing that himself, he knew he was headed for trouble where Charlotte was concerned.

"I find I like you, Highlander," Culth said.

"Odin still isn't going with you," Bryce said.

"I no longer want him. His escape has made him useless to me. I could never trust him again."

"Then why did you come for him?" Charlotte asked.

"You won't like my answer."

"I know your answer," she said. "You intended to kill the dog to prove to your men that no one, not even an animal, can betray you without suffering consequences. So now what will you do?"

"You tell me," Culth challenged. "You seem to have all the answers."

Bryce already had thought of a solution, but he waited to see what Charlotte would suggest. He had often been impressed by her acute grasp of fitting solutions in difficult situations, mostly because he had thought similarly.

"Since your leadership is in question—"

Culth quickly interrupted Charlotte. "How do you know that?"

Charlotte shrugged and lowered her readied bow though she kept it close to her side. "Gossip spreads as rapidly as fire. And I imagine that as soon as we had left your village, word spread that King Kenneth would not be honoring the promise of riches he had made to you. Add to that your men who never returned to the village and your dog running off. You definitely will need something sizeable to regain your clan's respect."

Culth took a step back as he sent Bryce a wary look. "Is she a witch who is able to see the past, present, and future?"

Bryce smiled. "I've wondered that myself at times."

"You are too intelligent to think such nonsense," Charlotte scolded.

"And you are too intelligent to ignore the possibility," Bryce said.

Charlotte stared at him a moment. "You may be right."

"What of my dilemma?" Culth demanded.

"There is a simple solution," Charlotte said.

"You believe so?" Culth asked doubtful.

"Of course," she said, "You strike a bargain with Bryce, pledging your services to the true king. You continue to allow King Kenneth to believe you fight for him and learn anything that will help the true king. And when the time comes, you battle for the true king. In exchange for your services, you have no worry that you will lose your land—"

Bryce took over from there. "And you will share in any wealth that is found."

"How do I know you speak for the true king?" Culth asked skeptically.

"I serve the true king and have been given permission to speak for him when necessary," Bryce said.

"Therefore, my word is his." Bryce stepped forward and offered his hand.

Culth did the same, accepting the offer without hesitation. "I give my word to serve the true king."

Both warriors clamped hands hard, sealing the pact.

"One other thing," Culth said. "I want to offer my condolences."

"For what?" Bryce asked guardedly.

"The lassie is going to make you a terrible wife!"

Chapter 15

Once Culth had retreated into the woods, Odin cautiously stepped in front of Charlotte and tentatively sniffed the air while she turned her attention to Bryce. "Do you think I would make you a terrible wife?"

"I haven't given it a thought," Bryce said. "Now let's be on our way. We've lost enough time today. We'll barely make it much farther before it's time to stop for the night."

His hurried and dismissive response turned Charlotte silent, for to her it spoke volumes. He might have wanted to kiss her, but he had given no thought to her as a wife. He simply lusted after her, no more. She felt a disappointment she did not quite understand. Why should it bother her? They didn't know each other all that well.

But then her father had simply looked upon her mother and had fallen in love.

Obviously, that hadn't happened with Bryce when he had first gazed upon her. But then he had thought her a lad.

She was foolish for letting it disturb her. He had more important matters to consider, and so did she. They had shared a kiss, that was all. She almost cringed recalling how she had told him that she wouldn't mind if he kissed her again.

He was lusting after her, and she was . . .

She shook her head. She would think on such nonsense no more. Determined, she picked up her pace, Odin following suit.

Conversation lagged between them for the rest of the day. Even when they made camp, not many words were exchanged. And she turned her back on him when going to sleep though sleep eluded her far too long and was interrupted far too often once it did claim her. Thus the reason for her many yawns the next morning when they continued on their way.

"You did not sleep well last night?" Bryce asked.

"I woke too often." She didn't wish to talk about her troubled sleep, especially with his being the cause of it. She hadn't been able to get him and the kiss off her mind. Why couldn't she have found it repulsive? Why had she enjoyed it so much?

Odin interrupted, prancing in front of her with a stick in his mouth. She took it and gave it a toss. He scampered after it, returning it to her in seconds.

The stick was much too similar to her thoughts; she could toss them away, but they always hurried back.

"We could stop if you need to rest," he suggested.

Her tired limbs screamed with relief, but her stubborn nature objected. She'd not show any weakness in front of the Highlander, not take a chance in having him think her incapable of completing this mission.

"That's not necessary; I'm fine," she insisted.

"No, you're stubborn," he argued.

"Is that why I would make you a terrible wife?" Her sharp retort was out of her mouth before she could call it back. It was a mistake she would probably regret, but she hadn't been able to stop herself. It was a question she itched to have answered.

"A stubborn wife can be a trial." He grinned.

That he found it amusing annoyed her. "Then it is good I will never be your wife."

"I am not looking for a wife."

"Nor I a husband." Charlotte marched ahead of him, Odin dropping the stick and joining her.

Bryce caught up with her in two easy strides. "That is good, for we don't have time to allow such interference."

He was right, of course, but why then did her heart ache, as if she had lost something dear to her. She turned the talk elsewhere, fearful she'd be unable to conceal her distress if they continued on about it.

"Is the village far?" she asked.

"An hour or more, though we should pass a croft before we reach it." No sooner did Bryce say that than they emerged on a meadow with a croft just beyond.

Charlotte hastened her pace, eager to known if the farmer had seen prisoners pass this way. The closer she got, the slower her steps, and it wasn't long before Bryce positioned himself protectively in front of her.

"Stay behind me," he ordered, his sword drawn and his steps cautious.

The farm looked as if it had been sacked, the garden trampled, barrels and benches smashed to pieces, the door torn from its hinges, and not an animal or inhabitant in sight.

Odin rushed ahead sniffing the ground frantically.

"What do you think happened here?" Charlotte asked, clutching her bow.

"A struggle? Though anger could be the culprit, the soldiers not finding what they searched for destroying what was here."

Odin barked just then, startling them both. Charlotte grabbed an arrow from the cache and readied the bow as Odin ran barking toward a small cropping of woods, a few feet from the house.

Bryce took a guarded stance a few steps in front of her, and it struck her that once again he had positioned himself protectively between her and possible harm. It warmed her heart and annoyed her all at the same time.

Odin rushed forward, barking, when suddenly it stopped, and he began whining.

Charlotte lowered her bow, his actions telling her that they had nothing to fear. "Children," she said to Bryce.

Sure enough, a lad around seven years and a lassie no more than four years stumbled out of the woods, each holding tightly to a parent's hand.

The man, slim and barely reaching Bryce's chin, stepped forward. "The soldiers grow bolder, take all our food, not caring if we can feed our families, and lately, they have been dragging off all males to serve the king. I spotted them in the distance."

The woman spoke up. "I made Evan hide with the children and me in the woods." Tears filled her green eyes. "I did not want to lose my husband."

"You both did the right thing," Bryce said. "How long ago did this happen?"

"The soldiers left about an hour ago," Evan explained. "We've remained in the woods to make certain they were gone."

"They most certainly will return," Bryce said. "Perhaps not today, but not finding anyone and its being obvious that someone resides here guarantee their return."

"I told you the same, Evan," his wife said, tears streaming down her cheeks and her young daughter reaching tentatively out to Odin, who was impatient to play.

"Where do we go?" Evan pleaded helplessly.

"The MacAlpin clan will open its home to you," Charlotte said, by now familiar with the invitation Bryce extended to anyone in need.

"This is our home." Evan shook his head. "How do I abandon our home?"

Charlotte stepped forward. "Your wife and children are your home; therefore, your home is always with you. Land is plentiful. That you can find elsewhere, or when the true king takes the throne, you can return here."

His wife again spoke up. "Listen to the lad, he speaks wisely. There would be no home without you."

Charlotte was glad the woman thought her a lad. At least she knew her ruse continued to fool the eyes.

Evan's son grabbed his arm. "I won't let you go."

"You are outnumbered," Bryce said with a laugh. "Surrender is your only choice."

Evan finally agreed, and while Bryce spoke privately with him, Charlotte helped Evan's wife, Lilith, gather what few things were salvageable. And Odin was finally relieved and the children delighted that they could play.

"The Highlander keeps his wife safe by having you dress as a lad?" Lilith asked.

"He isn't my husband," Charlotte was quick to correct and a trifle upset that the woman had seen through her disguise so easily. But that mattered not now. She needed to learn about her father. "This ruse helps protect me while on my mission to find my da. Perhaps you have seen him?" Charlotte went on to explain what she had learned so far about her da and, once finished, anxiously asked again, "Have you seen him?"

Lilith shook her head. "I am sorry, but if we spot soldiers, we hide. We started doing so when a father and son were dragged away by the soldiers from a farm not far from ours. And those who have passed by have warned us that it is being done much too frequently. But someone in the village might have heard something. Tongues wag constantly there though they have been more cautious of late, many not knowing who to trust."

"Thank you," Charlotte said. "I will seek information carefully."

Lilith reached out and laid a gentle hand on Charlotte's arm. She kept her voice low when she said, "Your ruse works well enough. It is the Highlander who gives it away."

"How so?"

"He looks at you as my husband looks at me, and that is when I noticed the curve of your hips and their gentle sway when you walk."

"My hips curve?" she asked incredulously. She never thought she had hips that swayed when she walked.

That was not only shocking to hear but too shocking to believe.

"You can see clearly when your hand rests at your waist, and there is softness to your lovely face that could only belong to a woman. I only tell you this so you are aware and will be careful." Lilith shook her head. "Things grow so much worse. I wish the true king would reveal himself and take the throne from this tyrant."

"He will," Charlotte assured her. "He will not let his people suffer much longer."

Evan called out to his wife and children.

Lilith gave Charlotte a quick hug. "Take care, and I hope I will see you again."

"I'm sure you will," Charlotte said, hoping the same, for she liked the woman.

They all gathered together, Odin quickly obeying Charlotte's command to sit, though he turned big sad eyes on the children, disappointed they could play no more.

"We must take our leave now," Evan informed his family. "Bryce explained where we are to go, where we will be safe."

"I can't thank you enough for what you do for us," Lilith said.

"My brothers and I were raised to serve the true king," Bryce said. "We act in his stead until the time comes for him to reign. We do what he would do— protect his people."

"God bless you, your brothers, and the true king," Lilith said, and after a flurry of good-byes and hugs, the family took its leave. And so did Bryce and Charlotte, only they traveled in the opposite direction.

They had traveled only a short distance when Bryce asked, "What you said about family, those were your father's words?"

Charlotte shook her head. "That is something I learned on my own. As I've told you, Da and I traveled around a lot, never remaining too long in one place. It upset me when my da would pack us up and move us. Then one day I realized that it didn't matter where my da and I called home, for without him, I would have no home."

"What brought about this discovery?"

"You're perceptive."

"Even more so since I've met you," Bryce said.

"I'm pleased I could teach you something," she teased.

"And pleased I am to learn," he said, "and I plan on learning much more from you."

The gleam in his eye had her looking twice at him, for she was certain she had caught a flicker of passion there. But he turned away too soon for her to be sure.

He returned to his question. "So what happened to your father to make you realize home was not a shelter but the person you love and who loves you."

"You feel the same?" she asked.

He nodded. "When I lost my parents, I had no choice but to find another home. It started with my brother Reeve, who I came upon just after the king's soldiers killed his family. He was only four years and I five. We walked many miles together, never leaving each other's side."

"Did you know where to go, or did you just happen upon your new home?"

"My mum told me of a close friend she had known years earlier and that if anything ever happened to her and Da, that I was to go to her friend—Mara." He grinned. "Mara is nothing like my mum though she is a good and loving mum. And I am grateful every day for her." He bent down as if he meant for no one to hear. "Just don't let her cook for you."

Charlotte chuckled.

"What of your father?" he asked. "What happened to make you realize that without him you would have no home?"

"He had gone into the woods in search of plants he wished to make drawings of and was gone longer than usual. I felt something was wrong and went in search of him. I arrived to witness two thugs beating on him."

"Don't tell me you went after them?" he asked.

"I most certainly did," she said with a toss of her chin. "They would have killed my da if I had not stopped them."

Bryce shook his head. "If I did not know you, I would think your story nothing more than a tall tale, but knowing you—" He shook his head again. "I know otherwise."

"I had them off my da in seconds and running for their lives."

"How?"

Charlotte leaned down, grabbed a good-sized rock, and pointed. "See that broken tree branch?"

Bryce laughed. "You'll never reach—"

Charlotte threw the rock before he could finish, hitting the crevice of the cracked branch, splitting it in two, and sending the broken branch hurtling to the ground.

Bryce stared in awe. "I would have never believed it."

"Leaving a child with not only a curious mind but a thirsty one, on her own much of the time can produce startling results."

"It would seem you have the ability to defend yourself against most anything."

Not against love and not against you.

The thought struck her hard, and if she hadn't caught her misstep, she would have stumbled as they continued walking.

"Everyone has a vulnerable spot," she said, knowing he was hers.

He thought differently. "Your da is yours."

If he only knew.

"And the true king is yours," she said.

They both nodded even though they knew that it wasn't the truth.

Chapter 16

The village they entered was like many of late, cautious. Skeptical eyes followed Charlotte and Bryce as they walked through, nodding greetings though many turned their heads. The atmosphere in the Highlands was changing rapidly, and with it, fear grew. No one knew whom to trust, and so none were trusted.

Tongues, though, never stopped wagging. It was the way of things. The way word was spread and more importantly how hope could be spread.

"While I would prefer we stay close, it wouldn't be a wise move," Bryce said, wishing there was another way but knowing this would be their best course of action. "Time is limited to us. If we stay too long, ask too many questions, we will become suspect. If, however, we separate, learn what we can independently, and take our leave within an hour, no one will be the wiser."

Though the plan was a solid one, Bryce hated suggesting it. He knew that if, in fact, Charlotte was a lad rather than a lassie, he wouldn't have such a difficult time with his decision. But since she was, he felt the need to protect her, and the thought of her going off on her own put the fear of God into him.

What if she got herself into trouble, a probability, and he wasn't there to help her? Damn, if it wasn't easier when he thought her a lad. And damn him for kissing her. The memory of that kiss had lingered much too long in his mind. He favored the taste of her and her innocent and eager response. He allowed that to interfere with what was necessary. And what was necessary was for them to separate for a while.

He had to let her go on her own, and the thought made him shiver to the bone. And it didn't help that the bruises on her face were vivid reminders of her previous altercations.

"A sensible decision, and don't worry, I'll be fine," she said, as if knowing his thoughts.

"Take no chances," he ordered sternly.

She grinned, and he shook his head. It was like asking the sun not to rise. He watched her dash off like a lad in search of adventure. She blended with the villagers more easily than he. He stood out a bit more, being a Highlander warrior of good size. It wasn't hard to see that fear ruled this village. It was on every weary face he glanced at, in every cautious movement that was made.

That the king's soldiers had passed through here was obvious. They had left behind their mark—despair and fear. Bryce tried trading worthless trinkets for more worthless items that could prove fruitful for future trades, but no one was interested.

He tried to keep his eye on Charlotte, but she was soon gone from his sight, and the longer she was, the more his worry grew. No matter that she had extracted herself from dangerous or difficult situations before, he worried a time would come when she found herself in an impossible situation.

He had become more attached to her than he thought possible, and that brought with it the worry and fear of his not being able to protect someone he cared for.

His quick perusals of the village proved fruitless. All kept silent, many looking anxious and some refusing to meet his eyes. There was nothing to learn here, and the sooner he and Charlotte left, the better he would feel.

Bryce made his way with hurried steps past and around the small cottages, his eyes alert for any signs of Charlotte or trouble.

He found both.

Charlotte was attempting to ward off a bear of a young man, while Odin kept two other attackers at bay with vicious snarls and barks.

"Put him down!" Bryce's shout startled the man so badly that he dropped Charlotte. She fell to the ground with a bounce, rolled, and scrambled to her feet.

Bryce expected her to run to his side, perhaps take cover behind him, but she didn't. After dusting herself off, she gave the big fellow a hard poke to his gut.

"Why did you tell me to be gone?" she asked with another jab.

The big fellow looked ready to throttle her again though that changed when Bryce took a forceful step toward him.

"You ask too many questions," the man admitted reluctantly.

"What's wrong with questions?" she demanded with another poke.

156   DONNA FLETCHER

His nostrils flared, and his thick hands fisted at his sides. "Rein the lad in; I'll not suffer another demand from him."

Bryce stepped between them. "Lay a hand on the lad, and you'll regret it."

"Be gone with you both," the man threatened with a raised fist. "You're not welcome here."

"Why?" Charlotte asked, poking her head from around Bryce. "Have you something to hide?"

"Enough!" Bryce shouted with a turn of his head to Charlotte, then turned to the large man. "We'll take our leave and disturb you no more."

"Hurry then and be off with you," the man spat.

Bryce turned, not surprised to see the look of dismay on Charlotte's face. He was quick to grab her arm and march her with haste out of the village, having to warn her twice to be silent. Odin was quick to follow. Once the woods devoured them, Charlotte yanked her arm free, and he knew she would give him a severe tongue-lashing.

He wasn't in the mood to waste time. He slammed his hand over her mouth as soon as she opened it. "Trust me on this."

Uncertainty flashed in her eyes, but not for long, and she nodded.

He removed his hand. "Something is not right. All you did was ask questions of him?"

"Not him, two others, who were not forthcoming at all. Then, suddenly, the large man and two others appeared. He swatted at me like an irritating bug and shouted for me to be gone."

"I found the same reluctance even for minor chatter.

It was as if—" Bryce shook his head, suddenly under-standing. He grabbed Charlotte's arm. "He and his two friends were trying to save us, trying to get us to leave. The fear I saw wasn't because soldiers had been there; it was because they were on the way." He shook his head again, annoyed with himself. "I should have real-ized it sooner. The only men there were too old to serve the king."

"You're right," Charlotte said, exasperated. "Fool I am for not having noticed it myself."

"The three men took a chance leaving their hiding spot to help us, and we would do well to leave this place now as I'm sure they did as soon as we took our leave."

They hurried off, not another word exchanged. It wasn't long before they heard the thunder of horses' hooves pounding the ground. They had only moments to find a place to hide, but it took less than that for Bryce to yank Charlotte under a thick blanket of bushes. It was a tight fit, with only room for her to lie atop him and Odin to stretch alongside him. The animal was trained well and knew when to stay silent. Bryce didn't have to warn Charlotte the importance of the same. She rested her face on his chest and stared up at him, her lips clamped tightly shut.

For all her bravado, her small body trembled with fear against his, and she clenched at his shirt, as if her hold on him kept her safe. He didn't hesitate to reach out and run his hand soothingly through her hair and down along her face to rest against her flushed cheek. She was soft to the touch from hair to cheek, and he continued to gently caress and stroke.

Her trembling eased, her body melting against

his, when suddenly the contingent of soldiers were upon them, or at least it felt that way. The ground beneath trembled violently from the pounding of multiple hooves that seemed only inches from their prone bodies.

Bryce wound his arms tightly around Charlotte. She tightened her grip on his shirt, squeezed her eyes shut, and buried her face against his chest.

At that moment, his need to keep her from harm overwhelmed him, and he knew he would do *anything* to keep her safe.

The ground continued to vibrate well after the troop had passed, and the trio remained as they were, tucked safely out of sight. Neither Bryce nor Charlotte dared say a word, both knowing that troops purposely left a few soldiers lagging to catch any and all who tried to hide from them.

Bryce remained with his arms snug around Charlotte, and she kept her face on his chest and her hand gripping his shirt. She had also tucked her small legs between his large ones, as if getting as close as she possibly could to him.

He certainly didn't mind. He actually welcomed the feel of her so snug against him. And oddly enough, it wasn't passion that dominated his thoughts at the moment. It was something he hadn't felt since he had lost his parents—a loving contentment.

He didn't want to question it, worry over it, or be rid of it. He wanted simply to linger in it, embrace it, and savor it.

It was Odin who stirred first, his large head poking up and sniffing the air. When the sniffing ceased, and he started panting, Bryce knew all was clear. And he had no choice but to let her go.

The thought sent his stomach churning. He didn't want to let her go; he wanted Charlotte by his side. Who would rescue her when she got herself into trouble? Who would see that she didn't do anything foolish? Who would take care of her?

"We should leave," she whispered, and he saw that she was gazing up at him.

He could get lost in those dark eyes of hers. He didn't know why. There was nothing special to the dark brown color, yet, to him, they were irresistible. He found his glance settling much too often on her eyes and found that once there, he did not want to look away. It was as if the dark color held him captive, locked him in, and he was helpless to escape.

Her stirring forced his musing aside, and he took command. "Let Odin go first, wait a moment, then follow."

Upon hearing his name and understanding, Odin crawled out of their hiding spot.

Bryce kept a firm hold on Charlotte when she suddenly giggled.

"All is well; Odin licks my leg."

Bryce unwound his arms reluctantly, and she slipped off him, to the side, and crawled backward out from under the bushes. He turned on his stomach and followed, getting to his feet and dusting himself off.

"We should make haste," Charlotte reminded.

He agreed, and, without saying a word, he took the lead and began walking. They walked in silence a good part of the day, finally stopping near to nightfall. Bryce had reminded himself all throughout the day that his mission took precedence over his unexplainable feelings toward Charlotte. Just as her need to find her father took precedence over all else.

He watched her from across the campfire. It disturbed him that her eyes were filled with such sadness, and he could not keep silent. "What troubles you?"

"We do not know if we travel in the right direction. We could be headed away from my da instead of toward him."

"It takes time to determine such things. Patience is needed when in pursuit."

"In the meantime, my da could be suffering."

"We've discussed this," Bryce admonished gently. "You need to have more faith in your da. He does in you."

"That's what troubles me," she admitted reluctantly. "He is confident that I will find him, and I have no such confidence. As the days slip by, I fear even more that I will never find him, save him from a terrible fate."

Bryce reacted without thought. He got to his feet and walked around the campfire to sit beside Charlotte. He took hold of her chin, gently lifting it. "You are much too stubborn for your own good."

"It is for my own good that I am stubborn," she corrected.

Sadly, she spoke the truth. With what he had learned of Charlotte thus far, she had required courage out of necessity. It had now become a duty for her, one she did not take lightly. She was as duty-bound as he was, and he suddenly felt the need to free her of such a heavy burden.

But how?

His fingers tightened on her chin, and he leaned down and kissed her. She startled at first, as did he, for he had not thought to kiss her, it simply seemed the natural thing to do. And it was, for they both eagerly tasted and enjoyed. Soon they were wrapped in each other's arms, the kiss fueling their passion.

Her slim arms wound around his neck, his hands went to her waist, and he yanked her up against him as he lowered them both to her blanket. His hands wandered of their own accord, caressing her body as if it belonged to him. And at that moment, it did, just as he belonged to her.

She was ever so soft and responsive to his every touch, and when he moved his lips to nibble down along her neck, she invited more with the tilt of her head. A soft, contented mewl spilled from her lips and fired his already heated passion. And made him all too aware that he wanted more from her—much more.

He paused to gaze into her dark eyes, which seemed to have grown as black as the night, and he knew at that moment that she would easily surrender to him.

"Why do you stop?" she asked, her voice heavy with disappointment and trembling with passion.

He could not take her like this, here on the hard ground, only to walk away. He had nothing more to give her than a night of passion, and she deserved more.

He rested his brow to hers, trying to find the right words, not wanting her to think that he didn't desire her when all he truly wanted was to strip her and himself bare and make love throughout the night.

But it wouldn't be love they made, for he had no time

to love, no time to give to another. Not now; not when so much depended on his mission.

She pressed her cheek to his. "It's all right. I understand. It is not a good time or place. Besides, we would come together only out of a need to feel close and not alone in our endeavors. It would mean nothing in the end."

Her last few words stung. Would that be how she felt? Would joining with him mean nothing to her? His arms fell away from her, and she moved away from him. They lay there, staring at each other, both at a loss for words or perhaps fearing to speak, fear of admitting the truth, fear of wanting more from each other.

Bryce sat up, not wanting to leave her side, arguing with himself that it was for the best. He was ready to get to his feet when he shook his head, turned to her, and took hold of her once again.

"Damn, but I enjoy kissing you."

With that, he kissed her again.

Chapter 17

Charlotte sat stunned from his quick, passionate kiss. His lips were devouring her one moment and gone the next, the campfire once again separating them. She didn't know what to do or what to think. Her mind was a jumble of thoughts that made no sense. And her body was still reeling from the intimate caresses Bryce had rained all over her only moments ago.

She was in an utter state of confusion, her body flushed with heat and her lips aching for more. She did the only sensible thing she could. She stretched out on her blanket and turned her back to him without saying a word.

She didn't trust herself to speak. She feared her own words, feared she would beg him for more—more kisses, more touches, and more—

Charlotte shut her eyes tightly against her wanton thoughts. How could she justify surrendering herself to him when they had shared nothing more than a kiss or two? Had she gone completely mad? And under the circumstances, was this the appropriate time for such a thing?

And more importantly, was it just a quick rutting she wanted or was she expecting more?

Leave it to her logical side to interfere though she was grateful for it. There was more to consider before she did anything she could possibly regret. And, the way his kisses had made her feel, it would have been much too easy to surrender to him.

She was also grateful for Odin. The large dog crawled over to her, making his way beneath her arm and planting his big body next to hers after giving her face a quick lick. She hugged him though she couldn't help but think she would much rather it be Bryce she had her arm wrapped around.

Odin gave her face another lick, as if understanding. She smiled, gave his face a kiss, and whispered, "Don't you worry; I love you and always will."

The dog responded, snuggling his face to her chest, and promptly went to sleep.

Not so Charlotte. She lay awake, her mind much too busy with thoughts. She ached for sleep to claim her and end her torment. It wasn't only the endless thoughts she wanted relief from, but the tingling sensations that rippled through her body. They returned every time her thoughts lingered on how Bryce had caressed her, so gentle yet determined.

And then, of course, she wished he was stroking her again.

She caught herself before she almost moaned aloud, clamping her lips tightly shut. She would not let him know that their short encounter had robbed her of sleep and filled her with even more desire.

With the passing hours, she feared that sleep would

never come, and so she kept her eyes tightly shut and repeated the single word over and over and over in her head—sleep, sleep, sleep, until the steady rhythm finally brought her what she wanted.

Morning came all too soon, and Charlotte lazily stretched herself awake, feeling as if she had not slept a wink. Being so tired, though, did have its benefits, she was simply too fatigued for mind chatter. Her only thought was on rest, which she would not get until this evening, when once again they made camp.

She was surprised when Bryce didn't comment on her slow start or her copious yawns. It took only a moment for her to realize why. He was moving just as slow as she was, and his yawns were as abundant as hers.

She smiled, satisfied that he had slept as poorly as she had and no doubt for the same reason. It gave her a boost to get moving, lightened her step, and kept a grin on her face.

"You're cheerful this morning," he snapped.

"I believe it will be a good day."

"How can you say that when gray skies greet us this morn?" Bryce grumbled.

"Showers can wash away troubles."

"Then we need a rainstorm," Bryce said and stomped off into the woods.

Charlotte worried that Bryce just might get that rainstorm, the clouds having thickened heavily after only a couple of hours. Not a drop of rain had fallen yet, but it didn't look promising.

"Where to from here?" she asked, not a word having

been exchanged between them since they left camp and her too curious to keep quiet any longer.

As she waited for Bryce to answer, Odin brought her a stick.

"Not now, Odin," she said, and dropped the stick.

The dog was insistent picking it up and nudging her hand with his nose.

"Not now," she said annoyed, though more at Bryce for not having answered her yet.

The dog refused to be ignored, and Charlotte finally grabbed the stick, ready to toss it, when her eyes popped wide.

She dropped to her knees, staring at the stick. "You found his messages."

Bryce turned at Odin's loud bark.

He raced to Charlotte's side, dropping down beside her. "What's wrong?"

"Odin saw what I didn't," she said with a tear in her eye. "He's found my da's messages."

Bryce took the stick from her hands. "I don't see anything."

Charlotte took the stick from him and pointed to what looked like nothing more than scratches in the bark. "These are symbols my da devised as a way for us to communicate if ever separated." She shook her head. "He did it right after I got lost, but there was never a reason for us to ever use them. I had completely forgotten about them."

"You wear your da's clothes, right?" Bryce asked.

Charlotte nodded knowingly. "Odin picked up my da's scent on the sticks from his clothes."

Bryce shook his head. "How could he have managed

to engrave the sticks when always being watched by the soldiers?"

It was an easy question to answer knowing her da. "No doubt he did it right in front of everyone."

"How is that possible?"

"My da loves to draw and would often sit and draw images in the dirt with a stick. It fascinated many how beautifully he could draw, and I imagine he entertained those around him with his talent, soldiers included, while his nails worked at engraving the symbols."

"Do you recall what the symbols mean?"

"It has been a long time, the symbols crudely made, no doubt due to my da's situation," she said. "What I can decipher is that he travels west. I believe there is an unfinished symbol here, but I cannot make out what it is."

Bryce stood and paced in front of her. "I don't understand why he travels west. The king has few supporters there."

"The other symbol could tell us more if it were legible."

"Your da will leave more messages. We need to make certain we find them."

Odin gave a bark.

Charlotte hugged the dog and rubbed behind his ear. "That's right, Odin, you'll find them for us, won't you?"

The dog answered with another sharp bark.

Charlotte stood, holding on to the stick. "Are we headed west?"

"We will be after I make one stop."

"Where is that?"

He didn't answer.

He seemed to give it thought, and his hesitation surprised and upset her. Had something changed between
them, and she hadn't realized it? She wanted to know,
and so she asked, "Suddenly you don't trust me?"

"It isn't that," he admitted, rubbing the back of his
neck. "I need to visit Clan Comyn, and they can be a
rowdy bunch." He hesitated again.

"Spit it out," she said, fearing he didn't want her
going with him.

"Going as a lad could prove difficult. It would be
best if all knew you were a lassie."

"That would restrict my movement and ability to
learn anything."

"You already know where your da goes," he reminded. "There is nothing you need to learn from the
Clan Comyn."

"There is always something to be learned," she said.

"They'll be expecting you to drink with them."

"I'll get around that."

"They'll be boasting about the women they've
known."

"Like you did?" she asked with a grin.

He didn't find her response funny, and it was with a
stern look that he said, "They'll offer you a woman for
the night and not take no for an answer."

Her grin faded in a flash. "They'll offer you one, too?"

It was his turn to grin. "That they will."

"You'll not turn them down?"

"It wouldn't be polite."

The thought of his bedding a woman other than herself infuriated her. As irrational as it was, she wanted to
reach out and strangle him. How dare he even conceive

the notion? Just last night he told her how much he enjoyed kissing her, and now he would go kiss another. She would throttle him first.

It was then the solution hit her and no soon as formed in her mind than it was out of her mouth. "If I go as a lassie, then I go as your woman."

"You'll be expected to share a bed with me."

Better me than another woman.

She kept that thought to herself, and instead said, "We'll manage." She wasn't sure how that would work, though she was curious to find out.

They only took a few steps when she called out, "Wait."

Bryce turned.

She didn't want to admit it, but it was for the best. She couldn't allow her curiosity of sharing a bed with him to interfere with what needed to be done. "I must remain disguised as a lad."

"Why?" he asked, sounding disappointed.

"It will jeopardize our mission," she said. "Gossip is the mainstay of most clans and villages. It is how news is carried, things learned. It wouldn't be long before news spreads about the mighty Highlander and his woman who wears lad's clothing."

"Others have learned of your gender."

"They understood why we maintained the ruse and are not likely to betray us."

Bryce shook his head slowly and reached out to stroke her cheek. "I hate to admit you are right, but you are. We need to continue this ruse. It would be unwise to do otherwise. But—" He took hold of her chin. "Promise me you will not do anything foolish."

"I never do," she said with a grin. "It is the fools I must contend with that cause the problems."

Bryce's hands gripped her shoulders. "Listen well to me, woman. I'll not see you place yourself in danger."

"Then close your eyes, for if it is necessary for me to do so to save my da, then I will."

He shook her. "You are impossible."

"I thought I was stubborn."

"And quarrelsome," he added.

"And you're"—she stopped, and her voice softened—"a good man for putting up with a troublesome lad."

He shook his head again and kept shaking it, and only stopped when his lips claimed hers.

Without thought or hesitation, Charlotte's arms went around his neck. She wanted this kiss, ached for it since last he kissed her. And she intended to savor every moment.

His lips were strong against hers, taking command, leading, and she followed willingly. How his kiss could do so much she didn't know, but it did. It not only sparked her passion but made her feel safe and protected. Nothing could happen to her when she was in his arms, nothing.

She wasn't aware of when he had slipped his arm around her waist and hoisted her up against him. She was too hungry for his kiss to realize anything. And he was too, for he fed the kiss until she thought she would burst from its fullness.

And still it was with reluctance that they both brought the kiss to an end.

"You will do nothing foolish, or I will throttle you," Bryce said, having rested his brow to hers.

"I would rather you kiss me," she said.

"You like my kisses, do you?" he asked teasingly.

She gave a faint laugh. "I more than like your kisses, and I favor your touches."

He drew his head back, and she almost recoiled, his blue eyes raged with such heated passion.

"Be careful what you say, for I have a thirst for you that needs quenching." He put her down, turned, and walked away.

She followed, though she kept several steps behind. He wasn't the only one with a thirst to quench.

The closer they got to Clan Comyn, the more Bryce's worry grew. The Clan Comyn were good people, but their warriors a boisterous bunch. They were fierce warriors and favored their mead, their games, and their women. And his reason for seeking them out was to see that they would support the true king.

It was no secret that the clan didn't favor King Kenneth though it did nothing to incite him. So it wasn't quite known who Clan Comyn would fight alongside when the time came, and Bryce was there to convince them to choose the true king.

The problem was that he hadn't expected to have to worry about having a wee bit of a lassie along dressed like a lad and who he found himself much too attracted to. He warned himself not to get close, not to kiss her, but that was like asking him not to breathe. And the thought that she had become so damn irresistible to him frustrated him.

Now he would worry even more about her, especially while at the Clan Comyn. He cringed when he thought of what she would be subjected to, the vivid tales of battle and conquests of women. He cringed again.

Charlotte should not be hearing such sordid things, but how did he stop it. She was right about the consequences of gossip concerning a woman garbed as a lad. It would definitely prove dangerous for her, more so than entering the Clan Comyn disguised as a lad.

He stopped and turned to Charlotte. "You'll not remain at my side when we arrive. I'll not see you forced to partake in whatever debauchery they subscribe to."

Damn, but he hated that she would be on her own again.

How did he protect if she didn't remain beside him?

His sudden realization came with a smile. "I trust that you can take care of yourself. I know that you are no fool, though I sometimes say otherwise. You are skilled with a bow and agile enough and have extracted yourself from difficult situations before."

Though he knew all that, it didn't make it any easier for him to admit it. His thought was to protect her, though, truthfully, his fear was losing her. He didn't know if he could live with himself if something should happen to her, and he hadn't been there to save her. And the thought of not having her around, never kissing her, never getting to make love to her—ripped at his gut and tormented his heart.

He didn't want to admit how much he cared for Charlotte, but it was getting more difficult by the day not to.

Let no woman have your heart until you are ready to give it.

His own words came back to haunt him. He wondered if he had been the fool to think that he would decide when to give his heart, when truthfully it was snatched from him without his even realizing it.

He finished his instructions with an adamant, "You will be cautious."

"I will, and, besides, I have Odin," she reminded. "What about you? What will you do when given a woman for the night?"

He heard the sharp sting of jealousy in her voice and was pleased to hear it. "We'll take our leave before nightfall."

She shook her head. "Not likely. From what you have told me of the Clan Comyn, they would be insulted if we don't stay the night and enjoy their generous hospitality."

He refused to admit she was right again. He had spoken from his own misgivings, knowing it would take a few hours of talk and festivity before he could even broach the subject of allegiance to the true king.

"We'll do what must be done for the sake of our missions," she said, with a shrug of resignation, and walked away.

Bryce caught up with her in two easy strides, and they continued on in silence.

He didn't know what would happen tonight though he did know one thing. There was only one woman he intended to take to his bed and that was—Charlotte.

Chapter 18

Badenoch was a beautiful area of the Highlands, mountainous land with forests of alder, a favorite tree of her da's. He used it to fashion bowls and spoons for them, and he'd take a young green branch, cut the ends, push out the pith, and make a whistle for her. It wasn't just any whistle, he'd tell her, it was magical; and it was, for he had made it for her.

She grew melancholy with the memories though she feared one memory in particular, one that might prove dangerous for her. She considered confiding it to Bryce, but once he heard, he'd no doubt forbid her from going any farther.

The incident had happened almost two years ago, when her da and she were in the area, though not for long. Bryce knew the Clan Comyn well, for they were a boisterous bunch, especially when full of drink.

Two men from the clan, having partaken of too much ale, had come upon her da in the woods gathering alder branches. It wasn't long before they were tormenting him, and it wasn't long or difficult for her to make fools of them, besting them both.

Her hair was long, then, and she wore a skirt and tunic, and they had been far into their cups, so she didn't think they would recognize her if they should spot her today. She, however, would know them. She never forgot a face that had meant her or her father harm, especially for the fun of it.

She would be extravigilant and spend most of her time with the young lads who tended the warriors' horses. They proved a useful source, seeing much and hearing even more. They enjoyed boasting about the warriors' exploits, intending to follow in their stead.

"Make sure to keep your face marred with dirt; else-wise, your beauty will shine through," Bryce said.

Charlotte almost tripped over her own feet; his words stunned her so much. He thought she was beautiful? Was he blind? Or could he truly mean it?

"And don't keep your eyes on another's too long, or he will soon be captivated by their potent dark color."

He made it sound as though the color of her eyes could stir passion.

He stopped abruptly, leaned over, scooped up some dirt, and rifled it through her hair. "I've never seen a blend of colors in hair like yours before, brown, gold, and honey." He shook his head. "It's as if the colors vied for dominance, and none won."

She was glad he expected no response, for she was at a loss for words. She was amazed that he had taken note of her hair color. It was rather odd, many having pointed out the obvious. Some even suggested that it was the devil's doing.

"Let's get this done with," Bryce said abruptly. "I want to leave with first light tomorrow, so make certain I know where to find you."

"Perhaps you will be too comfortable to take an early leave," she suggested, annoyance nagging at her over an almost certain possibility that he would have a woman sharing his bed this night.

"I'll be up before the sun; make certain you are too."

She followed behind his determined strides, grumbling quietly. She wanted him to assure her that he would couple with no woman tonight. She had been foolish to have alluded to it. He would do what must be done, as was only sensible.

Reason always prevails.

Not this time, Da, not this time, she thought.

It wasn't long before they spied the village of the Clan Comyn, and Bryce once again reminded her to be cautious and take no chances. She adhered to his words as soon as the chieftain and his two sons greeted him with wrestling handshakes, and she recognized the sons as the two who she had confronted and bested for tormenting her da in the woods that day.

Charlotte slipped away, not wanting to be taken note of, but she wasn't quick enough. She heard Toag, the chieftain, yell out for the lad to come join them. She was grateful for Bryce's response to the man.

"Leave the lad to go join his own kind. We warriors have tales to tell and mead to drink—"

"And women to enjoy," finished Toag.

The four warriors entered the keep just as the first raindrops began to fall.

* * *

Charlotte learned plenty in the three hours she spent with the young lads. They were more than willing to share stories of the Comyn warriors, boasting proudly of their clan's exploits. It seemed that Toag and his sons, Ewan, the older by two years, and Edgar, had different opinions about the true king. While Toag and Edgar thought it wise to follow the true king, Ewan disagreed. He believed King Kenneth a mighty warrior who would one day best the true king and end the ridiculous myth that seeded the Highlands.

The lads, with no exception, sided with Toag and Edgar, though they never dared voice their opinions. It would mean a thrashing from Ewan for sure. They even cast worried glances around the stable to see if anyone lurked about listening.

"Has anyone seen Albert?" one lad asked.

"If he heard, he'll tell on us for sure," said another.

"He's always getting us in trouble to win Ewan's favor," a thin lad with large brown eyes said. "Hope he's stuck out in the rain somewhere."

Charlotte didn't say anything though she thought she had seen someone sneak out a few moments ago. But she didn't concern herself with it. If the lad Albert had been listening and went off to inform Ewan, he'd probably find the large man too busy and into his cups to be bothered by gossip.

She settled down, eager for sleep, tired from not getting much last night and not wanting to think about what Bryce was doing. Otherwise, she would do something stupid, like go to the keep and spy on his every move.

Odin woke when she went to settle her arm over him. He had fallen asleep beside her over an hour ago.

He gave a soft whine, then stretched himself up and trotted out of the stable.

"Don't be long," she called after him, but she knew he would roam and take his time while seeing to his duty.

Her eyes drifted shut as soon as she stretched out on the straw and sleep was right behind . . . though not for long.

"Get up the lot of you!" the voice yelled.

She didn't need to look to see who it was. Ewan stood just inside the door, rain dripping down his ruddy face and off his clothes.

"Agate, get your useless ass over here," he demanded.

The skinny lad with the big eyes hurried to his feet, and Charlotte watched his face turn pure white as he ran over to Ewan.

The lad hadn't even stopped in front of Ewan when he backhanded him and sent him sprawling.

"You run your mouth with lies?" Ewan screamed. "You'll not be speaking another lie when I get done with you."

The lad scurried on his backside up against a wall, his face riddled with fear.

Charlotte reacted as she always did when injustice twisted at her gut. She quickly strove to protect the innocent. And it was easy. All she did was stick out her leg as Ewan rushed at the lad.

He went down hard, slapping the dirt with his full weight, his face bouncing off the hard ground. Loud gasps filled the air, and Agate's eyes nearly popped from his face, he was so shocked.

Charlotte quickly got to her feet and grabbed her bow, though she readied no arrow.

It took several moments for Ewan to get to his feet. No one dared approach him, not even Albert. He had disappeared into the shadows as soon as the warrior went down. Once Ewan finally made it to his feet, he shook his head and spat hay from his mouth.

If wise, Charlotte would have quaked with fear, the man looking ready to kill her as his face grew molten red with anger. But it mattered not to her. She stood her ground as he advanced on her and when he got close enough, though not too close, she poked him hard in the gut with the tip of her bow.

He went down on his knees, his hands grabbing his gut.

"Keep your distance," she warned sternly. "Bryce won't take kindly to your hurting me."

"I'm going to thrash you, you fool," he yelled, and struggled again to his feet and ran at her.

Charlotte sidestepped him just as he got close, and as he flew past her, she whacked him in the back of the head with her bow.

He stumbled, righted himself quickly, and turned with a fury. "I'm going to make you suffer."

Charlotte shrugged. "It isn't me who is suffering."

He growled like a crazed animal and came at her again.

With a quick vault to one bale of hay, then another, she avoided the man, who again wound up flat on his face in his attempt to grab her.

When Ewan got up this time, he did the unexpected, and Charlotte silently cursed herself for not having considered such a tactic. He grabbed Agate and slammed him back against his chest, wrapping his arm around the lad's slim neck.

He could easily kill the lad with one twist.

"Put that damn bow down and come over to me, or I will make him suffer in your stead."

Charlotte didn't have to think about it. She laid her bow down by her belongings and walked right over to him. "Touch me, and Bryce will see that you pay for it."

Ewan laughed when he tossed Agate aside. "You think a MacAlpin warrior frightens me. I'll teach you a good lesson whether he likes it or not.

Charlotte knew what was coming and she ducked, which angered Ewan even more, and the next furious blow he sent didn't miss. It sent Charlotte flying.

Her head was foggy, her eyes blurred, making it difficult to get to her feet quickly and avoid another blow. He was on her again, and she wasn't fool enough to think that she could survive his angry trouncing.

She wished Odin would return, then wished he wouldn't. There was no telling what Ewan would do to the animal while in such a rage.

Bryce. She needed to get to him. He would protect her.

She already felt blood dripping from her nose, or was it her mouth, she wasn't sure. And when he grabbed her by the throat and tossed her, the crack to the back of her head reverberated through the whole of her after hitting the wall.

Stunned again, she failed to move with agility, and her life depended on her getting to Bryce. When Ewan reached down for her once again, she did the only thing left to her; she grabbed him between the legs and squeezed hard.

He couldn't even scream. All he could do was suck

in air and fall to his knees. It gave her enough time to get up and run. Pain struck her, but she ignored it and kept running. Rain pelted her as she slipped and slid in muddy puddles, but she kept running. And when she heard Ewan let loose with a battle cry, she ran harder.

She burst into the keep with the large man right behind her.

Charlotte heard Odin then, growling and snarling, and she turned just as Ewan punched the animal in the head and sent him flying into the wall.

She didn't think of the consequences of her actions, and just as she launched herself at Ewan, she caught Bryce's eye across the hall and let out a heart-wrenching scream.

She didn't realize it was his name she had screamed.

Her stomach churned with anger as she latched onto the sizeable man and continuously pummeled him with her small fists, sharp, rapid, never-ending jabs that tormented and confused.

Charlotte was suddenly grabbed around the waist and flung off the man, her fists still flying.

"See to Odin!" Bryce yelled, yanking her off the man.

Relief flooded her when she heard his voice, felt his touch, and she stumbled over to the stunned animal, bravely fighting to get to his feet. She soothed him with soft reassuring words and kisses and urged him to stay where he was.

When finally he appeared stable, she turned to see Bryce standing over Ewan, his hand still fisted as he glared down at the large man lying motionless on the floor.

She could have kissed him right there and then. He was, without a doubt, at that moment . . . her hero.

Bryce walked over to where she knelt beside Odin. His blue eyes turned a tumultuous blue as he took stock of them both, and Charlotte feared what he might do.

He turned, and yelled, "Is this how you treat a representative of the true king?"

Toag walked over to Ewan, a tankard of ale in his hand, and tossed it in his son's face. It somewhat revived him, so Toag ordered Edgar to bring him another full tankard. He did, and threw the contents at his brother.

This time Ewan woke and staggered to his feet.

"What did the lad do that caused you to beat him?" Toag asked.

"I don't care what the lad did," Bryce said with a sharpness that had Charlotte cringing and the other men stepping back. "He had no right touching him. I and I alone decide when and if he is to be punished."

"He deserves a good thrashing, he does," Ewan said, finally having his full wit about him, which Charlotte didn't believe was much.

"I defend the true king," she retaliated.

That brought a hush to the hall.

Bryce glared at Toag. "You lied when you pledged allegiance to the true king?"

Toag shook his head. "My son is a fool."

Ewan went to object.

"I've had enough of your stupid notions," Toag snapped, and raised a shaking fist to his son's face. "Pledge your allegiance to the true king or be gone."

His father's words stunned him so badly that he stumbled back, away from him.

"Do it now, or I'll have you thrown off the land," Toag warned.

That was enough for Ewan; Charlotte almost thought he would make the dim-witted decision to take his leave, but he made the wiser choice. He held his hand out to Bryce and gave his word to honor the true king.

Charlotte thought for a moment Bryce wouldn't accept the warrior's hand. But after a brief hesitation, he took it. Though with the anger that stormed in his eyes, he looked as if he'd much rather beat the man senseless.

Bryce turned to Toag. "I want hot water, towels, and food brought to a private bedchamber where I may see to the lad and the dog."

Toag didn't object; his reply was swift. "It will be done, but let me have a couple of the women look after him and the animal, so that you may enjoy Lorna's favors. She's been fancying you all evening, and she won't disappoint."

"I've already been disappointed by your hostile hospitality," Bryce said. "The Clan Comyn has always been known for its fighting spirit and immense courage, but to pound on an innocent young lad"—Bryce shook his head—"it does not bode well for your clan."

Ewan was glaring at her, hadn't take his eyes off her, and when they spread wide, she feared he had recognized her.

"I've seen you before," Ewan said, pointing a finger at her.

"Where?" she challenged, hoping that confronting him would make him realize what he would have to admit . . . that he and his brother were bested by a lassie. And that she was that lassie. It sounded foolish to her mind. She couldn't imagine how it would sound coming from his mouth. She grinned at the thought, though soon winced from the pain in her jaw.

He must have realized the same, and her grimace must have pleased him, for he smiled, shaking his head.

"Enough nonsense," Bryce said, stepping to block her from Ewan's view. "I want that bedchamber now."

Toag waved a servant over and issued orders, saying last, "Make sure you bring plenty of food for the lad. He needs some meat on him."

"And a good-sized bone for the dog," Charlotte said.

Toag scowled but nonetheless nodded at the servant.

Charlotte spoke softly to Odin, who looked to have regained his wits. And she was relieved when he followed her and Bryce out of the hall. She worried that the stairs might be too much for Odin, but it was she who found the stairs too difficult. Her body ached with each step she took, and with each step she wished she could fall back into Bryce's arms. He would not object; he would hold her close, offer comfort, keep her safe and carry her the rest of the way.

She almost collapsed from sheer relief when they entered the sizeable bedchamber. Odin immediately walked over to curl himself in front of the hearth. She followed him, checking again to make certain he was all right. He licked her face furiously, letting her know he was fine.

It wasn't until the servant girl closed the door after promising to return quickly that Bryce did what she had been aching for him to do.

He swept her up into his arms.

Chapter 19

Bryce held her close, his heart beating wildly with relief. He needed this, needed to hold her tightly to him, needed to have her safe in his arms. His eyes had caught hers when she had rushed into the hall, and the desperation and fear in them ran his blood cold. But it had been her screaming his name as she launched herself at Ewan that had sent him over the edge.

He had run like never before, fearful Ewan would hurt her before he could reach her. He was never so relieved when his hands had finally settled around her waist, and he had pulled her off the large man. No sooner had he directed her to see to Odin than he had turned on Ewan, landing a severe blow that no man could withstand. His rage knew no reason, and he had wanted to mercilessly pummel him, but his need to see to Charlotte and the animal she so courageously fought to protect far outweighed the desire for revenge—at that moment.

Seeing her battered and bruised had hurt him more than if he had taken the beating himself. And that he hadn't been able to reach out and take her in his arms had infuriated him. All he had been able to do was take stock of her, and, when his eyes had taken her in from head to toe, his anger had almost exploded into an uncontrollable rage.

Blood had spilled from the corner of her mouth, and her nose and the right side of her jaw had turned a deeper purple than it already had been. He could tell by the way she had stood that she was in pain, and he had wanted nothing more than to comfort her though he had wanted to kill Ewan.

It had taken all his strength to treat her simply as he would have a lad under his protection.

He pressed his cheek next to hers and whispered in her ear, "You are safe now."

"The moment I saw you, I knew I need fear no longer."

That she had feared for her safety and he had not been there from the start to save her fueled his anger, which wasn't even close to subsiding.

"I should never have let you go off on your own."

She pressed her hand to his cheek and met his eyes. "You could not have stopped me. Besides, look what I discovered about Ewan."

"By almost losing your life."

"He is a bit witless, and a fool, but I doubt he would have killed me. Though I did fear for the lad he had intended to beat."

"You suffered for defending another?" Bryce asked incredulously, though it shouldn't have surprised him. After all, she had attacked Ewan for hurting Odin. And she had protected her da for so long that it had become sheer instinct to protect those she cared for or those in need.

"He was a skinny bit of a thing," she said. "I worried that he would not survive a beating."

He shook his head. Had she not taken stock of her own size? "And you're not a wee bit of a thing who could just as well not survive?" He gave another shake of his head. Of course she didn't think that way, and her response proved it.

"You are only as big and brave as your actions or as cowardly in size as your inactions." Her fingers over his mouth prevented any response. "I may have suffered a few bruises, but I had you to run to. You who I knew without a doubt would help me. The skinny lad had no one, and I could not, nor would I, see him suffer."

They heard voices approach the room, and Bryce hurried to place her on the bed.

"Say nothing," Bryce instructed sternly.

He had all intentions of seeing to her care himself as soon as the servants finished bringing all that he had requested. He could not take the chance of anyone's discovering Charlotte's ruse. There would be no telling the consequences here and elsewhere. And truthfully, he wanted no other touching her. He and he alone would see to her needs.

He saw her eyes round when the large washtub was brought in and began being filled. He was aware of her thoughts, for they mirrored his own. How did they ignore the attraction between them? How did he stop himself from wanting to make love to her?

Love.

Was it creeping up on him, winding its way around him and taking hold without his having noticed? He cast a quick glance over himself, almost believing he would see a vine of some kind having taken root and winding its way around him until it completely engulfed him.

He couldn't allow that to happen. He couldn't plant roots, not yet. He needed to remain free, and the thought disturbed him. He had given his life for the true king; his duty was to him whether he liked it or not.

Bryce finally closed the door on the last servant and latched the door.

His hands itched to undress her but ached to caress her, and it would be a battle of his own will to keep him from doing anything but tending to her wounds and seeing that she rested and slept well for the night.

He approached her slowly. He smiled and cringed at the same time when she jumped up off the bed, wincing and holding her hand out in front of her, as if warding him off. He cringed in empathy at her wince, and his smile was the humor he found in her thinking her small hand could stop him.

"I can see to myself. You can go join the revelry in the hall."

He saw lurking in her dark eyes what he knew she must see in his—growing desire. He tried to reassure her and himself. "We will tend your wounds, and you will rest."

"Are you sure?"

Her blunt query stopped him.

"We have shared a few kisses and only a handful of touches, and while I have never lain with a man or desired any particular man, instinct tells me that what I feel, the tingles that run through me, the churning low in my belly when you kiss and touch me is pure passion.

And I have no doubt you feel the same, for it shines as heatedly in your eyes as I'm sure it does in mine."

Though her direct honesty should not have startled him, it did. But then it was more what she admitted that startled. She was letting him know just how much his kisses and touches affected her. She left herself vulnerable to him, and that grew his passion even more.

He could not stop it; his desire soared. And as much as he wanted to walk over to her, take hold of her, and make love to her throughout the night, he could not. Her well-being came first. She needed her wounds cleansed and tended, and no doubt her body was aching from the pummeling she took. She needed rest if they were to leave early on the morn. And he intended that they do just that—leave at dawn. He had had enough of the Clan Comyn.

"I won't deny that I want you, but now is not the time or place—"

"Will there ever be?" she asked softly.

He took a step closer. "Do you want there to be?"

She nodded. "Very much."

Damn I am in trouble.

"I know you can promise me nothing, and I cannot promise or commit myself, so we seem to fit well for the moment. And if the moment is all we have, I will take it."

A spark of anger surfaced that she would think that they could be so intimate, then simply walk away from each other. But hadn't he done it before? Met a woman, enjoyed her, and walked away?

The thought of Charlotte walking away from him once they had made love fueled that spark and set his anger to boiling. It took him a moment to calm himself, too afraid he'd speak with anger. She had meant no harm in her words; she simply voiced the truth of their situation. And yet it disturbed him and angered him terribly.

He wanted more than just coupling with Charlotte, but the truth was he didn't know if he could give her more.

"Are you sure? You may regret it." He wondered if he would be the one with regrets rather than she. Did he truly think he would not want more after making love to her?

"The memories will outweigh any regrets."

Memories.

She already haunted his mind day and night. Whatever would it be like after they'd made love?

Bryce made a choice there and then. "We will be intimate, but not here, not this night. It is not fitting."

She laughed softly between winces. "And I am too full of aches to participate."

He walked over to her, his hand going to rest at the back of her neck. "I could bring you much pleasure without you doing a thing."

He gently kissed where her mouth was not bloody, and he felt her shudder. He thought she would melt against him, but, instead, she stepped away.

"I cannot do this."

Bryce looked perplexed, not sure what she referred to, and he reached out to her.

She stepped away again. "I know not why I desire you so badly; I only know that I do. You cannot tend my wounds or remain while I bathe, for I cannot be responsible for my actions if you do."

She never failed to stun him silent. Just when he thought she could say no more to surprise him, she did. Knowing that she desired him sent his own passion soaring beyond reason, and he knew she was right. He could not stay there.

"I have something I must see to," he said. "Bathe and be quick about it, for I shall return shortly and will want to see to your wounds."

"My wounds are nothing. I can see to them myself."

He grabbed hold of her before she could avoid his grasp. When she winced, he silently scolded his own foolishness and loosened his grip though he would not let her go. He worried if he did that, it would be too difficult, if not impossible, to grab hold of her again.

"You would let me tend you if necessary, would you not?" he asked.

"If ever there came a time that it was necessary for you to tend me, I would welcome it," she said with a smile and a wince.

"I must not make you smile, at least until you heal."

"That is not possible. You make me smile more than I ever have in my life."

His arm went around her waist, and he lifted her to rest against him, her feet dangling just above the ground. He rested his forehead on hers. "You stir me like no other."

"And you have awakened passion in me."

He kissed her gently, so as not to disturb her wound. "Let it slumber, for you will rest in my arms tonight."

"That could prove dangerous."

"You forget I am an honorable warrior," Bryce reminded.

"Even honorable warriors can fall prey to temptation."

He faintly brushed his lips across hers. "You challenge me?"

"I hope so," she whispered against his lips.

He let her go then; he had to. If he didn't, he might never let her go. He walked out of the room without looking back, though he said, "Be done before my return, or I will not only see to your wounds, but to bathing you."

Once Bryce shut the door, he leaned against the far wall and took a deep breath that pained his chest. It took every ounce of strength he possessed to walk out of that room. Even with her wounds, he wanted, needed, ached to make love to her. It was much better that he kept his distance, at least until the time proved right.

When and where that would be, he didn't know, didn't want to know. It would happen. He would make love to her, and what would follow he didn't know. At this moment, he didn't want to know.

He marched down the hall, his knuckles cracking from how hard he fisted his hands. He had not finished with Ewan, and he intended to see that he did.

Toag jumped off the bench and greeted Bryce with a hearty slap on the back. "The lad does well?"

"He needs tending, but first I wish to speak to Ewan."

"He can be a fool when mead takes hold of him. I ordered him to retire for the night."

"He did not detour to the stable?" Bryce asked.

"Why would he?"

"His pride has been wounded, and he would seek retribution as best he could," Bryce said.

When Toag did nothing but glare at him, Bryce turned and marched out of the hall.

The rain soaked him as he made his way to the stables. Even over the pounding rain, Bryce could hear the pleading cries of someone in pain. He hurried in and rushed Ewan before he could pound the skinny lad again.

"You don't learn, do you?" Bryce said, tossing him to the ground.

Ewan rolled to his feet and spat blood from his mouth before saying, "Plan on teaching me?"

"I doubt you'd be an apt pupil."

Ewan wiped his arm across his mouth, blood staining his shirtsleeve. "I think I need to teach you."

Bryce waved him on with both hands. "Come on. I'm right here waiting."

Ewan charged him head down, and the young lads cheered on the fighting warriors.

Chapter 20

Charlotte sat cross-legged on the bed. She cast a glance at Odin, who slept peacefully by the hearth, the half-gnawed bone he had enjoyed safely tucked beneath his paw.

She yawned, tired from her ordeal, and ran her fingers through her damp, short hair. She was grateful that she had been given a clean shirt to wear, large though it was, falling past her knees. The sleeves she had rolled up, so they would not cover her hands.

It felt heavenly to be clean and wear a clean garment, not that it would last long. Her ruse needed to continue, and there weren't many freshly scrubbed young lads around. So she would enjoy her fresh-scrubbed feel for at least tonight.

Her aches had diminished some after her bath, and her abrasions proved minor. She could do nothing about the darkening bruise on her jaw, which had joined what bruise was already there. It looked worse then it felt and would fade in time. She was much more concerned about her feelings for Bryce.

What confused her was why her desire for him had

suddenly soared. Why this relentless ache that needed soothing? The answer was there, she knew it; she simply did not want to admit it.

She feared that if she did not take this chance, did not taste of love, she never would. She was not even certain if it was love; though from what her father had described of his collision with love, it certainly sounded familiar.

That this was not the time to fall in love was an ever-constant reminder to her, yet how did she prevent it? How did she stop from falling in love? Wouldn't it be easier simply to allow her heart to lead instead of her mind?

She wished she had another woman to talk with. That was one thing she missed, moving around from place to place, establishing lasting friendship with other women. She only had her father's perspective on love, and she so wished for a woman's opinion.

She felt lost as how to deal with the escalating attraction between her and Bryce. She had fought against it, believing it for the best, but tonight, that had changed.

When Bryce had taken her in his arms, she had seen a look in his eyes she had never seen before. She knew there and then that love could be visible; she saw it shining boldly in his blue eyes. It had jolted her heart, and a comfort so overpowering had washed over her that she had wanted to linger in the soothing sensation forever.

She also wanted to explore it, to taste all it had to offer, and that was why she had let him know that she would not be averse to their making love.

Charlotte shivered and smiled at the tingles that tickled her body from top to bottom, a frequent reaction to her frequent thoughts of intimacy with Bryce.

Remain alert to all thoughts.

She certainly was paying heed to her father's words, but it was her father's dilemma that she should be paying the most heed to.

She sighed again, feeling more lost than ever and wishing that Bryce would return. Not that it would solve anything; she simply missed him.

The door opened as her thought finished, and she smiled. It faded quickly when she caught sight of him. Blood marred his shirt, straw stuck to a good portion of his plaid, his knuckles were scraped, red, and swollen, and his handsome face was damp with sweat though he had not suffered a scratch or bruise.

He stared at her a moment but said not a word. He dropped the bow, cache, and sack, all of which she had left behind, on the table. Then he walked over to the pail near the hearth and plunged his hands into the water. He scrubbed them clean and did not even wince though surely his scraped knuckles had to have stung. Her wounds had when she had cleansed them, and she had cringed often when doing so.

When he began stripping off his clothes, Charlotte turned her head, not that she hadn't already seen him naked. But that time he had thought her a lad, and she had had no choice. Now she did have a choice, and she believed the wisest thing for her to do would be to look away. He was simply too tempting naked.

With her glance averted and her mind cleared, she asked what she should have when he first walked in. "What happened?"

"I finished what you started."

It took Charlotte a moment to realize what he meant. "The lad—"

"Is fine," he said, "and will remain so until I can send someone to come collect him."

She smiled. "You offered the lad a home."

"I could not leave him here to suffer further abuse from Ewan, and no doubt he would."

"And Ewan?" she asked anxiously.

"He got what he deserved," Bryce said. "It will be a while before he's able to speak and able to see out of his one eye." He walked toward her. "And you?"

She knew he approached the bed, his voice growing closer. But she dared not look, not even a peek, or she feared she'd make a fool of herself. "I am fine, my wounds minor and my aches bearable."

"Look at me," he ordered sharply.

"Are you naked?"

"Yes."

"Then I will not look at you," she said emphatically.

"You've seen me naked before," he argued.

"When you thought me a lad; now you know me a woman. It would not be proper—"

She heard him walk around to the other side of the bed, and, as he did, she turned her head the opposite way. The bed gave way to his weight, and she felt him slip beneath the soft wool blanket beside her.

She turned then to glare at him.

"I told you that you would be sleeping in my arms tonight."

"You failed to tell me that you would be naked," she accused.

"Not something I planned on, but I much prefer."

"I don't," she said.

He smiled. "Why? Am I too tempting naked?"

She turned the question on him. "Am I?"

"Let's find out," he said, and reached for her shirt.

"Stop," she scolded, shooing his hands away.

He was quicker though he didn't rob her of her shirt. He grabbed hold of her waist and had her flat on her back and up against his side in seconds.

"In my arms is where you belong."

"For tonight," she reminded, relaxing against him. He was warm, his scent like that of freshly dug earth and spring rain. His chest, though hard with muscles, pillowed her head quite nicely. His hand stroked her back, dipping ever lower past her waist as he did.

His caresses sent tingles through her from his first touch, but when his hand slipped down over her backside and squeezed and then slipped slowly beneath her shirt, she knew she was in trouble.

A heavy pounding at the door had them both jumping apart and Odin standing. Charlotte ran for the chair by the hearth and plopped down in it just before the door burst open.

"Soldiers have just entered the village," Edgar informed them once in the room. "They look to have been traveling for some time."

Charlotte was grateful that Bryce asked, "Do they have prisoners with them?

"No," Edgar said. "There are about fifteen of them, and the rain has left them foul in temper. They demand food, drink, and lodging in name of the king."

"We leave immediately," Bryce said, throwing the blanket back and going straight for his clothes. "Can you get food for us to take?"

"Da has already arranged it."

Charlotte worried that Edgar would not leave. How then would she get dressed?

Bryce must have thought the same, for he asked, "Can you bring the food here to us? We'll be done gathering our things by then and can be on our way."

Edgar nodded. "I won't be long."

"Neither will we," Bryce said.

As soon as the door closed, Charlotte sprang into action. She kept the shirt on and slipped her tunic over it. She yanked her boots on and what was left of the bread, cheese, and meat on the serving platters she wrapped in a cloth and shoved it into the sack, which had little food left.

Odin nudged her hand, and she looked to see him with his half-chewed bone in his mouth.

She took it from him. "For safekeeping," she said, and shoved it in the sack.

He licked her hand in appreciation.

"Are you both ready?" Bryce asked.

Charlotte slipped her cache over her shoulder and grabbed hold of her bow, along with the sack. "Now we are."

Bryce stepped close, his hand going to rest at the back of her neck. "Are you sure you feel well enough for this?"

"I have no choice."

"There is no moon to guide us, and it rains. It will not be easy to put distance between us and the soldiers."

"But it is necessary," she reminded, "for many reasons."

Edgar returned with a sack of food and extra blankets. He guided them safely down a hidden stairway known only to Toag and his sons, then through a narrow passage and into the dark, stormy night.

The two men shared a quick handshake, exchanged whispered words, then Edgar was gone. So were they, disappearing into the woods at the back of the keep.

Charlotte ordered Odin to stay close and keep silent. The dog understood her commands and obeyed, not a bark or snarl out of him.

She in turn followed Bryce's brisk order. "Stay close."

If she didn't, she would surely lose him. The thick cloud cover and the steady rain made night visibility nearly impossible, so falling a step or two behind could prove dangerous.

After what seemed like eternity, Bryce stopped and turned to her. "Enough. I am not even sure of where we travel. It could be right into the arms of the soldiers. We need to take shelter until morning."

She almost fell against him in relief. Her body ached, and she was wet to the bone.

It wasn't much of a shelter, a tall pine so heavy and thick that the rain could barely penetrate the preponderance of branches. And a large stone that hugged the tree trunk helped block the windy rain. The trio sat huddled together, Charlotte in the middle.

Bryce wrapped himself around her, tucking her in the crook of his arm, then threw a blanket around them. She gratefully cuddled closer, and though he was as wet as she was, there was warmth to his body. It seeped inside her and helped to chase her chill.

He kneaded and rubbed her arm, sparking more heat to her cold flesh.

"We leave at first light," he said.

"We pick up the trail where we found my da's message?" She could not keep her voice from trembling.

"You are cold," he said, and, with a quick lift, had her in his lap and the blanket wrapped completely around them both.

Charlotte tucked her legs up, cuddling into a ball in his lap. He continued to stroke and knead heat into her, and his efforts as well as his combined body heat slowly began to chase away the deep-rooted chill.

"Our search does not go well," he said.

"It will now that we know about my da's messages."

"We don't know if we will find any more or even if he was able to leave more."

Her head popped up. "You are not suggesting that we give up?"

"It might be wise for us to return to my home, rest, regroup, and gather one or two of my brothers, then continue."

She got so upset, her heart started pounding, and the chill returned sending shivers through her. "No! I will not desert my da."

"That is not my thought at all."

"Then why suggest it?"

"It is the wisest thing for us to do at this point. We have run into obstacle after obstacle, and it grows more and more dangerous for you to be parading around as a lad."

"So it would be less dangerous for me after returning home with you to continue our mission as a woman?"

His hesitation made her realize his intentions.

She bolted up in his arms. "You intend to leave

me at your home and continue the mission with your brothers." She didn't give him a chance to respond. She poked him hard in the chest. "That will never happen."

She tried to move off his lap, but he clamped his arms tightly around her. She struggled for a moment, but her useless effort only served to aggravate her aches. She calmed and settled once again, deciding it was better to conserve her strength.

"I will search for my da with or without you."

"You know I will not leave you on your own."

"Then the matter is settled," she said.

He reached up and stroked her cheek with his finger, slowly turning her face to look at him. "At least tell me you will think on it."

Her annoyance with him deflated as soon as she looked into his eyes. It truly frightened her to see what she saw for a second time, and though she realized that she could be wrong, she knew she wasn't. It was love she saw, potent and powerful.

"It would be easy for me to lie to you," she said, "and tell you what you wish to hear. But I cannot. I will take no time to rest or be left behind. I will search for my da until I find him."

"You are a stubborn one."

"I am stubborn when it comes to those I love."

He smiled. "Then your husband will have his hands full."

"My husband will always have my hands to help him, to hold him, to care for him, to protect him, and to make love to him."

Her words sparked something in both of them, for their lips came together simultaneously. At first, it was a gentle kiss, a simple need to touch and linger in the inexplicable anticipation of what was to come.

Desire exploded in them both, driving them to taste like lovers long starved for each other. She didn't object when his hand moved over her breast and gave a gentle squeeze. She liked the play of his hands so intimately on her. It rushed heated tingles through her body.

It also gave her the need to touch him, and she ran her hand down inside his shirt to stroke his hard chest. Though wet, his heated flesh stung and made her want to touch him all the more.

He laid her back on the ground, his hand pillowing her head and his mouth going to nip at her nipples through her clothes. It felt good, and she could only imagine how it would feel if naked. And oh, how she wished she were. And oh, how she wished he would not stop, not ever.

She raised her legs to wrap around his hip, to move closer, to link herself with him so they could never be parted. He helped her, hoisting her legs up to settle around his hip. He then ran his hand down along her thigh and beneath her shirt and when it settled between her legs, she knew this was it. She would not stop him.

In the rain on this muddy ground, they would make love.

Fate had a different idea when suddenly the pine tree released an abundance of rainwater to pour down over them. They both jumped up.

Sopping wet, and their ardor cooled by the unexpected soaking, they sat there and saw that Odin still slept, the water having missed him completely.

They both laughed.

Chapter 21

They were up with first light as Bryce had wanted and on their way, forgoing food for safety. It hadn't taken him long to determine their whereabouts and point them in the right direction. Charlotte followed without objection, but then she had traveled with ease through the woods from the beginning. Her constant travels with her da had given her knowledge and awareness of the land that most never came to understand.

He admired her perceptive nature though it could prove difficult at times, like now. He wanted to take her home and see her safely ensconced with his family. Then he could proceed on his mission to find the spy and her da.

"I can hear you thinking."

Her remark had him halting in his tracks and turning to glare at her.

"You want to take me home and leave me there."

He saw no reason to deny the truth. "If you would just think on it, you would see it is for the best."

"For you, not for me," she said, and walked past him, Odin at her side.

Bryce shook his head and caught up with her.

"Don't bother to say a word," she said with a dismissive wave of her hand. "Go where you please. I travel west to find my da."

He laughed and caught hold of her arm. "I will go where I please, but you'll be coming with me."

"You can't force me."

"Yes I can."

"I do as I please," she said.

"In this insistence, you'll do as I say," he said. "And if you weren't so pigheaded, you'd see that what I propose makes more sense than aimlessly wandering the woods."

"We're not aimlessly wandering any longer. We at least know we need to go west."

"Toward my home."

"Then go there if you wish. I intend to continue on until I find my da."

"What of *us*?" He didn't like that he saw sadness in her eyes.

"There is no time for us," she said.

"We have this time right now. Will you walk away from it?"

"Do you ask me to choose between you and my da?" she asked.

"No. Never would I do that. And never would I make a promise I could not keep. We both have duties and missions that must be accomplished. The future is not ours to promise to each other. We have only this time here and now together."

"You're right. Here and now while we search for my da, and you search for your spy. This time can be ours. I will give myself freely to you. I want to make memories with you that will live long in my heart and, I hope, in yours. But it will be here on our journey, not at your home, where I will surrender to you—or I will not surrender at all."

"You give me an ultimatum?"

She shook her head. "I but speak the truth. We either work as one, or we work separately."

Work as one.

The revelation of working as one with her startled and yet intrigued him. And the idea of them working separately angered him. He had grown attached to Charlotte, much too attached, and he wasn't ready to separate from her, not yet—perhaps not ever.

No doubt she had wormed her way into his heart, and now that she resided there, he didn't want to let her go. He also knew that with so much uncertainty surrounding them, neither could promise forever. But working as one, thinking as one, loving as one could possibly be a step toward forever—a step he'd take, the chance he'd take.

He took a step toward her and reached his hand out to her. She took a step toward him and grasped his hand.

"We work as one," he said.

"We work as one," she repeated.

Their words resonated like a vow. And though here in the woods, their only witness Odin, Bryce felt the need to seal their words, and so he bent down and kissed her. Her arms instantly wrapped around him, and he knew there and then that their words had been a binding vow he would honor forever.

"We must keep moving," he said, after regretfully ending the kiss. He could have gone on kissing her, she tasted so scrumptious. If he had continued, he wouldn't have been able to get enough, he would have wanted more. And she would have given it to him.

The thought fired his already raging passion, but he did what was best. He moved away from her and started walking. She soon followed, and silence ensued as they continued their journey.

It was a few hours later that Odin stopped suddenly, sniffed the air, and took an alert stance. With Odin more on alert than guard, Bryce and Charlotte did not ready their weapons though their hands remained on them.

An old man slow in step and manner stepped out of the woods, a young lad of about ten years with dark brown hair and fine features following. No sooner did the lad spot them than he drew a dirk from his belt and moved to stand protectively in front of the old man.

The old man placed a reassuring hand on the lad's shoulder. "I do not believe they mean us harm."

"Do you?" the lad challenged, his dark eyes on Bryce.

"I have no cause to fight with you," Bryce said. "Though we were about to find a spot to have a respite if you care to join us. We have food to share should you be in need."

The lad's eyes turned wide as he swerved around to face the old man. "Food, grandda."

Bryce was impressed with the way the young lad patiently helped his grandda to sit and gave him food before taking any for himself. And he didn't grab for more food when he finished what Charlotte had given him though he obviously was hungry for more.

It also didn't surprise him that Charlotte insisted that the lad take more. It was easy to see she empathized with him and no doubt envied him. He had his grandda with him while Charlotte still searched for her da.

"I am Cadmus, and this is my grandson, Randall," the old man said. "We thank you for your generosity."

Randall nodded in agreement, his mouth full.

"Where does your journey take you?" Charlotte asked.

"To safety," Cadmus said.

"Away from soldiers," Randall added. "They stalk the villages and countryside for any manner of man or lad capable of carrying a weapon."

"When we learned they were close to our home, we left," Cadmus explained. "I will not have my grandson fight for King Kenneth."

"I will fight for the true king," Randall claimed proudly. "We hunt for his camp, and I will join in his fight."

"You are too young to go to battle," Charlotte said.

Bryce had not expected the lad's angry reaction. His hand shot out and sent her tumbling. Odin launched himself at the lad, and Bryce grabbed hold of him before he could do any damage. With a command to the dog to stay, Bryce was ready to get to his feet when Cadmus placed a hand on his arm.

"Let the lassie teach my grandson a necessary lesson."

Bryce was surprised the old man knew Charlotte to

be a woman, and it only confirmed his concern for her safety. He was about to intervene, regardless of the old man's request, when he saw that Charlotte had scrambled to her feet.

"You just proved you are not worthy to fight for the true king," she spat. "You push like a lassie instead of fighting like a man."

Randall's eyes popped wide, and his face flushed red.

Bryce looked to Charlotte, and she smiled. He remained where he sat and prayed she wouldn't get hurt yet again.

The lad launched himself at Charlotte, and Bryce had all he could do to keep himself from interfering. His confidence however in her grew as he watched her use wit instead of brawn to defend. She tripped the lad and sent him sprawling and outmaneuvered flying punches. She jumped from one rock to another, avoiding more senseless strikes, and finally gave him a hardy boot to the butt, sending him to land face-first and hard on the ground.

"That will teach you not to fight until you are ready," Cadmus said with a shake of his finger at his grandson.

"He's bigger than me," Randall said, getting to his feet and brushing dirt and mud from his clothes.

"Taller perhaps," his grandda said, "but he is a she. You were bested by a lassie."

The lad paled. "He can't be a she. He fights too well."

"I did not truly fight you," Charlotte said. "I avoided you, made you tire yourself out, lash out at me in frustration, until I finally seized the opportunity to end it."

Bryce expected anger from the lad, but instead was impressed by his reply.

"Teach me," Randall pleaded.

"The first intelligent move you've made," Cadmus said.

Charlotte introduced Randall to a few tactics while Bryce and Cadmus spoke. And when all was done, the old man and lad pointed in the right direction, Bryce and Charlotte continued on their way.

"How many defeats did you suffer before being able to successfully defend yourself and your da?" Bryce asked. The thought had crossed his mind as he had watched Charlotte deal with the lad. How many times had she suffered the same humiliation or worse?

"It is amazing how fast you learn when it means your survival."

"You need not worry about that any longer," he said. "You have me to protect you."

He was prepared for her to argue, say what she had said many times over—that she could defend herself. She, however, surprised him.

"It truly pleases me to know that."

It pleased him too that she finally didn't argue over it.

"I'm sure I won't need to trouble you with help that often, being able to handle most things quite easily myself. But it is good to know you are there for me."

There it was, her tenacious nature, though presented mannerly. What she was truly saying was, I can do it; I don't need your help. He was about to set her right when she spoke up, though her voice was softer than usual.

"You truly don't know how safe it makes me feel to know that you are nearby and will come to my defense without question." She smiled. "Even when I am the cause of the problem."

He laughed. "So you admit you can be troublesome."

"Occasionally."

He laughed again though it faded, replaced by the imposing voice of a mighty Highlander. "Occasionally or daily, your fault or not, I will always defend you without question or hesitation."

"I would do the same for you," she said just as soberly.

"You will not," he ordered firmly.

"I will too!"

"You will not place yourself in danger for me."

"I already have, and I will do it again," she said obstinately.

He was ready to debate the matter most strenuously when she spoke up again.

"We work as one, or do you forget?" She shook her head. "When you hurt, I hurt. When something troubles you, it troubles me. When someone does you wrong, he does me wrong. If someone harms you, he harms me. And may God help him, for I will kill him."

Bryce was stunned by her fierce declaration, especially her last few words. And he was even more stunned, for he felt the same way. He had wanted to kill Ewan for what he had done to her. Wisely, he had contained his rage though he'd made the fool suffer.

He noticed she was shaking her head.

"What's wrong?"

She stopped walking though she continued shaking her head. "I don't know when it happened. I can't believe I willingly admit it."

Fear gripped at his heart and throat, and he worried that he wouldn't get the words out. "What happened?" Had Ewan done something to her that she hadn't wanted to tell him? If he did, he would kill him and slowly. He took firm hold of her shoulders. "Tell me. Do not be afraid tell me."

She stopped shaking her head and stared at him.

"Tell me," he urged, fearing what she would say. "Tell me."

Chapter 22

"I'm falling in love with you." Charlotte was shocked that she openly admitted it but had felt compelled to do so. She was tired of keeping it secreted away inside, even to the point of denying it to herself. What good was love if you didn't embrace it?

Seeing the startled expression on Bryce's face, she wondered if she had blundered, speaking her feelings aloud. But it was done. She could not retrieve it, and she did not want to. She spoke not only the truth but from her heart.

Finally, his mouth opened, and she was eager to hear his words, but none came. Had she shocked him silent? She hadn't been wrong about seeing love in his eyes. It had been there more potent than she would have ever thought possible. Perhaps seeing it so visible had given her the impetus to admit her love for him though perhaps he did not feel comfortable or was not ready to do the same.

He opened his mouth again and looked as if he struggled to find the right words.

Her heart went out to him. Here he was, a mighty

Highlander warrior who fought fearlessly in battle, but found himself fearful when it came to love. She couldn't bear to see him suffer, and so she pressed her finger to his lips.

"It's all right," she said softly. "You don't have to say anything. I don't need flowery words and declarations of undying love. What I've seen in your eyes is enough."

His hand reached up, took hold of her finger, and moved it away from his mouth. "What have you seen in my eyes?"

"That you love me," she said boldly and without the slightest bit of hesitation. She had to smile, for the shocked look that registered on his face was priceless. "Have I told you something you have yet to learn yourself?"

He let go of her hand, took a step away, rubbed his chin, turned away from her, scratched his head, and turned back around to stare at her, his mouth open but no words forthcoming.

Charlotte laughed. "You are so in love with me that it has rendered you speechless."

He threw his hands up. "If you say so."

"Good, then it is settled. We are falling in love," she said. "Now we best keep moving. It would be nice to find fitting shelter for us to finally consummate our love."

She would have stumbled if his grip hadn't been firm when he suddenly grabbed hold of her. She looked quick in his eyes, and there, mixed with confusion, was love. It warmed her heart and made her feel secure, and she hoped that sparkle would remain there forever.

"I can make no promises to—"

"I know," she said before he could finish. "We have spoken time enough on that, and I understand more than most would. We take and give what we can for now; the rest is up to fate."

He kissed her then, and she welcomed it. She enjoyed his kisses and wished they could share them more often. Time and circumstances, however, interfered, and so she would welcome and enjoy their kisses whenever chance allowed them to steal one.

They were on their way once again, Charlotte feeling her step lighter than usual. She barely felt the aches and pains that tormented her now and again. And reminded her of the many altercations she had been in of late. Nothing seemed important now other than the relief of admitting that she loved Bryce. It had given her a sense of peace and filled her with joy.

That she had once again seen love for her in his eyes had made her even more confident of his love. She was glad she had had the courage to speak up and tell him how she felt, and she cherished and always would the memory of his shocked expression.

She wondered if he hadn't truly realized until that very moment that he loved her. Regardless, he did now, and when finally they made love, they would truly be making love. The thought sent tingles racing through her, and her smile widened.

The continuing gray clouds did not dampen her spirit or the muddy trail. She was in love, and it felt like the sun shone and the trail was no burden. That changed when the terrain turned rocky. She had no time for smiles or sunny thoughts; it was time to keep a firm watch on her footing.

Scotland could be a land of endless beauty and an unforgiving land. Her father had taught her that much could be learned from both. And so she had listened well to his lessons and learned the temperament of the land. It was for that reason that she paid close attention to where she stepped and what to avoid, especially with its having rained.

She and Bryce were halfway across the rough terrain when a light rain began to fall, and Odin gave a bark. They heard a shout then, a distance behind them. They both turned and spotted six soldiers on foot.

One shouted again, and it echoed across the land.

"In the name of the king, I place you in his service."

Bryce turned to Charlotte.

She spoke before he could. "We keep going. They no doubt will attempt to hurry their steps and will suffer for such a foolish move. We watch our steps and will soon find easier ground."

No sooner had she said it than they heard a soldier cry out in pain.

"My ankle. Bloody hell, I broke my ankle."

Bryce and she watched for only a moment as one other soldier tried to help the injured one and slipped and fell himself. While the other four looked awkward and foolish as they attempted to hurry their steps across the unforgiving terrain.

She and Bryce in turn were soon free of the treacherous patch of land, hurrying their footsteps and covering their tracks as they put distance between them and the soldiers.

"I doubt those soldiers will follow us," Charlotte said. "They will be too busy seeing to their injuries."

"If not them, there will be others," Bryce said.

"King Kenneth builds his troop to ready for battle with the true king." She shook her head. "How does he think those taken by force will fight for him?"

"He probably threatened harm to their families."

Thunder cracked and rolled around them.

"Not another night of rain," Charlotte said, still not fully dry from yesterday.

"We need to find shelter for the night."

"Hopefully, more than a tree to huddle under," she said. "A cottage would be nice, with a good fire."

Lightning lit the sky, and the loud crack of thunder that followed gave her a start. She hurried her steps, wanting desperately to be in a warm, dry place before the sky unleashed yet another storm.

She was not so lucky. The storm broke before they could find shelter. They walked until they were soaked and still found no place that would adequately harbor them. The dark clouds blotted the sky, night falling far earlier than usual.

They stumbled along, frantically searching for anything that could protect them from the thrashing rain.

Charlotte repeatedly wiped at her eyes, the rain making it almost impossible to see. Bryce grabbed her arm and pulled her along with him. She went eagerly, assuming he had found shelter. Catching a glimpse of Odin's backside slithering beneath thick bushes made her realize that Bryce intended to do the same.

"You can't mean this," she shouted against the storm as he stopped next to the bush that Odin had disappeared under.

"There is nothing else," he shouted back. "Now get down and crawl beneath it."

She shook her head. "No, I will find a tree to camp under."

"Under the bush," he ordered with a shout.

"I will no—"

She never finished. His arm went around her waist, and she was hoisted up and tucked flat against his side. He was on his knees before she could protest and had them both under the bushes in seconds.

There was little room to move, but the rain and wind could still be felt, but not with nearly the intensity of before. She had no choice but to rest her head in the crook of his arm and let her body relax against him. His arms remained firm around her, as if he expected her to attempt an escape.

She might be stubborn, but she was no fool. They couldn't have kept going. It was just that she so wanted more from this night.

She looked up at Bryce and innocently, without thought or intention, gently wiped away the rain from across his nose and cheeks. She spoke softly as she did, thinking nothing of her complaint. "I'm always wet of late."

His blue eyes turned intense, the color almost turbulent. Had it been her refusal to obey him or her words that angered him? With soothing strokes across his forehead, she continued wiping the rain away and the wrinkles that bunched along his brow.

"No doubt we both will heat each other soon enough," she said, already a nice warmth spreading through her. She tucked strands of his wet hair behind his ear and ran her finger down along his jaw to wipe away droplets of rain on his chin. "Before you know it, we'll be hot."

Raindrops doused his lips, and, without thinking, she kissed them away, lingering in her innocent efforts, or so she told herself.

Chilled at first, his lips began to warm, and though he hadn't responded, it didn't stop her from continuing. She actually was quite enjoying herself. And was pleased when more raindrops fell on his lips; this time, she licked them off.

Slowly and steadily, she made her way across his mouth, her tongue making certain to get each and every drop. It darted several times to the corners of his mouth to get tiny stubborn drops that clung tenaciously. But they were no match for her, scooping them up with the flick of her tongue.

With no more raindrops to wipe away, she gave him a gentle kiss, smiled, and glanced up at him. She froze as soon as she caught his eyes. Passion, hot and heavy, blazed in his blue eyes, and she wasn't sure if it frightened or excited her. But why be fearful? Wasn't it what she wanted?

"My turn," he said, and lowered his mouth to hers.

Chapter 23

Sanity vanished, along with fear, as soon as his lips touched hers. Nothing made sense, nothing mattered but his kiss. It took hold of her and held her captive, a willing captive. She would linger in the taste of him forever if she could.

It was a strong, demanding kiss, and she responded with the same strength and demand. Thunder rumbled overhead, but it was nothing compared to the thunderous passion that rumbled between them.

He abruptly pulled his lips off hers, and she tilted her head back and took a needed breath. She gasped when his teeth began to bite playfully along her neck, sending tingles all the way down to her toes. They were light and teasing and oh so tantalizing. His nips soon traveled up over her chin and along her lips before he once again stole her breath with a kiss.

Lost in sensations that were new and wondrous, she hadn't realized that his hand had settled on her breast. He cupped her, her small breast getting lost in his large hand, and gave a firm squeeze; and then his thumb teased her nipple hard. She so wished that there were no clothes to interfere with his touch. She ached to feel flesh against flesh.

He tore his lips away again, his breathing heavy. "We must stop."

"Why?"

"Look where we are," he said with a quick shake of his head. "This is no place for us to make love."

"We are together. What else matters?"

"A soft bed, a warm fire?"

"And what if we never get the chance to have that?" she asked. "What if this is our only chance to love each other?"

"There will be other times," he insisted, as if he decreed it.

"We don't know that. Tomorrow could change everything. What then? Do we remember this moment with regret?"

She rested her hand on his cheek. "I love you, Bryce MacAlpin, and I want to make love with you. Will you deny me? Deny us?"

He took firm hold of her chin. "You are the most remarkable woman. You make me mad with the want of you no matter time and place."

She smiled and pushed his hand away to nip at his lips. "And I am a woman you will never forget after this night is done."

"This night and you are already unforgettable," he said, and laid claim to her lips while his hands explored.

She did not hesitate to do the same. She might not be able to see him naked, the confined space allowing for no room to remove their clothes, but one touch of her hand on him, and she was reminded of when she first landed between his legs.

There was no doubt he was large. She had seen that with her own eyes, but to feel it for herself startled and delighted. And she took great joy in running her hand over the thick length of him time and again.

"Stop," he urged in her ear.

"You don't like—"

"I like it too much," he whispered, and nibbled at her ear.

Thunder crackled overhead and suddenly the sky opened ever wider and the rain drenched the land even more. It poured through the bushes, soaking them.

"Not again," Bryce said angrily and rolled over her, tucking her beneath him as he went. "Tonight we finish what we started."

She grinned and latched a hand on to each of his arms. "I was going to get on top of you and—"

He groaned.

"I shouldn't want to do that?" she asked innocently.

He grinned and rested his brow to hers. "When all is done and we are free, you can do that as much as you want."

"Truly?"

"You have my word."

"I hope this is not our only time together."

"It better not be," he said, and kissed her again.

They were soon two lovers lost amid a raging storm not only outside but within. Kisses and touches turned frantic, clothes were pushed up and aside, and there was no hesitancy, there was no need for it. Both were eager and anxious, and Charlotte not hesitant or willing to let him worry over her first time.

She whispered encouraging words in his ear, telling him she couldn't wait to have him deep inside her, to feel the thrill of being loved, to truly become one with him.

With each encouraging word, his hands explored, and she welcomed his intimate touches. Never had she felt so alive, never had she thought that a man's touch could bring such pleasure. The more his hand traveled beneath her tunic and stroked her flesh, and the more his fingers teased their way inside her, the more she thought she'd burst with the pleasure of it.

It wasn't long before she wanted *him* inside her and she encouraged him until finally . . . she gasped when he entered her and smiled. "Good Lord, that feels good."

"You haven't felt anything yet," he teased with a kiss.

Charlotte feared she was as loud as the thunder that rocked the night as he drove in and out of her, and she didn't care. She never knew anything could feel so fantastic and beautiful at the same time.

And when she erupted in a mind-boggling climax, she thought she had surely died and gone to heaven.

Bryce had never experienced such an explosive climax. It had rocked his whole body with such pleasure that, for a moment, he couldn't think at all or make sense of anything. All he could do was soak in the divine pleasure.

He had had no plans to make love to Charlotte. Not here in a rainstorm on the muddy ground, but it had been impossible not to. Their desire for each other could no longer be contained, and nothing could stop it, not the disagreeable weather or lack of proper lodgings. Nothing had mattered but making love.

With sanity being slowly restored, he eased himself off Charlotte, tucking her once again in the crook of his arm. He knew then and there he never wanted to let her go. And he knew there would come a time, he hoped soon, when he would make love to her in a proper setting.

Right now, he wanted to let her know how extraordinary it had been making love with her.

"That was better than I ever imagined it could be," she said on a sigh.

So many times she had startled him with her remarks, not only because they were often bold but because they so often reflected his own thoughts.

"Only true love could feel so"—she sighed again—"satisfying."

She was right about that. This intense, overpowering feeling that surged through and consumed him could only be love. And he was annoyed that love would strike now, when it was so inconvenient. He should embrace it and not worry over anything else, but there was more than just himself to consider, and as selfish as he wished he could be, it wasn't possible. He had his duty, and that duty prevented him from promising her a future.

She gazed up at him. "We will have these moments and take what we can, will we not?"

She asked, as if she feared he would say no. He wanted these moments between them as much as he wanted this fight to seat the true king to end.

"Every moment we can steal will be ours." He hugged her to him, and though their garments were riddled with rain and a chill permeated the air, they shared warmth.

Content from making love, they fell asleep wrapped in each other's arms.

Dawn brought the sun with it, and Bryce and Charlotte stretched the aches out of their cramped bodies once they were out from under the bush. Odin pranced around, having been up before them and eager to be on the way.

Bryce smiled, watching Charlotte kneel on one knee to favor the dog with a rub and a kiss. She looked a sight, her clothes still soggy and partially covered with mud. There were also patches of mud in her hair, while Odin did a good job of licking any dirt off her face. Bryce wished her bruises could be that easily wiped away.

She certainly looked a sight, but to him she was beautiful. The more he watched her, the more he seemed to fall in love with her. She wasn't the kind of woman he would have chosen to love, yet she was *everything* he wanted.

He almost laughed aloud, not making any sense and yet not caring. What mattered was that they were together, and he intended to see that they stayed that way for as long as possible.

"We better go," he said, the thought that he should be taking them home where she would be safe growing ever stronger. And with the direction they headed, home would not be far off.

Charlotte stood and, with a smile, hurried to his side and flung herself at him. His hands instinctively went out to catch her around the waist. She wrapped her legs around his waist, and he kept his hands planted on hers.

"It's a kiss I'll have from you this morn before we go anywhere," she said boldly.

Her smiling demand brought a grin to his face. "Is it now?"

"It is, and it will be the way we start every morn between us."

To know each day would start in such a glorious fashion made his grin grow wider.

"See, you like the idea."

"Aye, I like it very much," he admitted, and wasted no more time on words. He lowered his mouth to hers and kissed her.

Her arms tightened around his neck as she returned the kiss with force and hunger. Bryce realized that it was more than a kiss she was wanting. And he had to admit so did he.

Not a good time, though. They needed to get moving and keep alert. There was no telling if soldiers were nearby.

With much reluctance, he ended the kiss. "We have to go; we can't linger though I would love to."

Her cheeks grew fat with her wide smile. "So you want me as much as I want you."

Bryce knew he was in trouble. Charlotte wouldn't be shy about letting him know what she wanted, and that pleased him, but it also could prove distracting and dangerous for them both.

"You need to behave," he ordered, though certainly not sternly.

She sighed. "How can I when I've just discovered love?"

He didn't know himself since he felt the same. But there was one thing he knew would make her see reason whether she wanted to or not.

"Think about your da."

She wiggled her way down and out of his arms, which only served to strike an image of her naked on top of him, riding him with wanton lust.

"You're right," she said. "We'll steal moments when we can, and now is not one of them."

Oh Lord, did he want it to be. He wanted it badly. He wanted them naked and enjoying each other in every way possible.

"We better go," she said.

Bryce didn't say a word, didn't trust himself to. He turned and walked away from her. If he didn't, they both would be in serious trouble, for he would have her on the ground in no time, or perhaps up against a tree, or—He shook his head and swore beneath his breath. He had to stop the vivid images that raced through his mind and made him hard.

Next time, it would be in a proper bed that they made love and with no worries, another reason to head home.

Their garments dried as the sun remained bright and the day turned warmer than usual for spring. They kept a safe distance from each other, giving the impression to anyone who came upon them of nothing more than a warrior and lad traveling together.

Charlotte scurried after Odin when he went sniffing

sticks, and it upset Bryce to see the disappointment on her face when nothing came of it. She was determined to find her da, nothing would stop her. She would do the same for anyone she loved, especially her children. The thought provoked a sudden image of her round with his child and the sudden realization that it could be a possibility. She could very well be carrying his child, if not now, however, soon enough, for he had every intention of making love to her as often as possible.

"I'm beginning to think my da did not come this way," she said, walking up beside him.

"Or he has not had the opportunity to leave another message for you."

Her shoulders slumped with the weight of his words, and he was sorry to have added to her burden.

"The longer it takes to find him, the more I worry for his safety," she said.

"He's safe enough if he has yet to reach this secret prison."

"You're right," she said, her look slightly brighter. "It wouldn't be until he reached the prison that they would start torture."

"Even then, they might wait to see if he can give the king what he wants."

"That doesn't mean I can linger in my effort. It just means that there is time to reach him before he is made to suffer."

"There is a small village not far from here; perhaps the soldiers and prisoners passed that way."

"A friendly village?"

"You have seen for yourself how uncertain times have caused most to be extra cautious," he said. "And then there are the soldiers we need to be aware of, and it continues to trouble me to see so many so far north."

"The time draws near," she said. "The true king will need to make himself known soon and—"

"I will fight beside him." Bryce didn't need to remind her of his duties though perhaps he was reminding himself.

"I will help any way I can."

"You and your da will remain safe in my home." It was a command, no doubt, but he would not worry over her while he was needed elsewhere. He would see her situated in a safe place, and that was in the keep with his family.

"Where I will do what?"

"What women do."

She shook her head. "You forget that I have lived differently than most women. I have been free to explore and learn and do whatever I wished. And I don't wish to be confined."

"MacAlpin land is large enough for you to explore as often as you like."

"Alone?" she asked with a smile.

He laughed. "I don't know if I can promise that."

"As long as it is you that is with me, I won't object."

He was about to reach out and rub the smudge of dirt off her cheek when Odin suddenly stood in a guarded stance.

Bryce turned, as did Charlotte, just as a man came stumbling past the trees and collapsed on the ground.

Chapter 24

Charlotte remained on guard as she hurried to the fallen man's side, fearing that soldiers might have followed him. Bryce obviously felt the same, his glance darting cautiously about. Odin, however, thought differently. He went to the man and began sniffing his prone body.

Feeling somewhat safe that Odin hadn't remained cautious, Charlotte felt more at ease seeing to the man. Bryce got to him before she did and carefully turned him over. He was old and frail, too much so to be traveling alone on foot. And her thoughts immediately went to her da.

How was he surviving his ordeal?

As if he heard her thoughts, Bryce said, "He's not your da."

"He could very well be," she said, frightened by the thought.

"From what you have told me of your da, he is a man accustomed to walking great distances, over various terrains, and braving the elements. It will take much more than a forced walk to conquer your da."

Her da did have tremendous stamina for his years and a mind that was young and eager. He had often advised her not to let life beat at her, that she should fight back with all her strength and live courageously, no matter the circumstances. No doubt that was what he was doing now, and so must she.

She suddenly felt sympathy for the man, who was beginning to stir on the ground. His many wrinkles, stooped shoulders, and gnarled fingers told her that life had not been kind to him. She didn't think the soldiers had taken him for service to the king. He was too old and weak. Who or what could he be running from?

His eyes finally fluttered open, then popped wide when his glance settled on Bryce.

"It's all right," Bryce said softly, and moved a firm hand to his shoulder. "You are safe."

The man sighed and shut his eyes. When he opened them, tears fell. He tried to speak but had difficulty. His hand reached out to Bryce as he fought to speak.

Bryce took hold of it. "Rest. There is time to talk."

The old man shook his head and finally found his voice. "I am dying."

"Nonsense," Bryce said sharply. "You have survived an ordeal and will live to tell the tale."

"My time here is done, life is too hard," he said, more tears falling. "I have nothing. All I had is gone."

Charlotte had been taught to be strong, and she had never been allowed to wallow in pity. Her da often re-minded that life could prove difficult, but there was always something to learn from it.

"You are safe and you now have us," she said.

The old man smiled. "This is good, for I will not die alone."

Odin, as if sensing that the man needed comfort, licked his face and lay down beside him. The old man smiled again and hugged the large animal to him.

"Tell us what happened," Bryce said, taking one of the rolled blankets and, after gently lifting the old man's head, slipping it beneath.

The old man raised his gnarled hand. "For years, I forged the finest swords, but my hands suffered for it. I taught my son, and he did the same. The king's soldiers came one day and took him away. With my son's wife dead many years, I was the only one my granddaughter had left." She's a stubborn one and not long after her da was taken, she went in search of him. I have not seen her since."

The old man closed his eyes again, as if shutting away the harsh memories.

"The soldiers returned, and this time they took me." Tears once again began to fall. "They told me that my son was dead and that I was to take his place. I told them I was not strong enough to fight. They just laughed and tethered me to an old, though spry, man."

Charlotte's heart suddenly pounded in her chest. "White hair, short and slim, with a smile that showed good teeth."

"Yes, that is Idris," the old man said.

"My da," she said with a gasp. "You were with my da."

The old man's eyes turned wide. "You do search for him. He told me that his daughter would come for him. He said you were a stubborn one, much like him, and that you were more intelligent than most women and men. He had no doubt that you would find your way to him and free him. It is what keeps him going."

"How did you escape and not my da if you were tethered together?" she asked, and grew worried when he turned his eyes away from her.

"Charlotte isn't only strong, she's courageous," Bryce said, his glance going straight to her. "And she needs to know the truth about her da."

She appreciated his confidence in her, and she was grateful for the love she saw shining in his eyes. It warmed her heart to know she was not alone, that he was there to help her. It gave her the added strength to hear whatever truth the old man knew.

"The soldiers were merciless in marching us from sunrise till sunset with little sustenance to keep us strong," he continued. "They taunted and tormented us with jabs from the tips of their swords or sticks, or they would simply shove us, sending us stumbling."

The old man shook his head. "One day one of the guards pushed us too hard, and Idris and I went tumbling down. He yelled in pain, and the soldiers got upset. The fall had hurt his hand badly and wounded his ankle, and from their worried words, it seemed they were concerned that he would not be able to attend to whatever task they had expected of him."

Worry and rage rushed over Charlotte. Knowing her da suffered, and she was not there to help and protect him, filled her with such anguish that she wanted to scream.

She felt Bryce's hand on her arm before she saw it. It was a firm grip he had on her, one that not only meant to offer comfort but also empathy. He understood her grief, and he was letting her know that he shared it with her and that they would see this mission through and find her da.

She realized then that he had not asked if there were more prisoners. He had placed her concern for her da before his mission, and to her that was a sure sign of just how much he loved her.

The old man continued. "Your da and I talked, when possible, about trying to escape. Your da always felt one of us could possibly make it but not both. We agreed that if an opportunity presented itself, one of us would take it. Your da presented me with such an opportunity."

"That's my da," she said proudly.

"Writhing in pain, your da made the soldiers believe his injury was more serious than it was. They were quick to remove the rope that tethered us and quick to ignore me, so fearful that they would be punished for what had happened to your da."

"The soldiers must have searched for you," Bryce said. "How did you ever escape them?"

"Idris advised me how to avoid the soldiers, and I did, putting a good distance between them and me." He sighed. "But little rest and barely any food finally took its toll, and I have no strength left to travel any farther."

"Your name?" Bryce asked.

"Donald."

Bryce took the old man's hand. "You are safe now, Donald, and I will see that you remain so." He turned to Charlotte. "Give Donald food while I see to fashioning a carrier that will allow him to rest while we travel."

She did as he asked, the old man nibbling slowly at the cheese she had offered.

"You should leave me to die, as that is my fate now, and go find your da," he urged Charlotte. "He waits for you."

"My da would not want that. He would expect me to see you safe before I continued my search for him."

Donald tried to protest.

Charlotte wouldn't let him. "We waste time arguing; I have more questions about my da, and I need to know if there were any other prisoners with you."

The two began to talk.

Any protests Donald had of being left behind to die soon vanished after he was placed on the make-shift carrier, the bed cushioned with pine branches, then covered by a blanket with another blanket tucked around him. The comfort had finally eased his worries and allowed him to fall into a much-needed slumber.

Bryce had used a thick vine as a rein, slipping it over his head to rest across his broad chest. Charlotte could see that it was no chore for him to pull the man though it did slow their pace.

"What did you learn from him?" Bryce asked, as they walked, Odin trotting up ahead.

"Was that why you asked no questions?" she said. "You knew I would."

"You have a way of talking with people, of under-standing what they themselves don't always under-stand. I was confident you would learn all you could from him."

It had happened slowly, this understanding of each other, but she supposed that was part of falling in love.

You grew to know the person like no other, and once that bond was forged, there was no breaking it.

"I inquired about other prisoners, and Donald told me that my da had told him about another group of prisoners that had once been part of his group. Those prisoners, three of them, had been taken in a different direction only a few days before Donald showed up."

Neither one said a word, it wasn't necessary. Both realized what it meant. If her da traveled alone, then the spy Bryce searched for had been sent elsewhere. They would need to split and go in opposite directions in order to fulfill their missions.

They remained silent for several moments, neither wanting to voice the truth of the situation.

Charlotte finally continued. "My da's injury must have prevented him from leaving any more messages for me."

"Did Donald say if he or your da heard any mention of their destination?"

"No, he said the soldiers never spoke of where they were going though they made sure to remark how once there, my da and Donald would never see freedom again."

"Was he able to tell you where he last saw your da?" Bryce asked.

"You fear what I did, that he wandered so much that he lost focus and could not tell where he was or where he had been."

"It can happen easily," Bryce said, "especially to those unfamiliar with the land."

"He did better than I expected, though it was my da who actually told me."

"How?"

"He told Donald that his daughter would love to return to the area she so loved when she was young."

"And where is that?"

"Glen Loran."

"That is not far from my home."

"Then we can meet there when we're both done with our missions," she said, not truly wanting to voice aloud what they both knew must be done.

Bryce frowned. "What do you mean meet there? We travel together."

"But you now know that the one you search for isn't with my da. You must follow a different trail."

"And leave you to rescue your da on your own?" He laughed and shook his head. "That will never happen."

"But you have your duty," she insisted.

"A duty that I have determined needs more help than I presently have," he said, "which is why we will return to my home, have a brief rest, and—"

"No," she said adamantly. "There is no time to rest. I continue my search."

"You need to be reasonable."

"I need to find my da before it's too late," she insisted.

"The mission requires not only more help than just the two of us but a good plan, so that it will succeed."

"My da has been hurt," she said, as if it explained her urgency to reach him.

"That will give your da time as well as us."

It took a moment for her to understand his reasoning. "His hand will need to heal so that he will be able to work."

Bryce nodded. "It also gives us an opportunity to gather more men to help with the rescue."

Charlotte trusted him but not when it came to taking her to his home. She knew once there, he would want her to stay, and she could not do that. Her da was expecting her, and she would not disappoint him.

"You go gather who you must while I continue my hunt."

He shook his head. "We're not separating."

"It is the only way."

"No," he said sternly. "We remain together."

"Our missions dictate otherwise."

"Our missions are somehow linked, and we will see to them together."

Charlotte suddenly felt disheartened. Their duties stood between them, and unless they were careful, would separate them forever. He would continue to want to return home, and she would continue to want to hunt for her da. Though he offered help, it would be done his way. And his way was to see her safe and keep her from harm. While noble and no doubt loving, she would not have it.

Why argue with him, though, since it would do no good. If and when the time came, she would do what was necessary to rescue her da. She would face the consequences later. She only hoped she wouldn't regret it.

Donald was well rested by the time they came upon the small village and had insisted on walking, though with assistance from Charlotte. The carrier was discarded, and the trio entered the village, which was nothing more than a few crofts clumped together. The people there were as cautious as other villagers had been and kept their tongues to themselves.

Charlotte left Donald with Bryce to talk with an

older man, who, though apprehensive, was willing to cautiously chat. She insisted that she could learn more on her own than saddled with the two men.

The young were never as cautious as the older ones. Life had not yet hampered their spirit or desire to live. It was obvious that the soldiers hadn't been there, men and young lads still being in attendance. So she was quick to seek out the young lads and see what she could learn.

Charlotte was off on her own before Bryce could stop her. Though Odin went with her, Bryce felt uneasy about letting her go, more uneasy than ever since the incident with Ewan. It seemed that whenever she was out of his sight, she got into an altercation. She barely recovered from one when another followed. The injuries she had suffered had yet to heal, and yet she hadn't let them hamper her. He had seen her wince in discomfort now and then, but she had not complained once of a pain or ache.

"Stubborn," he mumbled, he and Donald moving along after having finished an uneventful chat with the older man. Whether he had nothing to share or had remained silent out of fear, he traded nothing more than mundane chatter.

Donald smiled. "Idris had said it would be his daughter's obstinate nature that would help free him."

"He knows her well," Bryce said.

"And loves her dearly."

"From hearing Charlotte speak of him, I have no doubt that there is a strong bond between father and daughter."

"One that will send her to him in spite of the danger," Donald said.

That was what Bryce was afraid of. He knew from their recent conversation that trying to convince her to return home with him had been a futile effort. She would do as she pleased. How would he ever get her to listen to reason?

He cast an anxious glance around for Charlotte. With the size of the village, she should have easily been recognizable, along with her dog. Where had she disappeared to?

Chapter 25

Bryce spotted her. She was flying through the air, limbs splaying, and landed with a hard bounce on the ground. She scrambled quickly to her feet as Odin hurried over to stand protectively in front of her, snarling and barking.

Bryce couldn't believe the size of the lad who suddenly came into view. He was a big one, more in width than height and no more than perhaps three-and-ten years. He was laughing, which did not bode well for him at all, not in front of Charlotte.

"Sit and wait here," Bryce ordered Donald, who sat with relief on an old tree stump.

"The big lad may have brawn, but she'll outwit him," Donald said, his eyes having followed Bryce's.

"Not before suffering for it," Bryce grumbled.

"She does what she must; do not deny her that," Donald cautioned.

"I'll not see her suffer," Bryce said, and turned away.

"He's as stubborn as she is," Donald grumbled though Bryce didn't hear.

Bryce couldn't believe that she ran with her head down, straight for the large lad. Odin ran alongside her, barking encouragement. He wanted to throttle both of them. Before he could reach her, she smashed her head right into the large lad's stomach and sent him reeling backward, to land with a solid thwack on his back. She had her booted foot firm to his throat before he could move, and Odin added to the capture by growling in his ear.

"It was a simple question. Now answer it, and I won't crush the breath from you," she threatened.

He capitulated fast enough. "No soldiers or strangers have passed this way. We are a small village with no want of quarrel."

"I don't believe you," she said, pressing her foot a bit harder to his throat.

He went to grab at her ankle, and Odin nipped at his hand. He immediately yanked it away.

"We have seen no one," he choked, and Charlotte eased the force of her foot. "But we have heard things."

Bryce wanted to rush to her side, grab her by the back of her shirt, and tell her if she ever did anything so foolish again, he would lock her away where she'd be safe. He shook his head. She'd never speak to him again if he did anything so foolish.

He took control of his anger as he stopped not far from them. She had things well in hand, and it would do no good to interfere. It would do him well to support her actions just as Odin had done, even though he much preferred to throttle her. If he was honest with himself, he'd admit that what he truly preferred to do was hold her close and keep her safe. That wasn't likely now and he sensed there would be future moments like these, and damned if that didn't alarm him.

Charlotte removed her foot and held her hand out to the large lad. Her keen instincts never failed to impress him. She always seemed to know the appropriate action to take in most situations even if it did frighten the hell out of him.

"Charles," she said, as the big lad took her hand.

"Edward," the lad said, and stood.

"I look for my da," Charlotte said.

"Why didn't you say so from the start?" Edward said.

"You never gave me a chance."

"For a skinny thing, you fight well and fear little."

"The only thing I fear is not finding my da," she said.

Seeing that the two were now agreeable, Bryce walked away. Odin must have thought the same, for he followed Bryce and seated himself next to Donald.

After only a few moments, Bryce watched a crowd begin to gather around the pair, and concern once again had him making his way over to Charlotte. The people seemed agitated and with Charlotte in the middle of it all, he didn't want things getting out of hand.

"So it is true?" a man asked anxiously of Bryce as he approached. "The soldiers are forcing men and lads into the king's service?"

Bryce answered honestly. "I'm afraid so."

"What are we to do?" a woman asked, teary-eyed, as she hugged a puny lad of no more than ten years to her, as if her loving grip could save him.

"Maybe the soldiers will not bother with us," one man said.

Donald had hobbled over to join them. "I would not count on that. The king prepares for battle and spreads his soldiers like a plague over the land, claiming all in its path."

"Is there nothing we can do?" another asked.

Edward spoke up. "We can go join those who fight for the true king, as I've been saying we should. There is little here for us, and the women and young ones will have even less if the men and lads are taken away."

"This is our home," one woman said through tears.

"Once the true king claims the throne, we can return to it," Edward said.

"And what if he doesn't?" someone shouted. "What if King Kenneth defeats him?"

"We have not seen or heard from this supposed true king," said another. "Where is he? Why doesn't he make himself known and help his people?"

"Is he a coward?" yelled another.

"Fools," Charlotte spat. "You would have the true king make himself known and risk losing all? He knows what is right, what he must do. Like King Kenneth, he gathers men, but not by force. Those who serve him do so willingly. He is a good man and will make a good king."

"You have met him?" someone shouted.

"My da has," Charlotte said. "He told me that he was a good man. A truthful and caring man who would do whatever was necessary for his people even if his people thought less of him for it. Never, never though, will he give up. He will sit the throne and keep his people safe."

She once again impressed him, talking with such

confidence of a man she had never met, though the fact that her da had could prove a problem. Few knew the true king's identity and for a good reason—to protect him.

"Our food runs low, and the land has not been good to us," a woman said, cradling a babe while a young lad clung to her leg and another older lad, his eyes filled with fear, stood beside her. "I fear my young ones will go hungry, and now I fear my oldest will be taken from me. I will go wherever I need to keep them fed and safe."

"There is food aplenty there and shelter and many to welcome you," Bryce said. "I know, I fight for the true king."

Edward stepped forward, looking around, then reached out his hand to a short, round woman, who pushed her way through the crowd. He slipped his arm around her shoulders. "My mum and I will go. I will fight for the true king."

Bryce placed a hand on the lad's thick shoulder. "He would welcome you, though you will be made to learn the ways of a warrior before you join the battle."

Others spoke up, some in agreement and others disagreeing. But it wasn't long before they all came to an understanding. They would go and take residence with the true king's followers. And those who could would fight beside him.

Bryce spoke with the men, explaining where they were to go and areas to avoid. It was decided that there was no time to waste. They would leave as soon as they all could get their belongings together. As usual, Charlotte thought as he did and was already having Edward help her retrieve the carrier from the woods where they had left it. She had asked Edward, as Bryce himself had planned to do, if he would look after Donald and see that he arrived safely.

By the time Bryce finished with the men, Edward's mother had Donald cozy on the carrier, with several bundles piled around him. Charlotte was saying her farewell when Bryce approached.

"You will stay well," she ordered. "My da will want to see you again."

Misty-eyed, Donald nodded. "You'll find him. He has no doubt you will, don't you have any doubt."

Charlotte leaned down and gave the old man a hug. "I will see you again."

"I hold you to that," he said, and waved her away.

When she turned and saw Bryce, she stared for a moment, her eyes filled with sorrow and unshed tears. She needed to be in his arms, where he could comfort her. He fought the urge to reach out and snatch her up, to let her release her sorrow and tears against his chest. But he couldn't, her disguise needed to be maintained for her own protection.

"Look after the stubborn lad," Donald said, and held his hand out to Bryce.

Bryce took firm hold. "Take care, Donald, and I will see you soon."

Donald gave his hand a yank to pull him closer, and Bryce leaned down.

"Let her do what she must, or she will never forgive you."

Could that be so? he thought, walking away. She was so intent on finding her da that at times she didn't see reason. He was used to commanding and taking orders, having had to do both over the years, along with his brothers. However, Charlotte wasn't, and Donald could very well be right. If he didn't let her have her way, she could possibly be stubbornly unforgiving.

His thoughts were interrupted by a couple of men with questions, which he took time to answer, but he was impatient to get to Charlotte. She had hurried off, Odin following her, and he knew she went to seek solitude so that she might shed her tears in private.

That she would be crying was bad enough, but that she should be crying alone broke his heart. His arms should be around her, comforting her, easing her worries, letting her know he was there for her and hopefully always would be.

In their short time together, he was already thinking of *always*. He could promise her nothing, and yet he was thinking of *forever* with her. He must be in love, for his thoughts were not those of a sane man.

He was relieved when he bid the last man farewell and hurried away from the chaotic village and into the woods. It was easier following Odin's tracks than hers, his steps heavy where hers were light and sometimes barely detectable.

They had wandered farther than he had expected, though he understood why when he found them. Odin was busy drinking from a rippling stream, and Charlotte was busy trying to scrub the caked mud from her hair.

She turned in a flash when Odin looked up. Her freshly washed face dripped with water, and her eyes ran with tears. He spread his arms out to her as he walked toward her, and she bounced up, ran, and flung herself into them. He no sooner had her snug in his arms than he scooped her up and walked to sit near the stream, resting her comfortably in his lap. Odin sat beside them, giving Charlotte's hand a comforting lick.

"My da is hurting this very moment, and there is nothing I can do for him," she said between sobs, her face pressed against his chest and her hands gripping his shirt.

"You are doing something; you search for him, and he knows it," Bryce said, his heart aching with every tear she spilled.

"I should have found him by now."

"You will find him," he insisted. "At least you know that he does not doubt you will come for him. You have heard this from someone who shared captivity with your da. You know that while he may be injured, he still does well. You know he waits for you and will wait as long as necessary with the same determination to survive as your determination to find him."

Her sobs grew weak, and though she lifted teary eyes to him, she no longer shed tears.

"Seeing Donald—" She shook her head, unable to finish.

Bryce finished for her. "Donald reminded you of your da, and it made you worry and miss him all the more."

She nodded, a couple of tears trickling from her eyes and her teeth biting at her lower lip, no doubt to stop it from trembling.

"I promise you we'll find your da," Bryce said with such a strong conviction that it brought a smile to Charlotte's face.

"You have been kind and good to me," she said softly. "I am very glad we have fallen in love."

Her boldness never stopped surprising him. He had yet to tell her that he loved her; still, she was so sure of his love. It did not bother her in the least that he had not spoken the words, but it bothered him. He should tell her and be done with it.

There was no difficulty in speaking the truth, yet he found it difficult to admit his love. There was so much standing in their way, and he worried—even though he wanted forever with her, would he have it?

She pressed her fingers to his lips. "I may not hear it from you, but I see it in your eyes. It shines bold and bright, fills me with warmth, and settles comfortably around me. "I am happy that you love me so very much."

How did she do that? How did she articulate what he felt?

She felt the same.

The thought struck him like a punch to the face. His love for Charlotte completely amazed him. Love completely astonished him. And to realize that she felt the same insanely wonderful thing for him made him love her all the more.

He needed her to know that she was right in what she saw, and so he showed her the only way he presently could—he kissed her. It was sweet and innocent. Light and soft. He did not want to make demands of her. He simply wanted to confirm what they both knew, that they were in love.

It didn't take long for the kiss to turn passionate and their bodies to flicker with desire. Neither dared let their hands roam. They simply fed on the kiss, or the kiss fed them; whatever way it was, it didn't end until their hunger was somewhat appeased.

Their lips parted reluctantly, Charlotte tucking her head beneath his chin to rest her cheek on his chest. He rested his chin on the top of her head, her hair still damp. And there they remained while their labored breathing slowed and their desire for each other dissipated, much too gradually.

Bryce knew they should get moving, but he didn't want to let go of her, didn't want this moment with her to end.

"We should leave," she said, though she sounded not at all enthused.

"Yes, we should," he agreed.

"I don't want to."

"Neither do I," he admitted.

She eased herself out of his arms, and he unwillingly let her go.

She stood looking down at him. "We must make our way to Glen Loran."

Bryce pushed to his feet and turned away from her for a moment, running his fingers through his hair, then rubbing his chin before turning around again. "What do we do if we come upon this prison? How do we penetrate its forces? How do we fight against its many guards?"

"If we hurry and stop dallying, we could reach my da before he is locked away, making for a more successful rescue."

"And if we don't reach him, what then?" Bryce asked, not wishing to discourage her but hoping she would see reason. "Old John wasn't only adamant but fearful when he told us that no one escapes that prison."

"He did," Charlotte said. "There is an entrance; therefore, there is an egress."

"But not a safe one. It will take planning and more men, and we still have to find where this prison is located."

"If we get moving, we could possibly find my da before all that is necessary," she said.

He grabbed her bundle off the ground and flung it over his shoulder to carry for her. "We will continue to search for your da, but if we turn up nothing soon, we return to my home and formulate a plan before proceeding any farther."

He waited, expecting her to argue with him.

She didn't. She picked up her bow and cache of arrows, then yanked her bundle off his shoulder to swing over her own. She walked off without a word, Odin trotting right beside her.

Bryce shook his head. This was going to be a challenge, and he had a nagging suspicion that he would wind up having to forcibly carry her home.

Chapter 26

They had to avoid two small troops of soldiers, had to forgo a campfire, and had to rely on their bodies' heat to keep them warm throughout the night. Though Charlotte had hoped for adequate shelter where they could make love without worry of the weather, it was not to be.

They rose with the sun, and it was another day of constant walking and remaining alert, with little time to spare for conversation or to steal a kiss. With signs that soldiers lingered in the area, they remained vigilant. It continued such for three endless days.

Charlotte found no messages from her da and, worse, the few people they met along the way hadn't come across soldiers with prisoners. It was as if her da had simply disappeared.

And so the argument began on the fourth day.

"We go home, gather help, and devise a plan," Bryce said, as they took to the road once more.

Her da had often reminded her of her stubborn nature; she was aware that it could interfere with making rational decisions. And Bryce's decision made sense. However, her guilt over not having saved her da from the soldiers coupled with not being able to find him turned her more obstinate than ever.

"I won't give up," she said, stepping past Bryce to walk several feet ahead of him.

"I'm not asking you to," he said, catching up with her in two easy strides.

She was glad she would never need to run from him, for he would certainly catch her in no time, his long, powerful legs more than a match for her short, thin ones. No matter how many times, out of sheer annoyance that she strode past him, he was at her side in an instant.

She almost smiled, for in a sense it was a good thing to know. He would always be there beside her. And while she was accustomed to spending much time alone, she found that she rather favored his presence. Actually, her heart sank at the mere thought of his not being beside her.

"Be reasonable," he said. "We do not retreat. We regroup and build strength to fortify victory."

"I know it makes sense, but . . ." She shook her head letting her words trail off, fighting the thoughts of how her da must be suffering.

Bryce grabbed hold of her arm, stopping them both. "I know how helpless you must feel, but think about how your da would respond to this situation. After time spent searching for you, would he continue or stop and reconsider?"

Of course, he was right, but that didn't matter; she felt that she had failed her da, and nothing he said would take that pain away.

He ran a finger beneath her chin and gave a lift. She hadn't even realized her head had drooped.

"You carry too heavy a burden. Stop struggling with it and let me lift it off you."

He didn't let her answer; he leaned down and kissed her.

She had never known something to be so welcoming. She needed this kiss from him as much as she needed to breathe. And though normally and instinctively her arms would shoot around his neck to pull him closer, this time they didn't. This time she simply stood there and welcomed his kiss.

It wasn't a demanding kiss that would ignite their passion. It was a kiss that asked for nothing but gave everything. It was a kiss of love.

Slowly, Charlotte's arms wound up around his neck as he eased her up against him. She lingered in his nourishing kiss, and, for a moment, all her worries slipped away. There was just Bryce and her, and their love.

When the kiss finally ended, she didn't want to open her eyes and once again be thrust back into her worries. She would much rather have remained in his arms, where her concerns dissipated, and she felt safe. It would be nice to think that she could live like that forever, but it wasn't possible. She had responsibilities; she had a mission just like he did. And soon, his mission would separate them. And then what would she do?

Do not be afraid to depend on yourself.

Her da had taught her that, and it had helped her face many a difficult time with strength. This time would be no different.

"I will let you help with my burden, but I will carry it," she said.

He grinned and gave her cheek a quick kiss. "You can be impossible."

"I beg to differ," she said. "I do what reason dictates."

"Then reason instructs us to go home."

"That would depend on how one reasons it," she argued.

And so the argument continued until they came to a fork in the road, a point in their travels where one road would take them home and the other would again have them searching for her da's trail.

It pained Charlotte to think they would separate, but she wasn't ready to give up on her da or drop her burden completely on Bryce. He had enough of his own concerns to worry about, she needn't add to them.

"Tell me you will be reasonable and do as I suggest," he said.

"Tell me you will let me do what I must?"

"I thought you would say that," Bryce said with a nod and a firm set to his jaw.

She realized too late his intention, and, besides, it would be a useless endeavor to try to outrun him. She was scooped up and flung over his shoulder so fast that everything around her spun.

Odin gave a protesting bark, but a sharp command from Bryce quieted him.

"You leave me no choice," he said, and walked with her slung over his shoulder like a sack of grain.

She debated fighting him, pummeling his back and kicking to get free. After giving it some thought, it didn't strike her as the best course of action. She could wait until he grew tired of carrying her, but she didn't believe she was a heavy burden to him and, therefore, he would not tire easily. By the time he did release her, they would be a distance away, and it would take her time to return to this spot.

"If you were reasonable, you would see that what I propose is our best course of action," he said, walking along, as if carrying her in such a fashion was a common occurrence. "I do understand your misgivings with it. But your da has proven that he is well able to survive until you find him."

"You're right."

"Finally, you admit it," he said on a laugh. "Then we can be done with this nonsense, and you will come home willingly with me?"

"You would assume so and yet you ask me if that is what I will do." She waited and when an answer wasn't forthcoming, she said, "We both know the true reason for my refusal to cooperate."

He continued to remain silent.

"I will say what you refuse to admit. You take me home and expect me to stay there."

"You'll be safe there."

"I'll be a prisoner."

"You certainly will not be a prisoner," he said sternly.

"I will join you then on the mission to rescue my da?"

"It is not necessary. I will see him safely returned to you."

It was her turn to be silent. He might think as he wished; she would make plans of her own.

"Your silence tells me that I will not be able to trust you when it comes to allowing me to rescue your da."

She saw no reason to lie when he already suspected her intentions. "You're right again."

"I will not waste time arguing this point with you. We will settle it once home."

"Good," she said. "Then there is room for debate, and I will sway you to my cause."

Bryce laughed. "You can try."

"I can succeed."

"And how will you do that?" he asked.

"I will make you see just how strong love can be, so that you will know that there isn't anything I wouldn't do to rescue you if you were in the same position." She poked him in the back. "And don't bother to warn me about putting myself at risk for you. I would fight the devil himself to see you safe."

He laughed again. "I have no doubt the devil would surrender posthaste just to be rid of you."

She gave him another poke, harder this time. "Make fun all you want, but one day you may be grateful for my tenaciousness."

"There is one place I'd welcome your resolute nature."

She waited to hear where that was, but instead felt his hand stroke her backside. She was about to snap at him when a familiar tingle rippled through her. She silently cursed his magic touch. And it had to be magic for her to respond so quickly. She couldn't say when she had first noticed it, or perhaps it had been like that from the first, and she hadn't quite understood it. All she knew was that his touch sent pleasant tingles through her.

Her response surprised her, though she meant it. "Put me down, and I'll show you just how determined I can be at making love."

She smiled when his steps faltered, knowing her remark had affected him just as potently as his touch had affected her.

"Be careful what you ask for," he warned. "You may just get it."

"I want it," she said. "I want you."

"Not a good time or place."

"It hasn't been for the last few days, and I grow eager to make love again."

His hand stopped stroking her. "When we get home—"

"How long before we reach your home?"

"Two or three days."

"Too long," she complained.

"We can't take a chance with soldiers spotted so frequently in the area."

"Don't you wish to make love before we reach your home? And what will your parents think of me when you take me to your bed? I like the privacy of only the two of us knowing what we share."

He stopped and swung her down off his shoulder and onto her feet. "My mum will assume I found the perfect woman to be my wife, and my da will not comment, leaving the decision mine. And you and I will do as we please regardless of opinions."

What pleased them was to enjoy each other while they could, then they would return to their respective missions. It was what followed those missions that had her more curious than worried. She didn't believe that, given how much they loved each other, they would ever part. But life as she had sadly discovered was unpredictable and did not always bring equals amounts of joy and sorrow. So there was no foreseeing what the future held; therefore, it was best they enjoyed and savored the time they had together.

"Now who's being stubborn?" She smiled. "We are more alike than we think."

He shook his head, grinned, and grabbed hold of her hand and began walking again. "We are different."

"Not as much as you think," she said. "And there is no reason to hold my hand. I will not run. I will go home with you."

"I like holding your hand."

She laughed. "Perhaps, but that is not why you hold it now."

"Give me your word you won't run?"

"I have said I wouldn't. Isn't that enough?" She hoped it was, for she didn't want to believe that he thought her a liar.

He released her hand, and she smiled.

"Now about shelter for the night," she said.

"We had best find something suitable, for I cannot wait any longer to make love to you."

Her smile spread, and, remarkably, the tingles returned without his touching her. "How wonderful it would be to come across an abandoned cottage. Not that I wish to benefit from someone's misfortune."

"We may very well find one though we still must consider the soldiers in the area. No doubt they search for crofts as well."

"Then what are we to do?"

"We have time until nightfall, we'll think of something," he said.

She dashed in front of him. "Time for a bit of privacy."

"Take Odin with you and don't be long. I'll wait here."

She hurried off, Odin following as he always did unless she or Bryce ordered otherwise. She went a good distance in and when she was nearly finished, she saw Odin's head suddenly rear up. He sniffed the air and immediately took a guarded stance.

Someone was about.

She motioned for Odin to be quiet and took a moment to listen. When Odin issued a small whine, she knew it wasn't her he was concerned about.

"Bryce?" she asked softly.

Odin whined again, and, with swift light steps, they both took off.

Chapter 27

Bryce spotted Charlotte running toward him. He ran at her, grabbed her by the arm, swung her around, and said, "Keep going."

She did exactly what he ordered, Odin quick to change directions along with her.

When they were a good distance away, still keeping a good pace, Bryce said, "There were two soldiers. Don't know if more followed. We need to get home fast. There are too many soldiers combing these parts."

"It isn't about enlarging his troops that King Kenneth seeks men and lads, is it?" Charlotte said. "It's about him searching for the true king. He wants him found."

"It would appear that way," Bryce said, hating to admit the implications of the obvious.

"Your home may not be safe."

"We are well fortified, and the Picts border our land. The king will not dare tread there."

"Why not?" she asked. "He claims the right to sit the throne, and all know that the rightful king is born of a Pict mother. King Kenneth should have no qualms about asking those of his blood to help him."

"Therein lies the problem," Bryce said. "King Kenneth is no descendant of a Pict."

"You have to get home and warn your people, so they will be prepared," Charlotte said.

"All those who fight for the true king must prepare," Bryce said. "Battle is on the horizon."

They kept up a hectic pace, taking time for only one brief rest throughout the day.

His legs began to burn, his body tire, and he could only imagine how Charlotte must be feeling, the bruises from her last two altercations still fresh on her body.

He needed to find them a place to rest for the night, and as soon as the sun rose tomorrow, they would leave, setting a pace as quick as today's.

The rain had left behind a chill that had grown decidedly colder, and it suddenly felt like winter had returned for one last sting. They had draped their blankets around them as they walked, but they could do with the warmth of a fire.

Bryce had hoped to come upon an abandoned croft where they could seek adequate shelter for the night, but so far there had been nothing. Being forced off the well-worn trail hadn't helped. Rarely had he come across a lone cottage in the woods.

Charlotte plopped down on the ground. "I can't go much farther."

Even Odin looked exhausted, spreading out beside her to rest his head on her thigh.

Worried, since she had never claimed she could not go on, he knelt beside her. "Does something pain you?"

"Everything pains me."

They both jumped at the sound of twigs cracking, and, without hesitation, stood back-to-back, his sword drawn and her bow ready. When Bryce saw that Odin hadn't moved, his worry faded though it did disturb him that Odin lay where he was, watching a squirrel scampering about. Usually, he would be chasing it, which meant the dog was fatigued.

He hated to say it, but he had no choice. He wanted them closer to home, closer to safety. "A bit more, then we'll settle for the night."

Charlotte groaned but started walking, and Odin reluctantly got up and joined her.

"A couple more days, and we'll be home," Bryce said. "Then you'll have a bed to sleep in."

"And sleep I will," she said with an annoyed toss of her head.

Bryce strode up beside her, and she stepped away from him.

"So then," he said, "you'll be sleeping in your bed alone?"

"No." She grinned. "Odin will be joining me."

He laughed. "There'll be no dog in my bed."

"And no woman either," she shot back.

He moved closer to her though he didn't brush against her this time. "Come on, lassie, you know you want to share my bed just as much as I want you to."

She sighed. "Can you imagine the pleasure of having a bed beneath us?"

"I can imagine the pleasure of having you beneath me."

She gave her head a tilt to look at him. "How about me on top of you? You did—"

"Stop," he said, taking a step away from her. The vision was enough to make him grow hard.

"It's only fair that we each—"

"Enough," he warned, thinking how much of a handful she would be in bed and growing harder with the thought.

He stomped past her, ending the debate, though the image of her naked on top of him refused to fade away.

A few hours later, with his thoughts finally his, they came upon a cottage the land had partially reclaimed. It wasn't what they had hoped for, but, with a little bit of work, it would lodge them sufficiently for the night.

Bryce got a fire going in what remained of the fireplace, so that Charlotte could keep warm as he worked. With the sun ready to set soon and the air continuing to cool, it would be a cold night.

Thick pine branches served as a partial roof and helped plug holes in what was left of the wattle-and-daub walls. Though it wasn't possible to enclose the structure, his effort would at least provide them with a snug area that would keep them from being fully exposed to the cold.

When Bryce finally finished, he wasn't surprised to see Odin curled in a ball, snug against a sleeping Charlotte. Crumbs, remnants of their meal, lay sprinkled around them. He had to smile. Hungry and exhausted, they had eaten, then fallen asleep.

He took some food for himself though he found he had less of an appetite than he had thought. When he finished, he cuddled up against Charlotte, wrapping his arm around her. He had hoped this night would end differently, but their frantic pace had completely worn them out.

He couldn't wait to get home, spend time with her while plans were made to search for her da. She'd give him a difficult time, no doubt, when she learned that there would be no debate about her remaining home. He'd handle that when the time came.

Until then, he intended to enjoy the time he had with her. He didn't know what the future held for them. He hoped that they would share it together. But there was so much standing between them that no matter what he wanted or how many promises he made, he wasn't sure if he could keep them.

Except for finding her da . . . that was a promise he intended to keep.

Morning came too soon and with it another long day of travel. Bryce kept them going at a rapid pace, and night, no doubt, didn't come soon enough for Charlotte, sleep claiming her before she had a chance to eat.

It was on the third day, the sun high in the sky with hours of travel yet ahead of them that she stopped.

"I've had enough," she said. "I ache from my head to my toes. I want a respite even if it is only a short one."

Bryce smiled, reached out, and scooped her up in his arms, then started walking.

"You can't carry me," she said, resting her head on his shoulder, "even if it does feel good. It's not fair. You will grow tired."

"I've told you before. You are no burden."

"Still—"

"Shush," he ordered. "It's not far now."

"We'll be there by nightfall?" she asked with a bit of desperation.

"Sooner."

"How soon?"

"Just over this rise."

Her head shot up. "You can't mean that."

He laughed. "That happy to be home?"

"No. No. Put me down," she said, squirming to be free.

He released her, and she stood in front of him, her hands planted on her slim hips. "I can't meet your family looking like this."

He glanced over her from top to bottom. She did look a bit the worse for wear. Her clothes were dirty and dust-covered, her hair lacked shine, and her face was spotted with grime, and though the bruises had faded, they were still visible. But to him, she looked beautiful.

He reached out and rubbed a spot of dirt off her chin, holding it up for her to see. "The dirt you wear and the aches you suffer are badges of your undaunting courage, wear them with pride." He smeared the dirt back on her chin. "Besides, no amount of dirt can hide your beauty."

The kiss wasn't planned, it never was, it simply happened. It was quick though thorough, the kind that let you know there was more to come but not just yet.

"We should hurry," she said when the kiss ended.

He smiled. "Eager for nightfall and bedtime?"

"Must we wait for nightfall to make love?"

His smile remained firm as he shook his head and took her hand. "How did I get so lucky?"

"You met me," she said, her small hand closing tightly over his.

They walked hand in hand up the rise, Odin scampering ahead of them. At that moment, Bryce felt more content than he ever had, and he wanted to keep a firm hold on it and never let it go.

As soon as Odin spotted children at play, he took off and Charlotte wasn't far behind. Bryce smiled and shook his head watching the pair. The big dog wanting nothing more than to join in play with the children, and Charlotte worried that the sight of him charging toward them would frighten the children.

His eyes rounded when he saw Reeve run forward, and his heart slammed in his chest when he watched Charlotte spot his attack charge. Odin was oblivious to it all, his only interest to play with the children. Bryce knew Charlotte would never let anyone harm Odin, and she picked up a speed that astonished Bryce and headed straight for his brother.

Bryce took off, but knew he'd never be able to prevent what was about to happen. He watched as Reeve positioned himself, ready to take Odin down with one powerful and possible deadly swing. He was amazed when Charlotte vaulted over Odin, rolled, and came up with her booted foot to Reeve's face, sending him flying up in the air to land with a bounce or two right on his back.

Before his brother could get to his feet, Charlotte had her dirk to his throat.

Duncan was hurrying forward as was his father, Carmag, though Mara, his mum sped past both.

"Get that dirk away from my son's throat," Mara ordered with a sharp tongue.

"Not until your son gives me his word that he'll leave my harmless dog alone," Charlotte challenged.

"He was set to attack the children," Reeve spat.

"Odin would never hurt a child. He only wanted to play with them, and if you weren't so ready to condemn and harm, you would have learned that for yourself," Charlotte said. "Now your word, or you stay where you are until I have it."

Bryce joined them, grinning, though not saying a word and ever so eager to see Reeve's reaction when he learned that a woman had bested him.

"You dare threaten me when surrounded by my family?" Reeve said, his face flushed red with anger.

"Odin is my family, and I protect him as your family protects you," Charlotte said.

"Give her your word," Mara ordered. "The dog already plays with the children, and they are delighted with him."

Reeve reluctantly said, "You have my word."

Charlotte slipped her dirk back in her boot.

"You protect him, so why didn't your dog help you when you attacked me?" Reeve said, once on his feet.

"He knew I required no help to take down the likes of you," Charlotte said.

Bryce cringed, though he continued grinning.

Reeve went right up to Charlotte. "You're a cocky lad who needs to be taught a lesson."

"Let him be, Reeve," Mara said. "He's just a lad, and I'll have him whipped into shape in no time."

Reeve laughed. "Now you're in for it, lad."

Charlotte turned to Bryce. "I don't think I like your family."

Bryce went to her, slipped his arm around her, and tucked her against his side. "I want you all to meet Charlotte, my woman."

* * *

Charlotte's heart soared with delight. Bryce had all but announced he loved her by claiming that she was his woman, and she couldn't have been happier. Though she wasn't sure about his family; they hadn't been at all what she expected.

She remained close to Bryce's side and wasn't surprised to see that eyes rounded, mouths dropped open, and silence reigned, though not for long.

Duncan laughed. "You were bested by a wee bit of a lassie, Reeve."

"She doesn't look at all like a woman," Reeve shouted at him.

Charlotte tensed, hurt by his remark.

Bryce gave her a comforting squeeze, and said, "Believe me, she's more woman than any man can handle in more ways than one, which she has demonstrated on you, Reeve."

Duncan laughed again.

Reeve whipped his head around to glare at Duncan, who didn't stop laughing though he calmed it some.

"There must be a good tale to why you're dressed like a lad and how you've come to learn to defend yourself so well," Mara said. "I'd like to hear it. And as soon as my son sees past his embarrassment, he'll no doubt realize you're no longer an adversary but a woman to be admired for her courage."

Charlotte saw the warning Mara shot Reeve, and though he remained annoyed, he did attempt to seek a truce between them.

"I'd like to hear the tale myself," he said.

Charlotte hoped they all would understand once they

knew her story. She didn't want difficulty with Bryce's family. It would not be wise, especially with her having longed for a family since she was young.

Charlotte left the support of Bryce's arms, wanting to offer something of a truce to Reeve as well. "Odin looks intimidating, but he truly is a lovable animal. Let me introduce you."

She called out to the dog before Reeve could object, and he came reluctantly, sitting next to her leg. She bent down beside him and rubbed behind his ears while he licked her face. She stood, looked down at him, and said, "Odin, this is Reeve, and he's a friend."

The dog walked over and licked Reeve's hand, then walked back to Charlotte, his big eyes begging to let him rejoin the children.

"Go have fun," she said with a laugh.

He ran off with a bark, and peals of delightful laughter filled the air as he once again joined the children.

Bryce turned to his mother. "We're in desperate need of food and a washing, Mum."

"Where are my manners," Mara said, scolding herself. "Let's get you fed first, then bathed."

Charlotte found herself quickly ushered inside the keep and deposited at a long table in front of a massive fireplace. More food than she had ever seen at one time was soon spread across the table. And chatter mixed with laughter as ale and wine were poured and consumed.

She noticed that Reeve was a handsome one even though a scowl marred his brow, and he was tall and slimmer than his brothers, though he did not lack for muscle. Duncan was a big one, with a slightly crooked nose and a scar in the corner of his mouth, though neither distracted from his fine features. Carmag was a good-looking man with gray threading through his dark hair, and Mara was plump, pretty, and had a sharp tongue though she did smile often. It was obvious they were a strong family, teasing and laughing easily with each other.

"My husband was tossed down by a woman?" Came a sultry voice that had everyone turning except Reeve.

The woman was attractive, with raven-colored hair and lavender-colored eyes and fairly tall. When she smiled, she turned even more attractive, and when she slipped her hands over her husband's shoulders, he turned his head and kissed her.

"Gossiping tongues, you can never trust them," Reeve said, after kissing her.

She laughed and slid in on the bench to sit close beside him.

"Reeve was tossed down by a woman?" A woman's voice asked anxiously.

Duncan jumped up and hurried over to help the woman down the last few stairs. Charlotte realized it had to be his wife, Mercy. She was so large with child that Charlotte thought she would birth the babe there and then.

Charlotte couldn't help but stare, the woman was beautiful, with dark hair and blue eyes, and she was petite. That they were in love was obvious. You could see it by the loving looks they exchanged.

Duncan helped his wife to sit, then sat beside her.

"How is Trey faring?" Bryce asked.

"He's back to his old self," Reeve said, "and gone

off to help Willow gather some of her things from her farm."

"You have yet to tell us about your encounter with this woman, Reeve," Mercy said.

"Mercy's right, I want to hear it all," Tara said. "Was she a big woman; she'd have to be to get the best of you."

Reeve hung his head.

Charlotte didn't wait to be introduced. "It isn't size that matters; it's having your wits about you. Reeve made it easy for me to conquer him."

Both women turned wide eyes on her.

"I'm Charlotte, Bryce's woman," she said with pride.

Chapter 28

Bryce smiled, listening to Mercy and Tara ply Charlotte with endless questions. She answered in her usual direct manner, and as she did, he could see admiration and respect for her grow.

He was glad his family liked her, well almost all his family. He figured it would take Reeve a bit of time to live down being bested by her. He'd come around eventually. He also liked that Charlotte had confirmed herself his woman, and how she rested against him without giving it a thought.

She was tired. He felt it in the slump of her body against his. It was time for them to get some rest. He gave a nod to his mum.

Her smile broadened, and she said, "Time to see about baths for you both."

Mara stood and hurried off as Odin made his way into the keep and rushed over to Charlotte. She gave him a hug and fed him some meat from the table.

Bryce was eager to get her upstairs and alone, eager to have soft bedding under them tonight, a fire to keep them warm, and shelter from the elements. He wanted to make love to her, he wanted to curl around her and hold her tight throughout the night and wake with her in his arms in the morning. And know that they did not have to spend the day walking endlessly.

He wanted time, brief as it might be, to love her, just in case it was the only time they would have together.

"We should talk, Bryce, while your mum helps Charlotte," Carmag said.

In his eagerness to retire with Charlotte to his bedchamber, he'd forgotten about meeting with his da and brothers to report on his mission.

"Tend to your duties," Charlotte said.

That they would be together shortly didn't stop Bryce from feeling reluctant about leaving her. They had not been long-separated since meeting, and he found he preferred it that way. He wasn't sure how he felt about being so attached to a woman that he was reluctant to leave her. And he certainly couldn't allow it to interfere with his mission.

"I will wait here for you," Charlotte said.

He didn't know how she did it, sense what he thought, but he liked that she was so attuned to him. He gave her a quick kiss and stood. That was when he caught the smug smiles on his brothers' faces.

"Say one word, and I'll beat the both of you," he warned.

"Your woman may have bested me, but it appears she has done the same to you," Reeve said with a laugh.

"Enough nonsense," Carmag cautioned as he stood. "We have important matters to discuss."

The brothers turned silent and, without another word being spoken, left the room.

* * *

It wasn't long before Charlotte found herself alone. Mercy had grown tired, and Tara had helped her to her bedchamber to see her settled for a nap. She had assured Charlotte that she would return afterwards to learn more about how the petite woman had bested her husband.

Charlotte was accustomed to spending time alone, and she was content here at the table in front of the fire, Odin asleep at her feet. She felt at peace as she so often had when she and her da were together.

It felt good to be in love, and she wanted to enjoy every moment of it. Life had changed too often on her, and with it had come sorrow. It had taught her to enjoy when she could, and, right now, she wanted very much to enjoy Bryce and the love they had discovered.

She did not know what tomorrow would bring, but she did have today, and it was a good day. She and Bryce would be together, they would make love, and she would fall asleep in his arms. Yes, it was a very good day.

Odin jumped up before a bell loudly tolled, reverberating throughout the hall. She and the dog ran out of the keep and into chaos. Warriors were gathering horses and weapons, and women frantically herded their children.

Charlotte stopped a warrior to ask what was happening.

"Soldiers attack a group of travelers seeking shelter here." He pointed to a group of women huddled around someone.

Charlotte ran over, pushing past the women to get to

the center. She was shocked to see Edward's mum lying
breathless on the ground.

As soon as the woman recognized Charlotte, she
reached out, grabbing at her. "My son, my son, please
save my son."

"The others?" Charlotte asked.

"They fight, and some hide," she said through labored breaths. "Edward pushed me into the woods and
told me to run for help." Tears started running down her
full cheeks. "Please, please help them."

Charlotte nodded and pushed her way out of the
circle of women. She spotted Bryce, his father, and his
brothers on the steps of the keep, their wives and Mara
behind them. From this distance, she could see he was
shaking his head at her.

She ignored him, eyed the horses, and anxious to be
off, headed for them, Odin on her heels.

"Charlotte!"

She didn't look Bryce's way. No doubt he'd order her
to stay behind with the women. She couldn't do that.
She felt responsible for the group under attack. And so,
with one swift vault, she was on the horse and, soon
after, out of the village.

"Damn, did you see the way she mounted that horse,"
Reeve said, shaking his head. "I wouldn't have believed
it if I hadn't seen it. It was almost as if she flew up on it.
I've got to have her teach me how she does that."

"Her foolish actions could soon see her dead, and
you stand here admiring her skills?" Bryce said with
anger. "When I get my hands on her, I'm going to throttle her."

Bryce didn't care about nor expect a response from his brother. What he did want was his help making certain nothing happened to Charlotte. And that's what Reeve and Duncan did. They mounted their horses and, with a troop of warriors, took off.

Charlotte had no plan though she knew it would be unwise to ride straight into the melee. She would be of more help in using the cover of the woods to make the soldiers believe they were under attack by a group of bowmen. She would do what she could, knowing Bryce and his warriors were not far behind.

She heard the clank of swords and screams of battle, and she directed her horse around the carnage to a spot where she would best serve those fighting. She was off the horse and had her spot picked while Odin pranced behind her, keeping watch. She drew an arrow from her cache and took aim, hitting her mark. She kept the arrows flying.

She moved only twice, when she saw Edward was in trouble. His mum's words came back to tear at her heart. *Please save my son.*

Charlotte didn't stop to think, she reacted. She dropped her bow and, with speed born of practice, ran straight into battle.

Bryce and his brothers came upon the battle to see Charlotte, ducking, dashing, and vaulting through the melee. Odin was right beside her, running down anyone who dared get near her.

"Damn, what a woman," Reeve said, and dropped off his horse and charged into battle.

Bryce remained mounted and headed straight for
Charlotte. Soldiers charged him, and his need to see
her safe had him slicing his way through anyone who
dared attempt to stop him.

By the time he reached her, she had Edward safe,
and his warriors had full control of the battle, bringing
it rapidly to an end. He almost reached out and grabbed
her, wanting to make sure she had suffered no injuries.

"I am indebted to you, Charles," Edward said, offering his hand.

In his quest to see Charlotte safe, he had forgotten
that Edward knew her only as the lad Charles; and then
there were the soldiers who had survived. He didn't
want them aware of her true gender. So once again he
was forced to keep his distance from her, and he didn't
like it. He didn't like it at all.

Duncan and Reeve took charge of the surviving
soldiers, Carmag and Bryce of the people and getting
them safely to the village. Charlotte joined in; though
he had ordered her home, she refused to go, insisting
she could be of help, and she was.

It took a couple of hours to get the weary and battered group to the village. Mara, Mercy, and Tara were
ready with food and lodging, and, with all that had to
be done, it would take at least until dusk to settle the
people.

After Charlotte saw that Edward was reunited with
his grateful and teary-eyed mum, Bryce approached
her. He didn't know whether to hug her or throttle her.
Instead, he grabbed hold of her arm and hurried her
away from the crowd to a spot where they could have a
modicum of privacy.

"You should have waited for me," he said, his voice low but his annoyance high.

"And wasted time?" She shook her head. "That would have made no sense. You were but a short distance behind me."

"You frightened me near to death when I saw you mount that horse and ride off. Don't ever do that again."

"I can't promise that," she said. "There may come a time—"

What troubled him the most wasn't that she had ended her response abruptly but that he understood what she meant without finishing it. There would come a time, and no doubt concerning her da, that she would do the same.

"You try my patience beyond measure."

"I do not mean to."

She remained calm while his annoyance grew.

"I don't know what to do with you," he said, frustrated.

She took a step closer to him, and whispered, "Love me."

"Bryce, we need help," his da called, and he silently cursed the interference.

"I suppose there is no point in ordering you to my bedchamber," he said.

"While I would be only too happy to retire there at this very moment, I'm sure my help here would be appreciated."

"Later—"

"Bryce!" his da yelled again.

He hurried off with a smile, pleased that she finished his words exactly.

"You're all mine."

* * *

Hours later, Charlotte dragged herself into the keep and, though delicious scents filled the air, she was much too tired to eat. She wanted to get clean and go to sleep, preferably in a soft bed. Tara was the one who took her to a bedchamber where a tub filled with steaming water waited.

Not caring about anything, she stripped herself of her clothes, which a servant instantly scooped up, and lowered herself into the tub. She had to pull up her knees to fit, but the water rose to cover her chest, and its wet heat felt most welcoming.

She didn't know when the servant and Tara had vacated the room but was glad they had. She wanted to rest in the luxury of the bathwater, scrub herself clean, then—she looked to the bed and sighed.

The water cooled all too fast, and she reluctantly scrubbed herself from head to toe, got out, dried herself thoroughly, and hurried beneath the blankets. She almost cried with pleasure at the comforting feel of the stuffed mattress.

She surely had to be dreaming, it felt much too exquisite, as if it weren't real. And in no time she was dreaming, having fallen asleep as soon as her head touched the pillow.

Bryce went to his bedchamber, expecting to find Charlotte there. What he found was a steaming bath and a table laden with food, but no Charlotte. A servant had informed him that Charlotte was given another room and had had a bath and was now sleeping soundly.

Had his mum intentionally kept them apart? Was she

implying that Charlotte wasn't a good fit for him? He shook his head. She would have been straightforward with him, told him directly if she hadn't liked Charlotte.

But then he hadn't had a chance to speak with his mum, so he didn't truly know how she felt about Charlotte.

Could Charlotte have been the one who requested separate rooms. And if so, why?

The question annoyed him though it was probably not having an answer that frustrated him the most. She had been only too willing about—later. Had something happened to change her thought? Or perhaps she was simply too fatigued and, not wanting to disappoint him, sought a separate chamber.

His mind went crazy with possibilities the whole time he bathed and ate though he ate sparingly, having lost his appetite.

He crawled into bed, disappointed. He might have been tired, but he wasn't too tired to make love to Charlotte. He hadn't liked the thought that their first time together was in a thunderstorm under a bush, though the memory caused him to smile. He'd never forget it, the tight space, barely room to maneuver, garments pushed aside, and the feel of her so snug and wet.

Damn!

He grew hard recalling the moment he had slipped into her and how she had reacted, so eager and receptive. He could only imagine her response in a more conducive atmosphere.

Damn!

If he didn't stop growing hard, he'd be out of the bed in no time and off to find Charlotte.

Why not?

Why not go find her? She had agreed they would get together later.

You're all mine.

That was what he had heard her say, what he had intended to say himself. She was probably expecting him, wondering where he was. She might very well be sitting there waiting and feeling disappointed that he had yet to show up.

He couldn't do that to her, couldn't disappoint her.

With a smile and a joyful hop out of bed, he grabbed a fresh plaid and wrapped it around him. And with eager steps was out the door.

He was glad it was late, everyone exhausted and in bed. He didn't want to meet anyone, especially his brothers and be asked where he was going. No doubt they would have to comment why mum had chosen to—

"So mum separated you and Charlotte."

"Damn," Bryce mumbled, and turned to see Reeve grinning. "Don't start."

"I asked a simple question," he said with a shrug, keeping his grin broad.

"You're asking for a fight."

Reeve laughed and shook his head. "No, I'm over-joyed knowing that you are where Duncan and I have both been."

"Where's that?"

"In the throes of fresh love."

"I didn't say anything about love," Bryce argued.

"Refusing to admit it, are you?"

"Go away, Reeve, or I'll have to—"

"Get Charlotte to fight your battle," Reeve said, laughing, while taking significant steps away from Bryce.

"You better back away," Bryce warned.

Reeve stopped laughing long enough to say, "You have a choice: chase me or go find your woman and love her. And I know my brother isn't foolish enough to make the wrong choice."

Bryce smiled. "You're right, he's not."

"Good night then," Reeve said. "And just so you know, Tara and I think that Charlotte is one amazing woman."

Bryce nodded. "She is, and I'm glad to hear you both feel that way."

The bedchamber wasn't far, and, once there, Bryce hesitated a moment, but only a moment. He opened the door slowly and peered around it. Odin's head was up, and as soon as he saw that it was Bryce, he yawned and returned to sleep in front of the hearth. The fire cast a soft glow to the small room, and Bryce could easily see that Charlotte was in bed, asleep.

He entered anyway, needing just to have a look at her. He had been so disappointed when he had entered his bedchamber, and she hadn't been there. He had actually missed her and was looking forward to seeing her again, holding her, kissing her, and loving her.

The fire's soft light highlighted her freshly scrubbed face, and lovely it was. He didn't know how he could have ever mistaken her for a lad. But then she had done a remarkable job in portraying one.

Her hair was still damp, and though she was curled beneath the covers except for one arm, he knew she was naked.

He stood there for a few moments before he made his decision. He unwrapped his plaid and let it fall to the floor. Then he crawled beneath the blanket and curled himself around Charlotte, so warm and soft, and he sighed with pleasure.

As much as he would have loved to wake her and make love to her, he didn't. He knew how exhausted she was; he felt it himself. But he could sleep with her, and that is what he did. Content having her in his arms again, he closed his eyes and slept.

Chapter 29

Charlotte didn't know what woke her; her eyes simply sprang open. She wasn't certain where she was at first though she was relieved that Bryce was wrapped around her. She waited to feel the breath of the chilled night air or for raindrops to splatter on her face. Then she realized where she was, and she sighed with relief that she was in a soft bed instead of on the hard ground. She cuddled her backside closer to Bryce and closed her eyes to return to blessed sleep.

Her eyes sprang wide once again, realizing that she was naked, and so was Bryce. It all came rushing back to her now. She had been waiting for his return so that they could finally make love without worry or troublesome weather to contend with. But she had fallen asleep, desperately tired from all she had been through.

She smiled, thinking that though he had found her sleeping naked in his bed, he had been unselfish enough not to disturb her. He was such a good man, and she felt so lucky to have him.

Though returning to sleep would be a wise choice,

it wasn't what was on her mind. Having thoroughly enjoyed making love with him during a raging thunderstorm under a bush, she wondered what delights waited for her making love with him in a bed and with nothing else to disturb them.

She grinned and bit at her lower lip.

Should she?

The answer came quite easily.

Of course she should.

With a wiggle and a twist, she turned around, a bit disappointed. She thought her action might wake him, her intention, but it hadn't. He slept soundly; but then, he was exhausted and rightly so. She wondered if she was being selfish in wanting to wake him, wanting to make love with him and concerned that perhaps he would be annoyed with her if she did.

After all, he had been unselfish. Shouldn't she?

Her grin grew ever wide.

No, she intended to be selfish.

Her hand slipped down between them and found his soft member, an impressive size in its sleeping state, and more than imposing when awake. She began to stroke it to life ever so gently, finding a natural rhythm as she went. With his head turned and his taut muscular neck quite inviting, she eagerly began to feast, kissing and nipping and enjoying the freshly scrubbed taste of him ever so much.

The rhythm she had set worked its way into her body, and soon her body was flowing with the seductive tempo close against him. He had already grown considerably in her hand, but now he grew even larger and she more wet as the cadence took command.

Her mouth moved to his, brushing light kisses along his lips.

When he took charge, she couldn't say. All she knew was that suddenly he took command, his lips taking hold of hers, his tongue forcing them apart and darting in to take full control.

His hands did the same, pushing hers aside as his body eased against hers, forcing her onto her back. His lips then left hers. Though she protested with a groan, he paid no heed, and, in a moment, she understood why. His lips captured one nipple and began to tease and torment, and she was soon writhing with pleasure. He did the same to the other, but it was when he traveled down her entire body, teasing, tasting, and tormenting that she knew she'd gone mad with the want of him.

She tugged at him. "I need you inside me."

He laughed softly, then worked kisses down along her body until finally he buried his face between her legs.

He had no sooner tasted her than she came, with such an explosive intensity that she screamed out his name.

While her tingling climax reverberated throughout her body, he slipped over her and into her. She startled for a moment, but as he began to move, his rhythm slow at first, then turning faster and more powerful, he sparked her to life again before the previous sparks could completely fade away.

She grabbed hold of his muscled arms, braced on either side of her, and hung on as he drove in and out with precise control. She didn't think it possible to feel such exquisite pleasure as she had before or more than she had; but mercy help her, she did. The pleasurably intense sensation grew rapidly inside her until she moaned wildly with the need for release.

"Please, now," she begged, eager for what awaited her.

He brought his mouth down on hers and kissed her with such a driving demand that she thought she would explode there and then.

"Not yet," he said after he tore his mouth away from hers.

And though he was already deep inside her, she ached to have him even deeper, and so she instinctively wrapped her legs around him. His thrusts took on a more frantic speed, and Charlotte welcomed it, ached for it, didn't want it to ever end and yet did. She wanted to share that explosive moment with him, and he didn't disappoint her.

They both erupted in exquisite pleasure. It rushed through her again and again and again. She kept a firm hold on Bryce and squeezed tight, as if holding firm she could make it last forever, keep him buried deep inside her forever.

Finally, he collapsed against her, and she wrapped her arms around him, though in moments she found his deadweight too much to bear. He realized it and rolled off her, though he slipped his arm around her and lifted her up and over to lie on top of him.

"Do not move," he said with labored breath. "You are right where I want you."

She rested her head on his hard chest. "And I am right where I want to be."

They let their breathing calm and the last sparks of pleasure fade away.

"You're not upset with me that I woke you?" she asked teasingly.

"Wake me that way as often as you wish."

"Be careful what you advise, or you may never get any sleep."

"Worry not; I have the stamina to make love to you as often as you wish," he said with playful bravado."

"Again, I warn you to be careful, for I may test your claim."

"And I shall rise to the occasion and be victorious each and every time."

She sighed, more than content with the moment.

"Why didn't you wait in my bedchamber?" he asked.

She raised her head and smiled at the love that shone so brilliantly in his eyes. She'd never grow tired of seeing it, and she hoped it would be there for more years than she ever dared expect.

"I thought I was in your bedchamber," she said, and grew concerned. "Did your mum purposely separate us?"

"It would seem that way though I don't know why."

"Perhaps she does not like me," she said, though she hoped that was not so. It would make matters so much more difficult than was necessary.

"I don't believe that to be so. I saw how her admiration for you grew along with the telling of your tale."

"She can still admire me though not think me suitable for you."

"It is not her choice." He yawned. "And I will speak to her about it."

Charlotte grinned. "I have only met your mum, but I can see how protective she is of her sons and how much she loves you all."

"A mother's way, I suppose. You no doubt would be the same."

Charlotte rested her head back on his chest, the steady rhythm of his heart a soothing cadence. "I will keep my children safe and defend them with my life." She yawned, her eyes growing heavy with sleep.

"It is good to know our children will be safe," he said, his words slowing as sleep crept over him.

"We do not know what the future holds for us."

"No one does, but I do know one thing . . ." He paused, fighting to stay awake long enough to finish. "I have no intention of ever letting you go."

Charlotte smiled, her eyes closing as well. "I love you too."

Chapter 30

Charlotte quietly slipped out of bed, into fresh clothes, a blouse too big and a skirt too long, and left the room without waking Bryce, Odin as always by her side. She wanted to return before he woke, hoping they could start the day with not only a kiss but making love. She intended to see if his stamina was as potent as he claimed.

She smiled at the thought and the remembrance of falling asleep on top of him. She didn't know how they had ended up in each other's arms, but it didn't matter. It was where she had wanted to be, and the way he had held her, so snug and tight, told her it had been where he wanted her.

She recalled with delight his way of letting her know how very much he loved her.

I have no intention of ever letting you go.

His words had warmed her heart and tickled her senses. One day, when he was burdened no more with missions for the true king, he would tell her that he loved her. She would be patient and wait; after all, her mission to find her da remained a priority. Their love would only grow stronger from the wait and make them appreciate it all the more.

Right now, however, she had to address something that troubled her. Though Bryce had every intention of seeing to it, it wasn't for him to tend to.

She entered the great hall and smiled. She had been right to assume that Mara would be up before anyone. She'd make certain all was ready for when her family woke, and it would afford them time alone.

"Good morning," Charlotte said upon approaching the table where Mara sat focused on the flames in the hearth.

Mara jumped and turned with a start. "I didn't hear you approach."

"I tread lightly," she said, letting an anxious Odin out of the keep before joining Mara at the table.

Mara motioned for her to sit. "A wise thing to do."

Charlotte wrapped her hands around the tankard of hot cider Mara offered her. "I'm also direct with my thoughts and opinions."

"Much like me," Mara said, crossing her arms to rest on the table in front of her.

"Good, then we can be honest with each other. Do you feel me unworthy to be Bryce's woman?"

Mara took no affront at Charlotte's blunt question and answered without hesitation. "You are not only a worthy woman; you are courageous where most would be fearful. I admire your tenacity in your search for your da. He is important to you and comes first above all else—" She paused and looked directly at Charlotte. "Bryce needs a woman who will understand that he is a warrior first and foremost, that his mission to support and protect the true king will always take precedence over all else."

"You mean that my mission to find my da interferes with his mission for the true king," Charlotte said.

Mara nodded. "Bryce needs to remain focused during these difficult times that grow ever more difficult. He can let *nothing* stand in his way."

"You can't mean that you think my love for him would be a deterrent."

"I've seen strong and courageous people destroyed by love and rulers toppled or never brought to power because love interfered."

"Bryce and I both are well aware that our missions must come before our love."

"But does your love for each other understand that, or will it rear its jealous head and interfere?"

"Did you feel this way when Duncan and Reeve found love?"

Mara grinned. "I welcomed their women with open arms though Mercy arrived shackled to Duncan and Tara, having been thought a death bride, gave me a stir. But your arrival" She shook her head. "You have a tenacity that reminds me of a friend who was more a sister to me. And she not only suffered greatly for it, but those around her did as well."

"What happened to her?"

"Her own tenacity brought about her death."

"I am sorry to hear that about your friend," Charlotte said, "and though we may be similar in nature, I am not her. I will not hurt those I love; I will protect them, with my life, if necessary."

Mara shook her head. "You echo my friend's words, though in the end, she failed."

"My da taught me that what strikes one as failure

could be victory for another. Perhaps your friend was more victorious than you thought." Charlotte stood. "I want to get back before Bryce wakes."

"Think on what I said, for I will not see Bryce suffer again."

"Again?"

Mara nodded. "My friend who suffered and caused others to suffer—was Bryce's mother."

Charlotte was about to sit down and find out more when Carmag called out good morning.

"We will talk more on this," Charlotte whispered, and turned to greet Bryce's da with a smile. "I was just going to wake Bryce."

"Take your time," Carmag said. "I enjoy some quiet time in the morning with my wife."

Charlotte nodded and left the pair sitting close together, holding hands, and whispering, though she didn't think they were exchanging whispers of love.

She hurried up the steps, her mind awash with what Mara had told her, though certain Mara hadn't told her all. And she intended to find out, partially to assuage her own curiosity but more so for Bryce. Obviously, there were things he didn't know about his true mother.

Charlotte's da had kept her mum's memory alive with the many tales he had repeatedly shared with her. He felt it was a way of keeping her in their hearts. Bryce had been young when he had lost his mum, and if Mara knew something about her, then she should share it with Bryce. This way he could keep a part of her with him.

First, however, she would speak with Mara and see what she knew about Bryce's mum and why she had failed to share the knowledge.

She hiked up her skirt and hurried along the hall, quietly opening the door when she reached it. She walked over to the bed and smiled. Bryce still slept. His chest was fully exposed, as was one leg; the blanket covered the rest of him. He looked much too appealing.

While she debated about waking him again, she shed her clothes, stood for a moment, and made her decision. Lifting the edge of the blanket, she crawled beneath and gently slipped over him.

His arms came around her, as if expecting her to be there. She bit at her lower lip once again, debating with herself. Should she do what he had done to her and drive him completely mad with passion?

It wasn't a long debate or a necessary one. She had already made up her mind as soon as the thought had come to her. She wanted her turn, and she intended to take it.

She started at his chest, kissing his hard, warm flesh, and slowly made her way down the length of him. She didn't notice when his arms had fallen away from her, though it was easy to see she had aroused him.

If she had woken him, she didn't bother to find out. She was much too intent on her course of action. Besides, she was quite enjoying herself and quite surprised by her own body's responses. Passion was budding in her, and she was eager to have it burst into bloom.

When her mouth settled over him, he bolted up, sending her tumbling off him and onto the floor.

"Damn it, woman, I thought I was dreaming," he scowled, peering over the side of the bed.

"You weren't," she said, getting quickly to her feet, "though the dream has now ended."

He hastily reached out, snatched her around the waist, and yanked her back in bed on top of him. "I loved the dream, I want to go back into the dream, I want to linger in the dream."

"But you're awake now," she teased with a laugh.

"I'll go back to sleep. Here, I'm shutting my eyes. I'm asleep. The dream needs to return."

A knock sounded at the door.

"Go away; I'm asleep," Bryce shouted.

"You can't be asleep, you're talking."

Charlotte recognized Reeve's voice and grinned.

"I'm talking in my sleep. Go away, Reeve, before I come out there and beat you."

"Too late, I know you're not asleep, and I need your help."

"Get Duncan to help you," Bryce yelled back.

"Mercy isn't feeling well. He won't leave her."

That had Charlotte jumping out of the bed and slipping back into her clothes.

Bryce followed, grumbling, and grabbed his shirt and plaid, casting a quick glance over Charlotte. "Those clothes are too big for you."

"That's what was left for me," Charlotte said.

"I'll see that you're found more suitable garments."

"I'll take care of it," she assured him. "Reeve needs your help."

Another knock shook the door. "Hurry up."

"I'm going to enjoy beating you," Bryce called out.

"Are you bringing Charlotte to help you?"

Charlotte had to laugh though she stifled it when she saw that Bryce hadn't found it funny.

Once he finished dressing, he reached out and

yanked her into his arms, giving her a sound kiss. "Tell me you will—"

She finished before he could. "Finish what I started as soon as we have a chance to be alone."

"Which will be soon, very soon," he assured with a nod.

He released her then and marched to the door and swung it open.

"That was fast; are you sure you satisfied her?" Reeve asked, grinning.

"You know I'm going to make you suffer for this, don't you?" Bryce said.

Reeve laughed. "You mean you're going to try."

Charlotte smiled at their brotherly antics but asked before they turned to leave, "Is Mercy all right? Is there anything I can do to help?"

"Her time draws near, and if she sighs, Duncan thinks there is something wrong with her," Reeve said. "But Tara has gone to make sure all is well. We'll all be gathering for the morning meal in about an hour. We'll see you in the great hall then."

Bryce hesitated, but she would not see him forgo his duties because he worried over leaving her on her own. He should know that she would keep herself occupied; though perhaps that was his worry.

"I'll see you then," she said with a smile. "I have Odin to see to."

The mention of the big dog assuaged his concern as she knew it would. She didn't follow far behind them as they descended the stairs, though they parted company once in the great hall. Bryce and Reeve left the hall while she cast a glance around to see if Odin had found his way back inside. Not seeing him, she went in search of him.

He wasn't hard to find. He had made friends with a short, wiry man sitting on a bench outside his cottage. He seemed to take pleasure in Odin's company. Though on closer inspection, Charlotte noticed that the man was sharing food with Odin.

"You must watch him," Charlotte said as she approached them. "He's quite the successful beggar."

The man laughed and rubbed behind Odin's ear. "He has manners and waits his turn." He patted the empty spot next to him on the bench. "Please join us. I'm Neil."

"Charlotte." She introduced herself and gladly accepted the piece of bread he offered as she sat. It was tastier than any she had ever had, which was why she finished it so quickly. "That was delicious."

He gave her another. "My wife, Etty, is the cook and a good one."

"Excellent cook," Charlotte said between bites. "And I can assure you that Odin will be visiting you often."

Neil laughed and, with a tilt of his head and a squint of his eyes, he said, "You look familiar."

"I doubt we've ever met," Charlotte said. "I only arrived here yesterday."

"I have not lived here long myself."

"Then perhaps our paths have crossed," Charlotte said. "I have traveled the area extensively."

He shook his head. "I cannot place where I have seen you."

"Perhaps it's my da you have met," she suggested, though she doubted it. "I have some of his features and inherited his short height and slim frame, though he has white hair and—"

"Idris Semple," Neil said with jubilant smile, "a man of great knowledge."

Charlotte was stunned, and it took her a moment to find her voice. "You know my da?"

"He was summoned to appear before King Kenneth. I served at the king's court."

"My da wouldn't let me accompany him there," she said, "though I didn't want him going alone.

"He is a wise man. We had good conversations, and I look forward to speaking with him again."

"My da is not with me," she said regretfully. "He was taken prisoner by the king's soldiers."

Neil shook his head. "I feared that would happen and warned Idris to get as far away as he could."

"He paid heed to your advice," she said. "We left our lodgings the day after his return from court. It took months before the soldiers found us." She said a quick silent prayer before asking her most important question. "I learned that he might have been taken to a secret prison. Would you know where it would be? "

He turned sorrowful eyes on her. "I have heard of such a prison, but I don't know its location, though—" He seemed to ponder a moment. "A man arrived here a few days ago, not too right of mind, and though he was offered shelter, he preferred to provide his own, far removed from others. Worried that he might be dangerous, Duncan spoke with him. He assured everyone that the man needed time to recover from being a prisoner of the king."

Charlotte jumped up. "Old John is here?"

"I do believe his name is John."

"And though he appears old, his eyes tell a different tale."

Neil nodded. "I thought the same myself about him."

"Where does he lodge?"

"Only Duncan knows that."

"Thank you, Neil, you don't know what a help you've been."

"I'm willing to do whatever I can to help Idris," he said. "I have great respect for your father."

"Again, thank you," she said, and ran off, Odin right beside her.

She would find Duncan, then Old John, and she would find her da.

Chapter 31

Charlotte hurried into the keep and found Mara busy getting the last of the morning meal on the table. She gave no thought to manners, interrupting Mara as she spoke with one of the servants.

"Where are the clothes I wore?"

Mara turned a smile though cold eyes on her. "I am busy with—"

"My clothes," Charlotte demanded.

"I had them burned. They were too filthy to ever get clean again."

"That was not a choice for you to make," Charlotte said, and turned and hurried out of the keep.

Odin kept up with her as they made their way back to Neil, who hadn't moved off the bench.

"I need a favor," Charlotte said.

"Anything to help Idris's daughter."

Charlotte emerged from Neil's cottage wearing a freshly washed brown shirt and beige linen tunic, belted at the waist with a leather strip, and a brown wool vest on top. Her worn leather knee-high boots remained.

She couldn't thank Neil enough, and he couldn't express how much it pleased him to help in finding Idris. As strange as it seemed, she felt her old self once again and, with confidence, rushed off to find Duncan.

He was where she expected to find him, with his wife Mercy in their bedchamber. Odin sneaked in alongside Charlotte and trotted over to the fireplace and plopped down.

"How are you faring?" Charlotte asked, approaching the bed.

"I'm fine." Mercy sighed. "Just a bit tired."

"She's needs to rest," Duncan insisted.

"I need for you to leave me alone," Mercy shot back.

Duncan look stricken, and Mercy breathed a heavier sigh.

"Where is Tara?" Charlotte asked, thinking a change of subject would be good.

"She went to see about getting me breakfast," Mercy said.

"Why don't you just join everyone at the table?" Charlotte asked.

Mercy threw back the covers. "A good suggestion."

Duncan blocked her from going anywhere, and Mercy's shoulders slumped in frustration.

Charlotte took hold of Duncan's arm and gently tugged him away from Mercy. "I need to talk with you."

Mercy grinned with appreciation and hurried into her clothes.

"Where is John, the man who arrived here and sought solitude from others?" Charlotte asked.

Duncan's brow furrowed in thought for a moment,

then answered, "I don't know exactly. He didn't want anyone to know his exact location so I left him in the woods to make his choice."

"Can you give me a general location?"

Duncan nodded. "I can, but why?"

"He knows where the prison is where my da was taken."

Duncan's eyes turned wide. "He escaped from the supposed secret prison?"

"It seems that way, and since he escaped, he can tell me where it is and how to get in and out."

Duncan shook his head. "I wouldn't count on his being forthcoming with the information."

Charlotte remained strong in her convictions. "I have no doubt he'll be only too glad to tell me."

"Sounds like you have a plan brewing," Mercy said, joining them.

"It is nothing for you to concern yourself with," Duncan said.

Mercy poked Duncan in the chest. "You forget I jumped off a cliff with you not once but twice. The second time fresh with your babe inside me."

"You did?" Charlotte asked, amazed. "You must tell me the tale."

Duncan reached out and grabbed his wife, hugging her to him. "You're right. I have forgotten how brave you are."

"Then you will leave me be?" she asked with a kiss.

"I'll never leave you be. I love you too much."

Charlotte watched them kiss and thought how lovely love could be. And at that moment she missed Bryce more than she ever had.

"Let's go eat," Duncan said.

"I need to know about John," Charlotte said, not the least hungry for food but starving to find him.

"I'll tell you and Bryce all I know over the morning meal," Duncan said, his arm firm around his wife's waist.

"I have no stomach for food," Charlotte said sharply. "I want to know where I can start my search for John."

"Bryce wouldn't want you going off on your own," Duncan said.

"I started off on my own," she protested.

"Perhaps, but you're not on your own now. You're Bryce's woman, and that makes a big difference," Duncan said. "We'll discuss it with him over the morning meal."

Charlotte didn't want to wait and was ready to argue with him when Mercy placed a hand on her husband's arm and smiled.

"This is all new to Charlotte. Why don't you go and see that Tara knows I won't need my meal brought here. And that I'll be joining everyone, while I have a word with Charlotte."

Duncan seemed only too glad to leave the women to themselves, and when he leaned down to kiss his wife, Charlotte heard him whisper, "Bryce has enough to burden him."

Did Duncan believe like Mara that she was a burden Bryce could do without?

"Pay him no mind," Mercy said, when the door closed behind her husband. "He feels guilty that Bryce has been doing more than his share of missions while he remains close to home because of me and the babe.

I've assured him it isn't necessary for him to remain behind though I'd be remiss if I didn't admit that I'm glad he is here." She shrugged. "I feel safe when he is close by. I suppose I think he can rescue me from anything, even a difficult birth, if necessary."

"I understand though it would have been difficult for me to comprehend if I hadn't fallen in love with Bryce. Now I find myself wanting to be with him more often than not."

"Then why go in search of your da alone?"

"Bryce has his own mission that needs his attention. While I fear for my da's safety the longer he remains a prisoner of the king."

"Yes, that could prove a problem," Mercy said. "The king is not a tolerant man, especially when he sets his mind on something."

"You speak as if you know the king."

"Unfortunately, I do. He's my father."

Charlotte's eyes rounded like full moons.

"My mum was his mistress, and he paid me little heed."

"I'm sorry for you. My da has been very good to me, and I miss him greatly," Charlotte said, and didn't hesitate to ask the question that she hoped could finally be answered. "Is there any chance you would know about this prison?"

Mercy shook her head. "No, he never discussed anything of importance in front of me." She smiled. "But I did hear Duncan discussing where he intended to take Old John."

Charlotte's grin spread from ear to ear.

* * *

Bryce couldn't stop thinking about Charlotte and how she had woken him this morning. The vivid memories filled his every thought no matter how much he tried to rid himself of them. He finally finished helping Reeve with settling some of the new arrivals in safe shelters since a storm brewed overhead.

He was looking forward to joining Charlotte at the morning meal, then retreating to his bedchamber to finish what she had started. It was all he could think about, and that disturbed him, since plans needed to be made not only to find Charlotte's da but the spy, who held important information to the mission. That was where his mind should be focused, and it would as soon as he finished this dream that haunted the hell out of him.

He stopped abruptly when he saw that Charlotte was not among his family gathered around the table in front of the hearth. He told himself that something no doubt had delayed her, and she would arrive soon.

When he reached the table, though, he had to ask, "Where is Charlotte?"

Each mentioned a place they had last seen her.

Duncan glanced down at his wife beside him. "She was with you last I saw her."

Mercy smiled sweetly at Bryce. "She told me to let you know that she goes in search of Old John."

"But she doesn't know where I settled him," Duncan said. "And I explicitly told her that we would discuss this with Bryce."

"Old John is here?" Bryce asked.

Duncan and Reeve shared the telling of the tale of the man's arrival and his need for solitary shelter and how Duncan had taken him to a remote area to live. Then everyone looked at Mercy.

"I overheard you speak of the area," Mercy explained with a shrug. "And everyone heard Charlotte's tale about her da and all she has gone through to find him. I would do the same if I had a loving da like hers."

"I would too," Tara agreed.

Reeve slipped his arm around his wife. "I would help you."

"And no doubt, Charlotte knows the same of Bryce," Tara said, snuggling closer to her husband.

Mara spoke up. "Bryce has more important things to see to, and Charlotte has proven she can well take care of herself."

Bryce looked at his mum, surprised by her remark, as was everyone else. Mara was the first to offer a helping hand and to protect when necessary. Yet she extended no such offer to Charlotte, and he wondered why.

"I'll not leave her to wander the land alone," Bryce said, sending a stern look to his mum. "Also finding Old John could aid us in our own search. As we discussed, I believe the person I search for could well be held at the same prison as Charlotte's da. Her search is also my search, and I will not leave her to do my chore."

Reeve and Duncan stood ready to help him.

"No," Bryce said, shaking his head. "I need no help with this."

"Do what you must," Duncan said. "Reeve and I will work on plans to continue the search."

Bryce confirmed with a nod and turned to leave.

His mum grabbed hold of his arm. "Let me get you some food in case you're delayed in returning home."

He smiled, pleased that she finally offered help, and told her he'd meet her outside.

Bryce went to his bedchamber, grabbed what few things he needed, and was outside in minutes, impatiently waiting for his mum. He thought of taking his horse, but with Charlotte not having much of a head start, he'd no doubt catch up with her in no time.

When his mum finally appeared, he took the sack, eager to be on his way, but her hand to his arm stopped him.

"Make sure this is what you want," she said, patted his arm, and hurried inside.

He stared after her a few moments, surprised that she hadn't embraced his choice in a woman as easily as she had his brothers'. He shook his head, deciding not to let it worry him; she would come around to liking Charlotte. With the thought, he took off.

Charlotte made her way through the woods, happy to once again be exploring. Mercy had told her that the area was fairly safe from soldiers. It was mostly woods and rocky terrain, not good for farming, so not inhabitable.

Habitable or not, she found the area rich with things to investigate, examine, and collect. Her da would love it here. She certainly did, and she wished she was free to take time to explore. She missed the days she had spent in the woods looking for specimens for her da or working together with him.

She disliked being confined indoors; even in the winter, she would pile garments one on top of another and venture out in the cold. Not that she hadn't attended to daily chores first, she just had been quick about them so that her time could be her own.

Her da had taught her to cook, and, though she wasn't fond of the task, she was good at it, like most things she did. It was her way—once she learned how to do something, she wanted to do it well. Even the things she wasn't fond of doing, like stitching. She found it tedious but necessary, and so became proficient at it.

But it was exploring that brought her the most joy, and she would find it most difficult if she was unable to explore at will.

Charlotte's musings often consumed her, but she always managed to keep alert in spite of them. So when Odin stopped dead in his tracks, so did she. She waited and watched while he sniffed the air, and as soon as his tail started wagging, she knew whose scent he had picked up. Her trail certainly wasn't difficult to find or follow. She hadn't meant it to be. She had assumed and correctly that Bryce would soon be after her. And perhaps she wanted him to.

"I expected you sooner," she said, turning, as Odin ran past her, his tail wagging.

She smiled at the sight of him emerging from the woods and her heart quickened its pace. Her stomach gave a flutter, and she almost laughed. She had never imagined that love could feel so wonderful. Tall and broad and swathed in his plaid, he was ever the mighty Highlander.

"I saw by your tracks that you were in no hurry and knew I would catch up with you soon enough," he said, and held up the sack. "Hungry?"

"Yes," she said, and hurried to him, throwing her arms around him and kissing him as if they hadn't kissed in forever.

His arm wrapped around her, and his hand roamed down along her back and over her backside to cup a firm cheek. "You've missed me that much?" he asked, after ending the kiss with much reluctance.

She had no trouble admitting the truth to him. "It is quite startling how much I miss you. It hasn't been all that long that we have known each other, and yet I feel as if we have not only been friends for many years but have been in love forever."

He stepped away from her and looked as if he collected his thoughts, and so she waited. Though love was new to her, she had no trouble admitting how she felt about it. It seemed easy since it made her feel so very good; so, regardless of what the future might bring, why not speak how she felt?

When still he said nothing, she spoke. "You once told me that love robs your sanity and interferes with everything. So have you gone quite mad yet?"

A slow smile spread across his face, and he stepped toward her. "I'm about to."

Chapter 32

Bryce never got the chance. Odin's sharp bark separated them before they got close. Their backs quickly connected in a protective stance, and they surveyed the area with vigilant eyes. Odin did the same, standing near them and looking about.

"He's watching us," Bryce said. "Whether he was lucky or stumbled across our tracks, he knows we came in search of him and now will make certain to hide."

Charlotte spoke up. "Old John, please, I need your help. I must know where that prison is. I must rescue my da."

He responded, his voice echoing from all directions at once. "There is nothing you can do for him. He is as good as dead."

"I don't believe that," she shouted back. "If you escaped, so can he."

"No! He'll never be free. There is nothing you can do," he cried out. "Now go and bother me no more."

"No!" she shouted frantic. "I will not stop searching for you. I will give you no peace until you tell me what I want to know." When there was no response she yelled, "Do you hear me? Never will I stop. Never!"

Silence filled the air, and Odin walked over and gave her hand a consoling lick.

Thunder erupted so suddenly that she and Bryce both jumped, and Odin whimpered and leaned against Charlotte's leg, shivering.

"We need to return to the keep," Bryce said. "A good storm is brewing, and I'll not be searching into the night out in such weather."

"The weather will not stop me from searching," Charlotte said adamantly.

"I know," Bryce said, reaching for her hand. "And I will help you, but not in a raging storm when we can be dry, warm, and snug in a bed."

She looked ready to argue.

"Don't make me carry you," he warned. "You know it's an easy task for me, no burden at all. And I want you tucked snug beneath me in my bed tonight."

She grinned with such a suggestively wicked grin that he grew hard.

"I'd prefer to finish what I started earlier this morning."

His hand rushed out and snatched hers. "Let's hurry."

She locked her fingers around his, and, as they ran off, he couldn't help but notice that sorrow lingered in her eyes.

A darkening sky, rumbling thunder, and flashes of lightning followed them all the way back to the keep. The rain just started to fall as they rushed up the steps and through the door.

The great hall was quiet, only servants stirred. Bryce

was glad, he wanted no interruptions. He snuck away to his bedchamber with Charlotte to spend the rest of the day with her and her alone.

He was reminded of Odin when the dog sprinted past him to plop down in front of the hearth. He thought about ordering him downstairs but knew it wouldn't sit well with Charlotte, and he was not about to upset her.

He didn't like it when she was upset, it ripped at his gut and made him feel like he wanted to tear apart anyone who caused her worry. It had disturbed him when she had pleaded with Old John for help and the man ignored her.

He had felt her pain, her disappointment, and her sorrow, and it had made him want to tear out the man's throat.

He went to her then, needing to take her into his arms and comfort her, and he knew that the best way to do that was to make love to her. He had thought to give her free rein to continue what she had started that morning, but that had changed when he had seen that she had tried to keep the sorrow from her eyes.

She needed him to love her, to take away her worry, if only for a few hours, and allow her some peace.

She turned to him with a smile she tried hard to maintain.

He reached out and took hold of her waist. "I'm going to love you."

"It's for me to finish what I started," she said.

"Not now," he said with a shake of his head. "Now is for me to show you how much I love you."

Her dark eyes turned wide, and her mouth dropped

open as if she intended to speak, but no words spilled
forth.

He took advantage and kissed her, his tongue darting in to lovingly tease hers. She melted against him,
and he felt, then, her first teardrop. He didn't stop kissing her even when he felt her tears against his cheek.
She needed this kiss from him; she needed it to linger,
to sustain her.

And he didn't fail her. He kissed her with an intensity that was meant to drive her pain away. When her
tears wouldn't stop, he raised her just enough to walk
her to the bed. Once there, he striped himself while
continuing their kiss; and then he striped her, stopping
only long enough to rid her of her clothes.

He lowered her to the bed, covering her with the
length of him and knowing instinctively that she was
as ready for him as he was for her; he nudged her legs
apart and slipped between them.

She welcomed his quick, deep entrance, tossing her
head back with a sharp yelp and a breathless sigh that
fired his already burning need. Soon they were lost in
the fury of the lovemaking. It knew no sense or reason
and needed none. It was just the two of them, lost not
just in depths of passion but in the depths of love.

Tears lingered on her cheeks after their fiery climax,
but none spilled. He kissed the few away and rolled
off her, quickly cuddling her close against him. With
a teasing laugh, he asked, "Was my lovemaking that
disappointing?"

She smiled and looked up at him. "My tears were
ones of joy."

"I was that good, was I?"

She gave him a playful poke. "I cried because I was overwhelmed with joy hearing that you love me."

"My heart would not allow me to restrain the words any longer."

"Then you are ready to give your heart to me?"

"*Give* my heart to you?" he laughed. "You *stole* it from me shortly after I discovered you were a woman."

"Then I shall keep it safe forever and ever."

He kissed her. "Make sure that you do, for it belongs only to you."

A single tear trickled down her cheek as they kissed again.

They spent the rest of the day in Bryce's bedchamber, talking, eating, teasing, and making love. He refused to allow anyone to disturb them, even chasing his mum away when she insisted an important matter needed to be discussed.

He had asked if it was a life-or-death matter, and when she admitted it wasn't, he told her he would speak with her tomorrow.

Charlotte worried that Mara would blame her for Bryce's not seeing to his duties, and while she certainly didn't want to be a deterrent, she wanted this time alone with Bryce. He might have admitted his love for her, and she had been more than open about her love for him, but that didn't mean that their future was sealed. They still both needed to attend to their missions. And though Bryce would attempt to leave her behind in the safety of his home when he went in search of her da, she had other plans.

Not one to sit and stitch or do womanly things,

though she was not averse to them, she planned to get an early start on the morrow and once again attempt to find Old John. He could tell her where her da was, and she intended to see that he did just that.

And though it would be nice to have Bryce with her, he had his duties to attend to, and she was certain Mara would see that he did. Besides, she needed Bryce to understand that she could not wait around for him to tend to her problems. She was used to tending to her own though it was good that he cared and would always be there to help her.

Tired from a night of endless lovemaking, she forced herself out of bed just before dawn, hoping to sneak out of the keep and be on her way when the sun peeked on the horizon. She also didn't want to run into Mara. While she knew the woman would no doubt have something to say to her, and she herself intended to learn more about Bryce's mum, today was not that day.

She hurried quietly into the garments Neil had lent her, thinking she truly had to see about stitching her own. She and Odin slipped out the door and down to the great hall, planning on heading through the kitchen to swipe some food for their day's trek.

She was surprised and a bit disappointed to find Mara there alone.

"You shouldn't be going off on your own," Mara scolded as she kneaded a mound of dough.

"How do you know I am?"

"It is what I would do."

"We are more alike than you care to admit?"

Mara didn't answer. Instead, she said, "You should

be more concerned about Bryce than chasing after this man in hopes of finding your da. He will worry when he discovers you gone and go after you instead of seeing to his own duty."

"Until he realizes that chasing after me will serve no purpose and let me do what I must." Charlotte quickly changed the subject with her next question. "Why do you keep the truth from Bryce about his mum?"

"When the time is right—"

"And who are you to judge that?" Charlotte asked with more curiosity than malice.

"It is for the best."

"Is it, or is it that your secret has grown far heavier than you had expected it to?"

Mara's stunned reaction proved that her assumption was correct, and suddenly Charlotte felt for the woman.

"Some burdens are easier when shared," Charlotte said. "If ever you wish to ease that burden, I don't mind carrying some of it for you."

Mara raised her chin, tears pooled in her eyes, and she battered the dough on the table.

"No one will eat that bread the way you pummel it," Charlotte said.

"No one will eat it anyway." Mara sighed. "Try as I might, I can cook nothing eatable. And I know my husband and sons fear each time I try."

Charlotte walked to the door, let an anxious Odin out, then returned to Mara, pushing up the sleeves of her shirt. "Before I go, let me show you the secret to making tasty bread."

* * *

Mara was just finishing stuffing a sack full of far too much food for Charlotte and Odin to take when Tara entered the kitchen.

"You're off again on your own, aren't you?" Tara asked Charlotte while pointing to the sack. And before Charlotte could respond, Tara asked, "Can I come with you?"

Again, Charlotte had no time to respond.

"Once I spent much time on my own, and I so enjoyed my walks in the woods. It would be nice to do that again though with someone, having spent more than my share of time alone."

Mara was the one to answer. "It is a good idea for Tara to go with you. Bryce would then know you are not alone. There is a shirt and tunic in my sewing room that you can use, and there should be a pair of boots here somewhere that should fit."

Tara grinned. "I'll be only a second." And she sped out of the room.

"What of Reeve?" Charlotte asked.

Mara grinned. "It will do him good to know that the world won't crumble around him if his wife is not here safe beside him."

Charlotte smiled and pointed to the first loaf of bread that had just finished baking. "Let me take some of that with me. The delicious scent will surely be good bait."

"But once he tastes it—" Mara shook her head.

Charlotte grinned and broke a piece off then split it in two popping one in her mouth and handing the other to Mara.

The woman hesitantly put it to her lips, then did as

Charlotte and popped it into her mouth. "That's delicious," she said, astonished.

"It's all a matter of kneading and coating the bread with the mixture of herbs that I showed you."

"No one will believe I made this bread," Mara said, as if she didn't believe it herself.

"Don't tell anyone until after they have eaten it," Charlotte advised.

"Don't tell anyone what?" Tara asked returning.

Charlotte handed her a piece of the bread.

"That's delicious," Tara said, and reached for more. "Bryce will be pleased that his woman is such a good cook."

"Mara made the bread," Charlotte said.

Tara almost choked. "Truly."

Mara beamed with pride.

"Don't dare tell anyone," Tara insisted. "Not until I'm here and can see their faces. Promise?"

Mara nodded.

"Oh, I can't wait for this," Tara said, and gave Mara a quick kiss on the cheek. "I never thought I would say this, but that was delicious bread you made, Mara."

The two women left a happy Mara busily making more bread.

Chapter 33

Bryce woke with a stretch and reached out to wrap himself around Charlotte, only to find her gone. He groaned and shook his head. He should have known she wouldn't wait. No doubt she was already on her way to try to find Old John.

He stretched himself out of bed and quickly got into his clothes. He couldn't keep chasing after her. He had his duties to see to, and he wondered if perhaps that was what she intended her early-morning absence to show him.

Should he let her be? She did well in speaking with people and discovering information, so perhaps she would do what others couldn't—get Old John to talk.

He pondered the situation as he hurried down to the great hall, eager to eat.

"What do you mean she went off with Charlotte?" Reeve yelled at his mum.

Duncan and Mercy shook their heads, and so did Bryce as he joined them at the table.

"And what are you doing sitting?" Reeve demanded. "We have our women to find."

"Your women are not lost," Mara said. "They took a walk and will return later."

"A walk?" Reeve shouted again, and turned, smacking Bryce in the shoulder. "Your woman dragged my wife off to find that madman."

"Actually, Tara asked if she could join Charlotte," Mara said, filling a tankard with cider and handing it to Bryce.

"Don't worry," Bryce said. "Charlotte won't let anything happen to Tara."

"You're not going after her?" Reeve asked, stunned.

"Not this time," Bryce confessed. "She needs to do this for herself."

Mara smiled and nodded as she passed around a chunk of bread.

"This is tasty," Duncan said, munching on it, and Mercy agreed with a nod, her mouth full.

"Etty should make this more often," Bryce said, agreeing with the others.

Reeve swiped a piece and gave his nod of approval.

Bryce placed a hand on Reeve's shoulder when he finally sank down on the bench next to him. "I do want to run after Charlotte and throttle her for taking off on her own, but I realize that isn't what she needs. As I said, she needs to do this for herself, and perhaps Tara does too."

"If I wasn't so large with child, I would have joined them," Mercy said, disappointed.

Duncan turned to his wife. "You most certainly would no—"

"Don't dare say it," Mercy warned. "If I could trek months through the woods shackled to you, I think I am capable of walking the woods with two women, one who seems quite able of protecting all three of us."

Bryce grinned. "That's my wife—" He sat, stunned that he had acknowledged Charlotte as his wife, and yet it seemed the most naturally thing to do. And only hoped the future would allow it.

"Well, of course Charlotte will be your wife," Mercy said. "Any fool can see that you both love each other."

Carmag entered the hall, preventing any further discussion. His expression was grim, and he told his sons that he needed to talk with them. They immediately stood and followed him to the solar.

As soon as Carmag shut the door behind them, he said, "A friend of Neil's arrived before dawn this morning. He has news of the supposed spy we've been concerned with."

"Is this fellow reliable?" Reeve asked.

Carmag walked over in front of the fireplace where his sons had gathered. "After meeting with him, I would say more than reliable, and he's asked to remain with us. He's brought his wife and three children with him. He says that the king is in a rage over the spy he discovered in his court. And that he plans on finding out just what information the person has passed on to the true king, and there is also talk that this person knows the true king's identity."

"How is that possible?" Duncan asked. "The only ones who know his identity are mum and those in this room."

Bryce shook his head. "That might not be true."

They all turned wide eyes on him.

"Charlotte told me that her da had met the true king."

He held up his hand to prevent any questions before he finished explaining. "I don't know the circumstances or even if it is true, or whether her da just got the notion in his head that a man he met was the true king."

"There is also Bliss, the Pict woman who helped heal Trey," Duncan reminded. "With her ability to see the future, she all but told us that day here in the solar that she knew who the true king was."

"She has returned home, and, besides, she would not have been received well by the king, being a Pict," Reeve said. "And hasn't this spy been in the king's court for some time?"

"Several months," Carmag answered. "The problem is: since we don't know exactly what this person knows, we don't know what danger it could mean for the true king."

"Which means we need to rescue this fellow and find out for ourselves," Bryce said.

The others nodded their agreement.

"Does Neil's friend know where the spy is being held?" Reeve asked.

"A secret prison," Carmag said, "and the mention of it caused him to shiver. It seems that those knowledgeable about the place fear it."

"We need Old John to tell us about that prison," Bryce said.

Charlotte sat on the ground along with Tara, enjoying the food Mara had packed for them. She had unwrapped the bread and set it on a nearby rock, the scent wafting into the air. She had to ply Odin with extra food so he would not try to devour the tempting loaf.

"You think it will tempt him?" Tara whispered.

"A man living on only what he hunts will certainly follow the delicious scent," Charlotte said, keeping her voice low.

"I'm glad I came with you," Tara said, no longer in a whisper. "I forgot how refreshing a good walk could be."

"It is refreshing," Charlotte agreed with a raised voice, hoping to attract John's attention.

"Why do you torment me," Old John called from the woods. "I told you to leave me alone."

"I don't mean to torment," Charlotte said. "And I can't leave you alone. I need answers that only you have."

"Answers that will do you no good," he said.

"Let me decide that," she said. "Now please come join us and share in our food."

"It is best I remain separate from others," Old John said. "But if you could leave some food, it would be appreciated."

"Isn't it time you gave up your solitary life?" Charlotte said. "And start living again."

"You don't know what you ask," he said.

"Then tell us," Tara said.

"You won't want to hear it."

"I've heard much heartache lately," Charlotte offered. "Just recently an old man stumbled out of the woods and into my care, having escaped the soldiers. He thought death his only choice, his son having been taken by the soldiers because of his ability to forge a fine sword and his granddaughter rushing off in search of her da, much like me."

"What? What is that you say?" And with that, Old John stepped out of the woods and approached them.

He was not bowed or slowed by age. This man had a proud posture and a fine step. Though gray filled his hair, he did not appear as aged as when Charlotte had first seen him.

"This man you speak of, do you know his name?" John asked.

"Donald," Charlotte said.

John stumbled as if struck and quickly lowered himself to the ground, his hands trembling. "Donald is my da."

Charlotte had never expected that, and neither had Tara; both their eyes turned wide, and their hearts went out to him.

"Your da survived an attack just yesterday on the group he traveled with. He is fine, and no doubt would love to know that his son is alive and well."

"My daughter," John said with a tear in his eye. "I must find my daughter."

"We could help," Tara offered.

Charlotte agreed with a nod. "Come with us. Talk with your da and talk with our men. There must be something we can do to help you find your daughter."

"I stayed away to protect them. I knew they would search for me, and I didn't want the soldiers harming my family," he said, shaking his head. "But my efforts made no difference, they still suffered."

Charlotte reached out and placed a comforting hand on John's arm. "It's time for the suffering to end. Your da will be happy to see you, to know not all is lost."

"But my daughter . . ." John shook his head, and a tear fell from his eye.

"Help me get to my da, and I will help you find your daughter," Charlotte said, giving his arm a squeeze. "I know how you feel, and I will do all I can to help you."

John wiped away another tear and nodded. "I will help you, and I look forward to seeing my da again."

By late afternoon, Bryce began to worry, though not as much as Reeve, who wore a path in the dirt in front of the keep.

"Why haven't they returned yet?" Reeve asked, as Bryce joined him.

He watched Reeve walk back and forth, his brow wrinkled with concern. He didn't want to add to his alarm by letting him know he felt the same. Why hadn't they returned? Had something happened?

Reeve stopped abruptly. "You feel the same. You think they should have been back by now too, don't you?"

Bryce nodded. "You're right. I had expected them to return by now."

"Something is wrong. We need to go after them," Reeve insisted.

"What? No faith in your women?" Duncan asked, joining them.

"I'd like to see if you'd be saying that if Mercy were with them," Reeve challenged.

Duncan grinned.

"Don't dare laugh," Reeve warned. "You know I'm right."

"You are right," Duncan admitted. "I'd be mad with worry."

"Then why make light of the situation?" Reeve asked, annoyed.

"Because your women are safe and well and headed this way," Duncan said, pointing past them.

Bryce and Reeve turned to see Charlotte, Tara, and Old John entering the village. Reeve went to run, and Bryce grabbed his arm.

"They return victorious. Give her the honor she deserves and stand here with pride and wait for her."

Reeve blew out a frustrated breath. "You're right."

Bryce and Duncan exchanged grins as Reeve started pacing once again. And when the trio was only a short distance from them, Reeve could contain himself no more and hurried to lift his wife off her feet and plant a solid kiss on her lips.

"You're not angry?" Tara asked, once he placed her feet on the ground.

Reeve shook his head. "Worried when I found you were gone. Just tell me next time so that I know where you go."

Tara wrapped her arm around his. "I love you more now than ever."

Reeve leaned in, and whispered, "Later you can show me just how much."

Tara laughed. "That's a promise."

Charlotte grinned as she passed Tara and Reeve, and when she reached Bryce, she gave him a quick kiss, and whispered, "Thank you for not coming after me."

He gave her a quick kiss back and answered with a whisper, "I knew you could do this on your own."

She smiled and took his hand as she introduced

John and told him about Donald being his da. It wasn't long before father and son were reunited, tears flowing freely from both as they embraced each other, not wanting to let go.

Food and ale were generous as father and son talked at a table in the great hall. Bryce knew that Charlotte was eager to hear what John had to say about the prison, but he knew that she also understood that father and son needed some time first. She would want it that way when she found her da, and so she would give it to another.

He sat with an arm around Charlotte at the table before the hearth, his family laughing and talking and he feeling more content than ever. He wanted to tell her that he had missed her in the short time she had been gone, but now wasn't the time. Her hand rested casually on his thigh, but her attention was fixed on where John sat talking with his father.

His thoughts might be on her, but her thoughts were on her da, and he needed to focus there as well and be ready to do whatever it took to rescue her father. He had promised her, and he would not break his promise.

"Is there any of the delicious bread left from this morning?" Tara asked with a smile at Mara.

"Not a crumb," Reeve said. "We ate it all and told mum to have Etty bake more. It was delicious."

"That it was," Duncan agreed, and Mercy nodded her approval.

"I got barely a crumb," Carmag said. "And after tasting it, I wish there had been more."

Tara laughed, and Charlotte joined in.

Bryce was pleased that the conversation had diverted

her attention and brought a bright smile and a laugh to her lips.

"What's so funny?" he asked, giving her a playful squeeze.

"Ask your mum," Charlotte said.

Mara's cheek burned bright red, and her eyes danced with joy. "I baked the bread."

Her husband's and sons' mouths dropped open.

"Impossible," Carmag said, and got a swat in the arm for it. "It's just that—"

"Don't bother to lie," Mara snapped. "I know that you all don't like my cooking." She waved her hand to silence them as each tried to disagree. "No lies, I said. I know my cooking isn't good."

"Then how did you get the bread to taste so delicious?" Carmag asked, wrapping an arm around his wife.

"Charlotte." Mara smiled, pointing at her. "She showed me what I was doing wrong and how to add a little something extra that would make it taste better."

Bryce beamed with pride and hugged Charlotte tight. "She's a woman of many talents."

Before any more praise could be heaped on Charlotte, John approached the table.

"It's time we talked," John said. "And the women don't need to hear what I have to tell."

The women, all but Charlotte, got up and left.

Bryce eased his arm from around Charlotte and took hold of her shoulders. "This is where you leave it to me now. I'll see to rescuing your da."

"No!" she shouted so loudly that the other women stopped and turned.

Charlotte jumped up off the bench. "I've told you time and time again." She slapped her chest. "I will not be left out of this. I started it, and I will finish it."

"You don't want to go where I've been," John said.

"I don't care if I have to go to hell and get my da; I will."

"Then it's hell you're going to," John said, shaking his head. "And it's worse than you ever imagined."

Chapter 34

Charlotte stood firm. There was no way she would be left out of planning her da's rescue and the rescue itself. He expected her to come for him. He was waiting for her, had left messages for her, had stayed strong knowing she was coming for him. And she would not disappoint him.

John was the one who finally said, "Let her hear what I have to say, then she'll understand why it would be wise for her to remain here."

Bryce ran a reassuring hand down her arm. "Are you sure you want to do this?"

"Do you truly need to ask?"

He shook his head and kept firm hold of her arm as she climbed over the bench beside him to sit. She took his hand and locked fingers with his to remind him that they did this together as they had vowed they would. She was relieved when he smiled at her and gave her hand a reassuring squeeze.

They loved each other, and no matter what happened, nothing could change that.

"This prison is like no other; it cannot be seen," John said.

"What do you mean?" Reeve asked.

"It is but a mound with tentacles in the earth, no more. The entrance is also the egress. One way in and one way out. Every chamber feeds off one narrow hall, and at the end is the chamber from hell." John stopped, reaching to pour himself a tankard of ale.

His hands shook so badly that Duncan reached out and filled it for him.

He gave a grateful nod, drank, then proceeded. "The stench was so bad, I can still smell it. The screams of those being tortured still linger in my head. The cries of agony from those left to suffer in their tiny cells loiter in my nightmares."

"Why were you taken there?" Charlotte asked, her stomach rolling at the thought that her da could be suffering horribly at this very moment.

John shook his head. "I was forging swords for the king one moment, then suddenly I was taken to this hellhole, put in a cell and left to rot, to wait—" He shook his head again. "I don't know why. One of the guards mentioned something about waiting for another prisoner to arrive, and once they were done with us, we'd do whatever the king wanted."

"You weren't tortured?" Reeve asked.

"I was made to watch them torture others day after day as they burned the eyes out of prisoners, ripped patches of flesh off them, and . . ." He stopped, unable to detail any more or not wanting to. "They laughed, telling me my turn would come soon enough," he continued with a nod. "I would have preferred death to what awaited me."

"How did you escape?" Charlotte asked, more anxious than ever to free her da from hell.

"Sheer luck," John said. "One of the guards was distracted when he returned me to my cell and forgot to lock me in as he rushed off when another guard called out frantically to him. I slipped out and closed the cell door behind me, knowing they would not come for me until the morrow. Then I went quietly and, with my back to the wall to blend with the shadows, made my way to the entrance and freedom." He gripped tight to the tankard. "I never looked back."

"Do you know the location of the prison?" Bryce asked.

John nodded. "I made special note of it so that I would never go near it again."

"You can map it for us?" Reeve asked.

"I can," John agreed. "And I will do anything to help you if you will help me find my daughter."

"We'll help you, but first we must see to freeing Idris," Bryce said, making no mention of the spy they sought.

"I don't know how you will ever be able to get in or out of the prison; the place is impenetrable," John said.

"We could attack the place," Reeve suggested.

"No," Charlotte said, quickly rejecting the suggestion. "The guards might kill the prisoners before we can reach them."

"She's right about that," John agreed. "From what I saw, none would be allowed to live if the guards thought they might be made free."

"Map the area for us," Charlotte suggested. "Perhaps once we see it, we'll have an idea as to what to do."

They talked over the map until supper, John having left well before that, his da tired and he wanting some rest himself. Supper was soon to be served in the hall when Duncan stretched out of his seat.

"I'm going to get Mercy," he said. "I'll be back shortly.

Tara entered the hall just then, and Reeve smiled at her, but she paid him no heed and, as she headed toward the kitchen, she said to Duncan, "Stay where you are. Your wife is in labor and has been for hours. We'll let you know when the babe arrives."

Charlotte jumped up. "Can I help?"

"Have you birthed any babes?" Tara asked.

"Several." She beamed proudly.

"Good, then go and help Mara," Tara instructed, and disappeared into the kitchen.

Charlotte gave Bryce a quick kiss on the cheek. "Wait to discuss my da until I return." And with that, she was gone.

Bryce looked to Duncan, who stood frozen, completely stunned by the news. Bryce nodded to Reeve, who stood, and, with a firm hand to Duncan's shoulder, eased him down on the bench.

"She didn't tell me," Duncan said, still stunned.

"Could you have done anything?" Bryce asked.

Duncan stared at him a moment, then shook his head.

Reeve filled their tankards and raised his. "To Mercy, a strong woman who will birth a strong babe."

Bryce raised his tankard, and Duncan joined in though he downed the whole thing and held it out to Reeve to fill again.

* * *

Charlotte smiled at the little bundle in her arms. She was petite, with a thatch of black hair. Mara joined her, holding another bundle.

"Where she is small, her brother is large," Mara said, grinning proudly from ear to ear. "Two grandchildren. I cannot believe it."

"Neither can I," said Mercy from the bed.

Tara had just finished getting her settled, clean sheets having replaced the soiled ones. The women had bathed her, combed the tangles from her hair, and slipped her into a fresh night shift. All was in ready for the new da to meet his son and daughter.

"Your delivery went surprisingly fast for two babes," Charlotte said.

"It didn't feel that fast." Mercy laughed. "Though I am grateful I did not linger long in labor."

"I hope I pop babes out as easily as you," Charlotte said, in awe of the little girl in her arms. Having been an only child, she had always longed for a brother or sister or both. It was lonely growing up without a sibling to play or tease or sleep beside.

"I was only blessed with Trey," Mara said, swaying the babe in her arms. "But the good Lord saw fit to give me three more sons, and I love them all the same."

"Who will go get your son Duncan?" Mercy asked.

Mara walked over to her and eased the babe into his mum's arms. "I will though I'll leave it to you to tell him the wonderful news."

"Bring his brothers and da as well," Mercy said. "I want everyone to share in the good news."

Mara nodded and left the room. When she entered the hall, the men jumped up. "All of you come with me," she ordered.

Duncan hurried alongside her. "Is Mercy all right? Do I have a son or daughter?"

Mara nodded.

"Which is it?" Reeve asked, annoyed. "A son to grow into a warrior like his da or a daughter Duncan will forever worry over?"

Mara nodded some more and stepped aside after leading them into the room.

Reeve went to his wife, Carmag to Mara, and Bryce joined Charlotte, whose joyous smile brought a smile to his face.

Duncan went to the bed, where his wife sat, a babe in each arm. "There are two?"

Mercy's smile grew ever wider. "One of each. A son and a daughter."

Duncan collapsed to sit on the bed. "Two? You birthed two babes?"

"And quite easily," she said proudly.

Duncan finally emerged from his fog and turned a huge grin on his family. "I have a son and a daughter." Then he got up, gave Mercy a kiss, and cuddled beside her so that he could take one of the babes in his arm.

Congratulations rang out, and everyone filed by to get a look at the new babes before drifting off and giving the parents privacy.

Charlotte was disappointed that her da's plight wasn't discussed any more that night. Not that she begrudged anyone the thrill of the twins being born; she simply worried that her da would suffer unspeakable torments before she could reach him.

It wasn't until she was alone with Bryce in his bed-chamber that the discussion picked up again.

"Tomorrow, we'll talk and begin to plan how to rescue your da and the spy," Bryce said.

"You believe he is being held in the same prison?" Charlotte asked.

Bryce shook his head as he removed his plaid. "In all the excitement, I forgot to tell you that we learned that the spy was taken to the secret prison."

"From who? When? Can I speak with this person?" Charlotte asked, popping up in bed, ready to jump out.

Bryce gave her a nudge back. "Tomorrow is time enough."

"There is no time to waste," she urged, and tried once again to get out of bed.

Bryce lowered himself over her, pinning her to the stuffed mattress with his naked body. "There is nothing that can be done tonight. Tomorrow is soon enough."

She intended to argue until she felt him hard against her. And while she shouldn't be thinking of making love with him when her da needed her help, she knew that Bryce was right. There was no more she could do tonight.

"Seeing the babes tonight makes me think—"

"Let's have a slew of them," she interrupted, wrapping her arms around him.

He grinned and brushed his lips teasingly across hers. "We have matters to attend to first, and, besides, will you be able to remain confined while waiting for the birth?"

"Why must I?" she asked.

"I thought you would say that," Bryce said, shaking his head.

Her grin faded. "You talk of a future with me. Is that what you want?"

"It is what I've always wanted but wasn't sure if I could give you a future."

"But nothing has changed. We still have our missions. We still don't know what the future may hold."

"I've finally realized," Bryce said, "it will always be that way. Each day begins anew. We know not what it will bring, but we do know that we have each other, that is what truly matters. So there is no reason to wait for our missions to end, for another mission will take its place. We take a chance each and every day, but not with our love, for that is something that will forever remain the same, strong and vibrant and growing more potent every day. I know not what the future holds for us; I only know that I want to spend it with you."

She kissed him quick. "And I feel the same. I want to wake every morning to you by my side. I want to see your smiling face throughout the day, hear you bark orders I rarely obey, make love whenever our passion strikes, have lots of babes, and fall asleep in your arms every night."

"We should start working on those babes right now," Bryce said, and whipped the blanket out from between them.

"What do you mean a week?" Charlotte asked angrily. "We can't wait a week to rescue my da. He could be suffering horrible torture right this very moment, and what do you do? You talk about getting men together and mounting an attack that will surely kill him if the torture doesn't."

"There aren't many choices," Reeve said.

Charlotte slammed her hands on the table in the great hall. "We go now with a few men, to lure out what guards we can, and sneak into the prison to dispose of the others one by one."

John shook his head. "They are too well guarded. An alert would be sounded and the prisoners put in danger."

Bryce was worried. Charlotte had grown more agitated over the last two days as they attempted to formulate a rescue plan. She was impatient and understandably so, but this had to be thought out and a sound plan implemented, or it could prove disastrous.

He allowed her to participate in the planning but in no way would he allow her to take part in the rescue. From what John had told them about the prison and the guards who took such joy in the torture, he had no intention of allowing her anywhere near the place.

He knew she'd be angry, but she would see the wisdom of his decision. At least he hoped she would.

"There's one thing no one has mentioned," Reeve said. "How do we know for sure her da is there? Perhaps he has yet to arrive."

"From all we have learned, that was where my da was being taken, and by now, he should be there," she insisted.

"But we can't be certain," Reeve argued.

"I'm certain," Charlotte snapped, and no more was said on it.

The talking and planning continued until finally Charlotte threw her hands up in frustration and marched out of the keep, Odin on her heels.

"She's better off not being part of this," John said.

"I know," Bryce said, his eyes on the door closing behind her, "but she feels she owes it to her da."

"Give her time, she'll see reason," Duncan said.

Reeve shook his head. "She's a warrior at heart, and you can't keep a warrior from battle.

Bryce woke up drenched with sweat, his nightmare still vivid in his mind. He immediately turned to reach for Charlotte, she having slipped from his grasp in his dream and he not able to find her. His hand touched an empty space beside him. He bolted up in bed and cast an anxious glance around the room. *Nothing.* He was the only one there. He rushed out of bed and into his clothes and went in search of her, his fear building with each step he took.

He told himself that Odin might have needed to be let out, but he could not find the dog anywhere. He was somewhat relieved since it meant she wasn't alone. But any relief was short-lived since they both managed to get into trouble together.

Not having checked to see if her bow was gone, he returned to his bedchamber, almost colliding with Duncan as he did.

"What are you doing up?" Bryce snapped.

Duncan raised a brow. "Someone's angry. Fight with Charlotte?"

"No!" Bryce said much too sharply, and shook his head. "I can't find her. I woke up, and she was gone. I'm going back to my room to see if her bow is missing."

"You think she took off to rescue her da on her own?" Duncan asked with concern.

"That's exactly what I think she did," Bryce said, confirming his fear aloud.

"I'll wake Reeve and da," Duncan offered.

"No, nothing can be done until morning, and I may still find her."

"But you truly don't believe that, do you?" Duncan said.

Bryce shook his head and walked away. He grew even more concerned when he found that her bow and cache were gone. He wanted to storm after her, but instead he sunk down on the bed. He'd not get far in the dark, and neither would Charlotte though she did have a head start.

There was a rap on the door, and it swung open.

Duncan walked in. "We should get the others and be ready when dawn breaks."

Bryce nodded and reached for his sword.

Chapter 35

Charlotte watched, stretched out on her belly, from a rise in the distance. It hadn't taken her long to find the place John had mapped for them, two days' travel at the most. And after only a few hours of steady watching, she learned the guards' pattern. Only one guard remained outside at all times, and there were three who alternated the shifts. She assumed more were inside.

She wished Bryce was with her. She believed together they could successfully free her da and the spy as well. They worked as a pair, knowing what the other would do without a word's being exchanged. It bothered her that he hadn't intended to include her in the rescue. He knew how she felt about it, and she knew that his worry over her safety was what brought him to the decision.

He should have known better . . . known her better. He could not lock her away because he feared she would come to harm. He had to allow her to be who she was, the tenacious lassie he had fallen in love with.

Odin gave a low whine, and his tail wagged against the ground where he lay stretched out beside her.

She smiled, knowing who approached, and perhaps she had delayed her plans, knowing Bryce would be on her trail soon enough.

She turned. "It took you long enough."

He walked straight at her, reached down, yanked her up by her tunic, and marched a distance away from the prison, Odin happily trailing.

"I should throttle you," he said once he placed her feet on the ground.

"Why be angry with me when it's your own fault?" she asked, taking a defiant stance though unable to keep a smile from her face, so very pleased was she to see him.

"And why is that?"

"You have to ask?" she said.

"We made a vow to do this together."

That he remembered made her smile grow though it faded some when she asked, "Then why, when you pledged your word, would you have left me behind?"

"*Love.*"

He didn't shout it, but the force with which he spoke nearly had her stumbling backward.

"I expected peace, joy, contentment, not this wild insanity that plagues me at every turn. You invade my mind much too often, I ache to kiss you whenever I see you, even when you're not in sight. And I cannot stop thinking about making love to you. And sleep?" He shook his head and laughed. "I need to be wrapped around you to sleep soundly."

He threw his hands up in the air. "And I don't remember any of this happening. It was as if it was always like this, that there was always you and me." He shook his head again. "Stop smiling. I shouldn't be spouting love when we have your da to rescue."

"I have waited patiently to hear this from you."

"Patiently? Hah!" Bryce laughed. "You are by no means patient."

"When it comes to you I am," she said. "I knew you loved me, it was only a matter of time before you realized it yourself and finally embraced the inevitable."

"Then why drive me mad with worry and take off on your own? Did you truly believe you could succeed in rescuing your da alone?"

"I knew you would follow," she said, "and I feared the longer we lingered, the more my da would suffer." She raised her hand, stopping any response. "Don't tell me you didn't think the same. My da wasn't brought to this prison to conjure. He was brought here to *make certain* he would conjure for the king. And once they learned he could not perform as they wished, he would suffer horribly."

"You forget one thing," Bryce said. "You don't know for certain he is here."

She pulled a stick from her belt. "I knew my da would find a way to let me know that he was here."

Bryce reached for the stick, looking over the crude markings. "What does this mean?"

"It means he's here."

"Then we wait," Bryce said. "Reeve and Duncan shouldn't be far behind.

"No troop of warriors?"

Bryce shook his head. "Not appropriate for such a mission."

"Why didn't Reeve and Duncan come with you?"

"Plans needed implementing so that all will be ready."

"When will they be here?" Charlotte asked.

"Tomorrow sometime, and we will proceed the following day," Bryce said.

Charlotte shook her head. "Two days. To my da and your spy, that is two more days in hell."

"We can't do this on our own," Bryce argued.

"We've taken on other difficult challenges and succeeded," she reminded him.

"Not this difficult. The way in is the way out, which makes for an impossible escape and for almost certain capture."

"If John got out, then so can my da."

"John got out by sheer luck."

"Then sheer luck will get my da out," she said emphatically.

He grabbed hold of her as if he could hang on to her forever. "No, it won't be luck that gets your da out. It will be your sheer tenacity. Now show me what we're up against."

Charlotte took Bryce to the rise, and they kept a watch on the entrance to the prison. Charlotte explained to him the routine of the three guards who alternated shifts. She expressed concern over not knowing how many guards were inside, worried that it could prove troublesome.

As dusk fell they both pulled back and put a good distance between themselves and the prison, not wanting the guards to take notice of them.

Odin was sound asleep, while Bryce lay wrapped around Charlotte, talking.

"This is not the end," Bryce whispered in her ear, "but the beginning of more to come."

Charlotte rested her hand over his where it lay across her stomach. "I know. You will join the many battles to see that the true king sits the throne."

"I will do what I must."

She turned around in his arms and rested a gentle hand to his cheek. "As do I for my da and as I will do for you . . . always."

Bryce was about to protest, but she stilled him with a kiss.

She rested her brow to his, and whispered, "We know not what tomorrow brings, but we have this night, you and I, and it is memories we should be making."

Neither would say what they both thought. Tonight could be the last night they ever made love. They both would face death in their attempt to rescue her da and one or the other might only survive. This was a night for them to remember always.

The night sky, brilliant with twinkling stars, served as their canopy, the campfire gave them warmth, not that they needed it, as passion already heated their bodies, and the night creatures provided a lovely tune.

Bryce immediately took control, and Charlotte surrendered. She understood he needed it this way, needed to show her that he was a true warrior who could protect and love her no matter the circumstances.

As much as she would have preferred to be stripped of her garments, she knew that was not a wise thing to do. And so they made love, possibly for the last time, as they had the first time, though without the rain pummeling Bryce's back.

Their never-ending kiss added to the fiery passion that burned deep within them, and touches were not hesitant or demanding. They simply addressed the aching need in them both.

Somewhere during it all, it turned more potent, as if they both realized this could be it; this could be the end, the last time they were together. They both demanded from each other, and they both gave willingly. And when Bryce slipped into her, she welcomed him like never before and urged him deeper than ever before.

Even after she climaxed, he didn't stop, and so she was rocked by another climax more powerful than the first. And as the sparks exploded within her, he drove into her with a force that brought her to life once again, and this time they both exploded together, making a memory they would never forget.

They lay breathless in each other's arms afterwards. No words were exchanged, no words were necessary. They knew at that moment their love had been sealed for eternity, and no matter what tomorrow brought, no one could take it from them.

Charlotte woke resolved. This was the day she would rescue her da. She felt in her bones, knew she couldn't wait any longer. If she did, she feared she would find her da dead.

She told that to Bryce when he stretched awake. "It is imperative I rescue my da today. He has no more time."

"We must wait for my brothers," he said, trying to reason with her. "Extra hands will serve us well."

"I fear I have waited too long already," she said. "I

must go now, or I will never forgive myself if I wait and discover that I had delayed too long."

Bryce sat up and reached out to take hold of her arm. "A few hours, no more."

Charlotte was about to argue when Odin turned and took a guarded stance.

Charlotte and Bryce grabbed their weapons and positioned themselves back to back, an instinctive reaction that had served them well on many occasions.

Odin relaxed his stance, and his tail started wagging just as Reeve and Duncan came into view.

Charlotte was never happier to see them. It meant that they could put their plan into action and finally rescue her da. She hurried over to them and gave them each a tight hug.

"I am so glad you are here," she said, taking Bryce's hand as he joined them.

"Everything set?" Bryce asked.

"The warriors are ready," Duncan said with a nod.

"Do you need time to rest?" Bryce asked.

Reeve and Duncan shook their heads.

"Let's get this done," Reeve said.

Bryce nodded and explained the plan to them. One of them would dispose of the guard while another snuck inside to locate and free the prisoners. The problem was that from what John had told them, the entrance was narrow, tight for any large man. It would be difficult for one of sizeable width and height to blend with the shadows and attract no attention.

"That's why it must be me who goes in," Charlotte said.

"No!" Bryce said.

Reeve nodded. "She's right, Bryce. She's a good size and no doubt could move around with more ease than any of us."

"And would you let Tara go if it were her?" Bryce asked.

"No," Reeve answered honestly, "though I doubt she'd be stopped if it meant the life of one she loved."

Charlotte pressed her hand to Bryce's chest. "We always knew this day would come though never spoke of it. I need to do this for my da, and you need to let me."

Bryce grabbed hold of her and almost hugged the breath from her, then held her at arm's length. "You take no chances. You draw the guards out and let us do the rest."

Charlotte nodded.

"I mean it, Charlotte, draw them out and leave it to us."

"First my da, then the guards," she said, not wanting to lie to him.

"It will take too long and be too dangerous," Bryce protested.

"Not if I take Odin. He knows my da's scent and will lead me to him."

Bryce was ready to argue when Reeve clamped a heavy hand on his shoulder. "Let her do what she must. She has proven her worth many times over."

"I can do this, Bryce," she said. "I must do this."

He hugged her even more fiercely. "You better come back to me."

She laughed. "Hell itself can't stop me from returning to you."

Duncan laughed. "Hell won't want such a stubborn lassie. It will just spit her out."

"I'll be waiting right outside to catch you," Bryce said.

They all waited impatiently for the guards to change, allowing them more time to carry out their plan before the next shift change. Once the new guard was disposed of, Charlotte snuck inside, with Odin in the lead. She knew the narrow hall might not allow for use of her bow, but she had taken it anyway, feeling safer with it in hand. Her dirk was tucked in her boot, and Bryce had insisted she take an extra one; she hadn't argued when he tucked it in her other boot.

She almost gagged from the stench that hit her like a blow to the face, and she worried that Odin might not be able to sniff his way through it, but he had no problem. She had ordered him, before entering, to go slow and remain quiet. He did so as he made his way slowly down the narrow passage, lit occasionally by a lone torch.

She listened for the sound of approaching footfalls and kept a keen watch for any moving shadows.

Charlotte jumped when a heart-wrenching scream pierced the tunnel, and even Odin stepped back and pressed his big, shivering backside against her legs. She reassured the animal with a comforting pat that all was well and slipped an arrow from her cache to hold with her bow.

She was relieved when Odin turned down the third passage to the right from the entrance and stopped in front of the second cell.

Charlotte almost retched from the odor that assaulted her. She put her hand in front of her nose and sniffed her skin. She could smell Bryce on her and a hint of their lovemaking had lingered along with it. It gave her a shot of courage and propelled her to hurry and be done with this, to return to him so they could love and so that he could finally meet her da.

"Da?" she called out quietly.

Nothing, and she was about to try again when she heard, "Charlotte?"

"Da," she said through the small square hole in the door.

"Good God, Charlotte, you made it. You've come for me," her da said tearfully. "But you must hurry."

"I'll work on the lock," she whispered, and slipped her dirk from her boot. She bent down and, remembering everything her da had ever told her about the workings of a lock, set to work. It was a simple matter of hitting the right part, and it would open.

"You haven't much time. A guard will be coming soon for me," her da said. "I have kept track of his comings and goings."

She knew then what she had to do. She ordered Odin in the shadows and before she melded with them, she whispered to her da, "Do you know of a recent prisoner brought here, a supposed spy in the king's court."

"Next cell to my right."

Footfalls and the jingle of keys could be heard, and Charlotte stepped into the shadows to wait, her bow ready.

Chapter 36

Bryce paced impatiently in front of the prison. "She should be out by now."

"Let it be," Duncan warned. "She knows what to do."

Reeve hurried toward them. "I spotted a troop of soldiers headed this way."

"How long before they reach here, and do they have more prisoners?" Bryce asked.

"Twenty minutes at the most and no prisoners," Reeve said.

Bryce looked from one brother to the other. "If she's not out here shortly, I go in."

Just then, Odin burst out of the entrance with one cloaked figure and a short, wiry man following him, with Charlotte the last one out.

Not a word was spoken. They followed the plan, which meant they followed Reeve at this point. When Bryce and Duncan saw that no guards pursued them, they hurried off to trail the escaping group, though not before Bryce quickly informed Charlotte that soldiers approached the prison.

Horses awaited them when they reached the spot

where Charlotte and Bryce had camped for the night. When they all mounted, they took off as if the devil himself were after them. Bryce had no doubt the soldiers would find their trail. He only hoped that they could reach the area where MacAlpin warriors waited before the soldiers caught up with them.

It was a harrowing ride, with Duncan taking the lead not long after they started and Reeve cutting back to see if the soldiers had yet to discover that the prison had been penetrated. It wasn't good news he returned with almost an hour later.

He rode up alongside Bryce, who had only recently slowed their pace. "One of the surviving guards happened along the soldiers and told them of the escape, that three guards were dead, and the prisoners gone."

Bryce shook his head. "How did the other prisoners escape?"

Reeve grinned. "I don't know, but I sure would like to hear what Charlotte did."

"We need to send warriors to see if they can find those prisoners," Bryce said. "They no doubt will need help, or they will be captured again."

Reeve nodded. "I'll go ahead and arrange it and meet you where we planned. But you better pick up your pace and keep it quick. The soldiers don't lag; they're not far behind."

Bryce rode to the front after Reeve had turned and left. He sent Duncan to the back after informing him of what Reeve had told him. And they once again rode like the devil was on their tail.

They forged ahead, taking no time to rest, and

trusted that Reeve and the warriors would be ready when they got there.

Hours passed, and riders and horses tired, but still they kept going, and, just a short distance before they reached Reeve, the soldiers were spotted not far behind them.

Duncan called out to Bryce, alerting him.

Bryce waved for the others to pass him and pointed to the rise up ahead. Then he fell back to join Duncan and take a stance against the soldiers if necessary. He was furious when he saw Charlotte do the same. But he could do nothing about it now, and she was good with a bow. And he should have realized she would not leave him behind. She would never leave him behind just as he wouldn't leave her.

The soldiers were gaining ground, and Bryce cursed aloud when Charlotte stopped her mare, turned, and took aim with her bow. She hit one in the shoulder, knocking him off his horse; the second arrow took another man down. She wasted no time with another arrow. She turned and caught up with Bryce, who was riding toward her.

Bryce shook his head as he turned his horse to join hers and sped to Duncan a few feet ahead. Just as the trio caught up with the two escaped prisoners at the bottom of the rise, MacAlpin warriors crested at the top.

With battle cries and the waving of swords, they descended the rise and headed straight for the soldiers. The soldiers, seeing that they were outnumbered, turned and rode off, the MacAlpin warriors riding after them.

Not wanting to take any chances, Bryce kept his group riding though not at the previous speed. He wanted to at least be near MacAlpin land by nightfall. Then it wouldn't take them long the next day to reach home.

Again, no one spoke, everyone much too anxious to put as much distance between them and the soldiers, not to mention the prison, to slow down. It was a couple of hours before nightfall when Bryce finally brought them to a stop, and it was with grateful sighs that they all dismounted.

Charlotte didn't waste a minute; she ran to her da. He opened his arms wide to welcome his daughter.

Bryce watched with a smile as father and daughter were finally reunited. She did resemble her da in height and form and had some similar features. He saw the pride on Idris's face and the joy in the way he hugged her tightly again and again.

"I knew you'd come for me, Charlotte," he said through tears. "I knew you'd free me. I knew you would have the courage and tenacity."

"I got them from you," she said, tears spilling down her cheeks.

They hugged again, then Charlotte reached her hand out to Bryce.

"I want you to meet my da," she said, tugging him closer, then turned to her da. "And da, I want you to meet the man I love with all my heart."

Idris smiled, and tears filled his eyes once more. He looked up at the tall warrior and nodded. "A good choice, daughter. A good choice indeed." And offered his hand to Bryce.

Duncan interrupted any response when he called out, "Bryce you better come over here."

Charlotte and her da followed him, Duncan having sounded upset.

"What—" Bryce stopped dead and stared at the woman who was no longer hidden by the dark cloak.

"Holy shit," Reeve said, walking past Bryce.

Charlotte looked from one brother's shocked face to the others', and finally asked, "You know the spy?"

They all nodded, though only Bryce spoke. "This is Leora, the woman our brother Trey loves and had intended to wed, but whom we all thought dead."

Charlotte waited along with the brothers for Leora to speak. But she looked with wide, frightened eyes from one to another and dropped to the ground in a dead faint.

Bryce saw to it that Leora was made comfortable on a bed of pine boughs and allowed her to rest. They could get no answers from her since she cried every time they tried. Charlotte had been the one to suggest that they allow her to rest. After all, she had been through an awful ordeal.

He and his brothers agreed that there was no point in looking for answers from her until they returned home, where others would be present to hear her story.

The three also wondered and worried how Trey would take the news that the woman he loved was still alive and was thought to have spied against King Kenneth. No doubt he would have many questions, as they all did, but for now they would ask nothing of her. They simply wanted to get her home.

And Leora wanted the same. When she had woken

from her faint, she had asked for Trey and begged them to take her home to him and cried if any questions were asked of her. She ate little of the food offered her and fell asleep just as night claimed the land.

Reeve took first watch, not that they thought any of the soldiers had made it past their warriors, but were more concerned that other soldiers might be lurking about.

"Do you think Trey will be home when we arrive?" Bryce asked, joining Reeve for a moment.

"We were expecting him home around this time, so he could very well be there."

"I wonder how he will feel about Leora's returning."

"I don't know, but she certainly has a lot of explaining to do." Reeve shook his head. "And if she were my woman, I don't know if I would trust anything she said. I mean, why let the man who loves you think you're dead?"

"She's going to have to be watched carefully," Bryce said.

"You don't trust her either."

"I can't help but wonder what she was doing in the king's court. Why she led us all to believe she was dead? And why spy on the king? If she even is a spy." Bryce shook his head too. "None of it makes any sense."

"Let's hope sense can be made of it," Reeve said. "And that Trey seeks answers before he gives his heart to her again."

"That's what I'm worried about," Bryce said. "He's already given her his heart, and, broken or not, I fear it still belongs to her."

Bryce bid Reeve good-night and told him to wake

him in a few hours and he'd take the next shift. He hoped to talk some with Idris, become acquainted with him.

Idris wished the same, but exhaustion had already claimed his weary body. He was sound asleep. Bryce would have to wait until they got home to talk with the man.

He made his way to where Charlotte lay beneath a blanket by the fire and joined her. It was soon obvious that sleep eluded them. Not wanting to disturb anyone, they went to Reeve, and Bryce offered to take first watch.

Reeve didn't argue, though he turned to Charlotte before taking his leave, and asked, "How did the other prisoners get free? You didn't have time to free them all."

"But they had time to free themselves," Charlotte said. "One key fit all the locks, so after I freed my da and Leora, I freed the man in the next cell. I told him to free the others and make sure the cell doors were closed so no one would suspect them gone. I also explained that one guard or more would follow us out and once they did, they should make their escape. I left a dirk with the strongest one in case it was needed."

"I told you," Reeve said with a laugh as he walked away. "She's a true warrior woman."

"That she is," Bryce said, slipping his arm around her.

They sat braced against a large rock, holding hands. Silence lingered for a while between them until Bryce finally broke it.

"There is something I need to tell you," he said.

"I'm listening." She snuggled against his side.

He was reluctant to discuss the matter with her but knew it was the only fair thing to do. She had a right to know. He wanted her to know in case it made a difference.

"You hesitate to share a secret with me?" she asked, once again having the uncanny ability to know what he thought.

"It is a heavy secret that could place a burden on you."

"I advised someone recently that a burden can be less burdensome when shared," she said. "And you offered to lighten my burden once, so let me help lighten yours."

"You stubbornly refused my help," he reminded.

"But I grew wiser, and, in the end, I accepted."

He leaned down and brushed a light kiss across her lips. "And glad I am that you did."

"Besides, there should be no secrets between us . . . ever."

Bryce shook his head. "There is a secret and one that I must keep from you."

"Does it have to do with the true king?"

Bryce grew alarmed. "What do you know?"

"Only what I've surmised, which was rather easy," she admitted with a smile.

"Tell me what you have surmised."

"Part of the myth says 'four men ride together and then divide' and I'm assuming that you and your brothers are those four men. And in a sense you are dividing as one by one you fall in love and pledge yourselves to others."

"I never thought of it like that."

"The four of you thought that it meant you would literally separate?" she asked.

"That is what it says."

"Myth language is veiled. You must get past the veils to see the truths."

"There is nothing veiled about the part that says 'among them the true king hides.' "

She shook her head. "He cannot hide amongst those who know him, so what it means is that he waits among those who protect him."

"Since you are aware of this, then you must know my secret."

She nodded. "I determined it not long ago though I waited to see if you would tell me yourself."

"Then hear it from my lips," Bryce said. "One of the four MacAlpin brothers is the true king of Scotland."

"I will guard your secret well and will help you with all your missions to see that the true king claims the throne."

Bryce yanked her up and into his lap and gave her a quick kiss. "Missions or not, king or not, without you, nothing matters to me. I love you, Charlotte, more than I ever thought possible. And we will wed soon."

"You have not asked me if I wish to wed you," she said with a teasing smile.

He laughed quietly. "There is no need. I know you wish to wed me. I see it in your eyes as you see my love for you so strong in my eyes."

"Truly? You see how much I wish to be your wife in my eyes?"

"That among other things," he teased.

She pressed her lips near his ear. "My desire for you lingers just as potently in my eyes."

He turned and took her face in his hands, kissing her with a hungry need before tearing his mouth away. "You need to leave me now and go to sleep."

She sighed. "I distract you from your watch."

"Much too much."

"I cannot wait until we're home."

"Believe me, neither can I," he said, and lifted her off him.

She didn't move. "If I promise to be good and simply sit beside you, can I stay?"

"I'll have your word on that."

She laughed. "You don't trust me?"

"I don't trust me, so I'm holding you responsible for our safety this night."

"You have my word," she said, and sat beside him though their bodies didn't touch.

After a few moments of silence, Charlotte said, "Whether king or warrior, I love you with all my heart and will stand beside you always."

Bryce wrapped his arm around her, pulled her close, kissed her, and whispered in her ear, "Let's wake Reeve to take the watch, then find a secluded spot in the woods."

Lovers eager to be off on a tryst, they went and woke Reeve.

Read on for an excerpt from
the fourth and final book in
The Warrior King Series,
WED TO A HIGHLAND WARRIOR,
coming Winter 2012
from Donna Fletcher
and Avon Books

Highlands of Scotland, 1005

Bliss waited, not sure of her fate.

She often wondered why she could see the providence of others, yet, when it came to her destiny, she was blind. At times it made sense to her. After all, it was a burdensome lot to unwillingly peer into the future and see not just happiness, but pain and sorrow. Certainly, if she saw that for herself, life could possibly become unbearable. Even knowing the destiny of others brought a burden—one that, at times, Bliss would much rather not carry though she had no choice.

This gift, as her people, the Picts, called it, or curse as others often referred to it in whispers, had been part of her as long as she could remember. There had never been a time she had been without her knowing, and while she could see small, incidental moments in her future, she could not see the whole of it, the important moments in life that had others seeking her knowledge.

If her knowing wasn't enough, there was also her ability to help heal. Her touch held power; not that she understood it, but she did not question it. Like her knowing, it had always been a part of her, and she had always willingly shared it with those in need.

At the moment, though, her instincts warned her that this was where she must stop and wait. Why, she did not know. She truly had no time to dally. There was an ill woman in need of healing, and she was still a day's journey away. But to ignore fate's warning could prove unwise.

Bliss hugged her dark blue wool cloak more closely around her. Winter's bite was sharp in the air, leaving no doubt it would be a bitter one. She wished, however, this year she need not spend the cold days and dark shivering nights alone. Being one-and-twenty years, she had thought for certain, though she had never foreseen it, that she would have a husband and children by now. She didn't, and she worried that she never would.

Respected for her abilities by her people, she also found it a deterrent to finding a mate. Most men feared her knowing, one fellow being adamant about it, saying, "There would be nothing I could keep from you—nothing."

Bliss realized then that she wanted no husband who would hide things from her. She wanted honesty and trust from the man who would be her husband, or she would remain alone.

The crunch of leaves alerted her to heavy footfalls, and it was easy to tell that more than one person approached. In an instant, she knew that soldiers headed her way. Normally, she would detect their presence much sooner, giving her time to flee to safety.

Why had she been cautioned to wait for those who

could very well do her harm? Could they possibly be in need of healing? Or had she been mistaken? She dismissed the foolish thought as soon as it entered her head, reminding herself that fate knew well life's course, and she need not fear.

Three king's soldiers broke past the trees and into the clearing where she stood. Apprehension fluttered her stomach, but she remained confident that all would be well.

"We've found ourselves an angel," one young soldier said with a grin.

"She is a beauty," remarked another with a sneer that warned that his thoughts bordered on carnal.

All too often, men remarked on her beauty so much so that the words no longer meant anything to her and certainly not from this lot. Someday, she hoped to find a man who would look past her features and see her true worth. But at the moment she needed to wait, for she sensed that these soldiers were not why fate had her linger.

A sudden ill wind blew around them, scooping up leaves and twigs and swirling them in the air before carrying them off on a rush of wind. A fast-moving mist followed, sweeping in along the ground. It would not be easy to take a step or find one's way if it grew any thicker.

Gray clouds rushed in overhead, warning of an impending storm, or was it a portent of someone's arrival?

Bliss shivered, sensing someone's approach, someone of great power and strength, someone who would stand before these soldiers with courage and someone she was destined to meet.

"What is a beautiful lassie doing out in the woods all alone?" the youngest soldier asked, inching closer.

"I wait." Bliss let her cloak casually fall away from her arms to reveal the drawings on her wrists.

Another soldier gasped. "She's a Pict."

"We don't mix with pagans," said the older soldier, who had remained a distance from the other two.

"Why?" the young soldier asked boldly.

The older soldier slowly shook his head. "They are strange ones."

Bliss sensed that the younger soldier would not pay heed to the wisdom of the older one. He was brash in his bravado and intent on proving his courage. Warnings from the older soldier, to him, were nothing more than fear and old superstitious nonsense.

"Because they paint symbols on themselves?" the young soldier asked with a shake of his head and a laugh. "There will be no more Picts soon enough."

Bliss's fair cheeks flared red, and her pale blue eyes darkened ever so slightly. "Mark your words wisely, young lad, for Picts have walked these lands far longer than you know and will continue to claim these lands long after you're gone."

"Is that a threat?" the young soldier demanded, his chest expanding as he drew his shoulders back and approached her with swift steps.

He didn't in the least intimidate Bliss. She stood firm, her head up, her pride and courage evident. "It is the truth."

"And I say with as much truth that the likes of you and your kind will be no more," the soldier challenged, his comrades encouraging him with cheers.

"You can say or claim all you wish, but the truth is written and cannot be erased," she said confidently.

"She's a seer," the older soldier said with a shiver. "Stay clear of her, or she will steal your soul."

The young soldier scurried away then, tripping over his feet as he went, his pretentious bravado failing him.

"What do we do with her?" the other soldier asked, taking several cautious steps away.

"She might prove helpful to King Kenneth," the young one suggested.

"Fool," the older one spat. "The king has his own seer, and he keeps his distance from the Picts; being pagans, they cannot be trusted."

Bliss felt a sudden catch in her stomach though she moved not a muscle. It intensified as the unknown man continued his approach. From how palpable his strength, he was no doubt a warrior. They were an easy lot to sense, their potency far-reaching. Though there was a force about this particular one that caused her to shudder. Passion tickled at her flesh, and a heady scent soon followed, wrapping around her like a lover's strong embrace.

This was the man she was meant to meet, and why fate had her wait. A tingle of anticipation ran through her and, without warning, as was the way of it, a sense of knowing struck her like a mighty blow. Only this time it was about her.

She could foolishly doubt it, but it would do no good. The sense of what was about to transpire was much too strong, too rooted in her knowing. Still, it was difficult to believe, and yet she knew without a doubt that fate had her wait here—she took a deep breath, not sure if she was ready—to meet her future husband.

"What do we do with her then?" the young one asked anxiously.

Her answer spilled from her lips, shocking her. "My husband has come to get me."

He walked out of the mist then, as if summoned, emerging slowly, the fog dissipating around him with each confident step he took. He was a formidable figure: tall, his shoulders broad, his body lean, his eyes intense, his long auburn hair blown wild by the irate wind and his long, slim fingers resting heavily on the hilt of his sword. A Highland plaid, the colors a near match to his dark hair, draped proudly around him, and a black wool, fur-lined cloak hugged his wide shoulders.

The three soldiers shuddered, and a shiver ran through her.

Trey MacAlpin.

Bliss knew this man, had helped heal him and kept the secret that he and his three brothers shared—one of them was the true king of Scotland and would soon take the throne.

"Husband of mine, finally you arrive," she said, walking over to him though her legs trembled. She stretched her hand out, knowing he would not refuse her.

His hand reached out, taking hold of hers tightly and drawing her intimately up against him as only a husband would. The vision came swiftly and left with the same haste. There was no time to consider it. She had to pay heed to the present, and so she tucked it away to examine later.

The young soldier wanted more confirmation, and asked, "This Pict is your woman, your wife?"

Trey didn't hesitate. "Bliss is my wife."

Bliss spoke the words that would seal their fate. "Trey is my husband."

"You are on MacAlpin land," Trey warned.

"King Kenneth owns all land," the young soldier challenged. "And all on the land serve him."

"I serve the true king," Trey boldly announced.

The young soldier stepped forward, his bravado regained and his hand going to the hilt of his sword. "There is only one true king, and perhaps it is time you served him."

"Take another step, lad, and it will be your Maker you'll meet and be serving," Trey warned with a cold, hard stare that froze the fellow in his steps. "Go back to your king and tell him that the time draws near, and soon he will be king no more."

Anger had the young soldier taking a hasty step forward as he shouted, "There is only one of you and three of us."

"Unfair odds for sure, but I have no time to wait for you to fetch more soldiers," Trey said without a trace of a smile.

Bliss marveled at his confidence and courage. But then his bravery wasn't foreign to her; she had felt the heart of it pulsing through her when she had helped heal him. She knew then the strength of this man and what he was capable of; but there had also been a moment when a shiver of fear had run through her. He was also a man heavily burdened, and it had troubled her heart to feel his sadness.

Now it troubled her that she had not sensed the connection between them sooner, but then Bliss had learned at an early age that fate often worked in mysterious ways, and it wasn't for her to question.

The young soldier looked quickly to the other two soldiers, his hand already beginning to draw his sword from its sheath.

"MacAlpin warriors are superior swordsmen," warned the older soldier.

"I heard tell that one took ten soldiers down on his own, without an ounce of help," the other said.

"That would be my brother Reeve," Trey said proudly.

"And another brother survived wounds that would have killed most men," the older soldier said. "Some say he cannot die."

Trey nodded. "That would be me."

The two soldiers took a step back, and the young one spat at them. "Cowards you are. Death claims everyone, and it will claim him today."

Bliss raised her voice before the soldier took a step. "Death will claim someone this day, but it will not be my husband."

Her prediction caused all color to drain from the young soldier's face, and his sword slipped down into its sheath as his hand drifted off the hilt.

"Now be gone, and take my message to your king," Trey commanded.

They obeyed, disappearing into the woods without a backward glance.

Bliss smiled when he turned his attention on her. "It is good to see you have healed well."

"With your help, *wife,*" he said, smiling.

Her heart gave a catch, as if his smile had stolen a beat. Certainly, Fate had had a hand in his defined features, making him the handsomest of men. But it was his eyes she found the most compelling, for she could not be sure if they were blue or green. They seemed to change from one color to the other right before her eyes.

She shook her head. With more important matters at hand, she had no time to be musing over her husband's good looks.

Husband.

How did she explain this to him?

First, she had to take a step away from him. His arm around her waist felt too intimate. It made her want to step closer to him, rest her body to his, run her hand across his chest, feel his heart beating as rapidly as hers, and wonder if love could truly come from their strange joining.

Bliss slowly slipped out of his embrace, and she thought she detected his reluctance to let her go. "I should explain—"

"Not necessary. You followed your instincts, and it worked well."

"Yes, though—"

"I am honored to be your husband, if only for a short time."

"And I am honored to be your wife."

"We still pretend then?" Trey asked, stepping closer.

Her thoughts turned foggy. She had spent time healing him and had not felt a tug, a pull, a tingle of interest in him. But then she had no visions of him as her future husband. She couldn't help but wonder why now it was different? Why had fate chosen this moment and this way to bring them together?

She sighed and rested her hand on his arm.

He placed his hand over hers, his warmth not only running through her but his strength. He was a man of great courage and conviction and a man who loved deeply—and a man who was still recovering from the loss of a love.

Whatever was Fate thinking, sending her a man who still loved another woman?

"You are upset," Trey said. "You tremble."

She stared at him a moment, for she did tremble, but inwardly, and he had felt it. "I must explain."

"No need. I understand how difficult this incident must have been for you. I will see you safely home."

She shook her head.

"I insist."

Bliss continued shaking her head, though not because he insisted on escorting her home. "I must tell you something."

"I'll listen as we walk."

He reached for her hand and closed his fingers firmly around hers. Bliss could not help but think how his innocent gesture sealed what Fate had decreed.

She tugged at his hand when he went to walk, forcing him to stay put. With a more adamant tone, she said, "We are husband and wife."

He nodded, appearing not at all upset by her resolute words, and clearly not understanding what she was trying to convey to him.

"Aye, we should continue to appear so in case other soldiers approach us."

She shook her head a bit too frantically, worried that he would fail to understand the truth. She poked his chest repeatedly, hoping to make him pay closer attention. "You"—she tapped her chest—"and I are wed. We are truly husband and wife."

Next month, don't miss these exciting new love stories only from Avon Books

A Blood Seduction by Pamela Palmer
Quinn Lennox is searching for a missing friend when she stumbles into a dark otherworld that only she can see. She has no idea of the power she wields . . . power that could be the salvation or destruction of Arturo, the dangerously handsome vampire whose wicked kiss saves, bewitches, and betrays her.

Winter Garden by Adele Ashworth
Madeleine DuMais's cleverness is her greatest asset—one she puts to good use as a spy for the British. When she meets Thomas Blackwood, her partner in subterfuge, duty gives way to desire and she discovers their lives are no longer the only things in danger.

Darkness Becomes Her by Jaime Rush
Some might say Lachlan and Jessie don't play well with others. But they're going to have to learn to, and quickly. Because they are the only two people in the world who can save each other— and their passion is the only thing that can save the world.

Hot For Fireman by Jennifer Bernard
Katie Dane knows better than to mix business with pleasure, but when she finds herself working side by side with Ryan, the sexy heartbreaker of Station One, playing with fire suddenly feels a lot like falling in love.

*G*ive in to your Impulses!

These unforgettable stories only take a second to buy and give you hours of reading pleasure!

Go to *www.AvonImpulse.com* and see what we have to offer.

Available wherever e-books are sold.

AVONIMPULSE

IMP 0811